FEELS LIKE FALLING

To Joanne

Enjoy often

Kristy Woodson Harvey

FEELS LIKE FALLING

MICHELLE McGRIFF

URBAN BOOKS
www.urbanbooks.net

URBAN SOUL is published by

Urban Books
10 Brennan Pl.
Deer Park, NY 11729

ISBN 1-59983-009-4

First Printing: November 2006
10 9 8 7 6 5 4 3 2 1

Printed in the United States of America

To Uncle Samuel, Cousin Michael, Uncle Son-Son, Uncle Ike, Uncle Preston, Cousin Tim, and all the other brave men in my family who fought and currently are fighting the battle with cancer.

Acknowledgments

I would first like to thank Dr. Maxine Thompson for all her hard work on my behalf over this last year. Meeting her was a coincidence; getting to know her has been a pleasure.

As my writing takes me to new places, I've started seeing that those who work with me the closest seem to be the last people I get to meet face-to-face. I'm speaking of those who really put the book together: my editors and publisher, the cover designers, and the like. I want to thank all of them so very much for the hard work they do for artists like me. I realize that it's business, and I'm not naïve about what goes on behind the scenes, but I apprceiate the respect I've been shown since coming on board. I appreciate that I'm seen as a person and that my voice is allowed to show through on the pages of my books.

Again, my Guerilla Readers—Tammy Branch, Joy Goodding, Stephanie Wilkerson-Hester, Renee Williams, Shirley Bain—did not fail me on this one. Going over the draft of *Feels Like Falling*, even in the roughest form, they did not complain. I love them all. As hard as I'm sure it was, they all resisted the urge to "edit," yet they each gave me enough feedback to complete this project and in the end had confidence that it was going to be read-ready for the publisher. I think I'll send my Guerilla Readers all red pens just for the heck of it.

As always, I'm grateful for the wonderful women at Kelly Temporary Services—Connie and Margau—for providing me with a flexible work schedule so that I can complete my writing projects on time.

Portland, Oregon, has been a wonderful muse for me and my writing and the best move I could have made in my writing career—that and the Progressive Lens bifocals I bought last year.

Although I've stepped back from much of my online time, I still want to give props to all those doing their thing in the on-line book clubs, reviewing groups, and other forums that promote reading from the heart.

UNCERTAINTY

Sebastian shrugged into the jacket of his tuxedo. He smoothed back his hair again out of reflex, yet knowing not a strand was out of place. The mirror didn't lie; he looked damned good.

About that time, Ta'Rae moved up behind him, sliding her arm around his shoulder, turning him to her.

She was dressed in black—a spaghetti-strapped number that showed off plenty of cleavage.

He couldn't resist and kissed her neck, inhaling her perfume. Her diamond earrings, bought for her on their last anniversary, tickled his nose as he gave her one more sniff for good measure, causing her to give way to flirtatious giggles.

"Don't make me get naughty," she teased.

"You can get naughty any time you get ready," he flirted back, lightly biting her smooth neck. She pushed him away quickly—before things went too far.

"We're going to be late if you keep this up," she reminded him, looking at her watch.

"Ahh, let 'em eat cake," he answered smugly, all the while knowing he wouldn't miss tonight for anything in the world. He'd worked too hard for this award, and he knew he deserved it—everyone knew it.

Ta'Rae's graceful movements were like dance steps as she slid from his tempting arms.

They were good together, the two of them. . . . No, they were perfect together—that, Sebastian knew. There was nothing they couldn't conquer if they paired their minds—he believed that.

In their many years together, the two of them had conquered all things put before them, won all battles. Some fights they didn't realize they were in until they had conquered them, hindsight being their only remembrance. Yes, the Yorks were flying high without a net.

Tonight's award—the big thank-you, complete with a plaque installed in the lobby with his name, thanking him for his contribution to the hospital's success and for his large donation to the children's wing—more than spoke of his generosity and goodness as a human being.

And good things happened to good people.

Sebastian smiled at his beautiful wife as she bent over, reaching for her shoe.

"Yeah . . . And it's all good," he said audibly.

Ta'Rae glanced over her shoulder at him, moving her hips back and forth more than needed while buckling her shoe.

"You better stop that flirting before I insist that you get naked, Mrs. York." Contemplating jumping her and grabbing a quickie before the ceremony, Sebastian waited for his body to dictate his next actions.

Will we have sex, Sebastian? he asked himself.

She's definitely willing, came the internal response.

Stepping toward her, his intent was suddenly and quite uncomfortably derailed by the familiar ache in his lower belly. Maybe it was nerves; maybe that nagging ulcer again. He grabbed at the pain. Ta'Rae noticed.

"What's wrong, sweetie?" she asked, quickly putting on her Physician's Hat, which was just slightly different from her Mother's Hat; either way, he wished she had neither. All he wanted was a wife; however, Ta'Rae was a very talented general practitioner, and he would never begrudge her career choice, made long before they met.

"Nothing," he lied. "I guess I'm just a tad nervous about tonight."

"Don't be," she purred, moving close to him and needlessly straightening his tie. "You are the man," she added, her slang far from street potent—she was the most unethnic black woman he had ever met. "And when we get home, I'm going to show you just how much a man you are," she promised, making a move on him.

Sebastian grinned, hoping their night would end with a follow-through on her commitment made. He hoped his foreboding thoughts would not win out over his wonderful mood.

"It's time for your physical, Dr. York," his secretary had reminded him just the other day.

But there was no time for all of that . . . not with this award thing coming up.

The pain was worsening by the second.

"You sure you're okay, honey?" Ta'Rae asked again.

Sebastian pulled her into an embrace. "Why don't you ever call me 'baby' anymore?" he teased, knowing how she hated the use of that particular term of endearment. She always said it sounded stereotypical and more like a cliché than a true expression of affection.

Ta'Rae moved her face, avoiding his kiss. "I'm all made up, dear," she fussed, avoiding the pet name he requested. Sebastian shook his head and chuckled under his breath.

"I guess I better make a pit stop," he finally admitted.

"I'll wait downstairs. I want to make sure Precious has her last-minute instructions," Ta'Rae said, referring to their daughter, Precious, who was still a little huffed about not being included in the evening.

The limousine was waiting outside by the time Ta'Rae, grabbing her mink, had finished with Precious. Sebastian came down the stairs.

"Thought you had gotten stuck in there," she commented, regarding his apparent last-minute case of the jitters sending him to the bathroom.

His face showed disconcertment, but then again, *sometimes a trip to the bathroom could be like that.* She chuckled at the thought.

Precious was sulking in the den, still upset at being left out. "You'd be bored out of your mind."

"You treat me like I'm nothing more than a child," Precious fussed.

Ta'Rae shushed her with a quick kiss on the cheek. "You are. Now stop trying to grow up way too fast. Enjoy your childhood. Blink and it'll be gone."

"Be good for Mommy and Daddy, okay, sweetie," Ta'Rae requested. Glancing over at Sebastian, Ta'Rae could tell he still seemed to be having some stomach discomfort.

"You okay, Sebby?" she asked again.

He nodded but did not smile.

"Be good. We'll check in during the evening," he added, speaking in Precious's general direction. She rolled her eyes in irritation.

Stepping outside, the cool air hit his face. The sight of the stretch limousine brought a pleasant reality, one that helped him push the pain back, way back . . . so far back in his mind he didn't give attention to it again for the rest of the evening. As a matter of fact, he didn't think much about the pain again—until it was too late.

The five stages of grief:
Denial
Anger
Bargaining
Depression
Acceptance

DENIAL

Sebastian found himself in his office, moving his pencil in the air as if conducting an orchestra with one hand while holding his earphones to his ear with the other.

He always enjoyed Beethoven and now, suddenly more than ever, he wanted to hear it full blast, but he knew his patients would think him mad if he were to engage them in his lunacy. But surely, he felt mad, because it was the only emotion he'd yet to experience since hearing the final diagnosis from his doctor.

Cancer.

"So, am I dying?" he'd asked, his voice holding to its normal deep pitch—the practiced tone that he'd used since becoming a doctor himself.

Thinking of the physicians from daytime TV, he'd learned the volume they used; he'd practiced the perfect bedside manner they had. He'd mimicked those television doctors nearly to perfection.

Striving his whole life to be above the norm, he'd

sacrificed his youth, his fun and games, to be a serious student. He'd saved his hard-earned money to pay his way through college, supplementing his financial aid and scholarships so that he wouldn't have to ask his low-income single parent for any monetary assistance.

He'd not played the field when his buddies were sowing wild oats, "wolf calling" the honeys. He married the woman of his dreams, Ta'Rae Ams, a tall, beautiful, talented med student, and together they built the perfect life. They had a daughter and named her Precious, in simple but factual explanation of what she meant to them. As soon as she was old enough, Precious went into a private parochial school, where she studied next to the other kids who lived within similar income brackets.

Their home was in one of the most expensive areas of Northern California—Sausalito. They each drove the latest, the most expensive, fresh-off-the-showroom floor cars every year. They ate at only the best restaurants, and outside of Ta'Rae's family, they only hung out with the "in" crowd.

He lived the life he'd seen on television, and now what? Was he being written out of the script? Sure, they were snobs. But what was wrong with that? They earned it. Did he deserve to die for that?

"I'm forty-five years old. Do I deserve to die because I wanted only the best for my family?" Sebastian had asked his doctor after hearing the reports from the endocrinologist; oncologist; and doctor of internal medicine, who had performed a battery of tests.

"You are not making sense, Sebastian. You know that none of what you're saying connects," Phil, his personal physician, said in response to Sebastian's soliloquy.

"Are you going to talk to Ta'Rae soon?" Phil had asked. Sebastian stared at him for a moment, as if allowing the words to sink in.

"As in . . . get my affairs in order. Is that what you're saying to me, Phil?" he had asked.

Phil looked down at his notes and then back at his patient. His friend.

Sebastian could see pain on Phil's face.

"Sebastian, we've been friends for years. Giving you this news has not been the easiest thing to do," Phil admitted, his fingers squeezing his eyes closed underneath his glasses.

"I know, Phil, and I'm sorry," Sebastian said, calmly touching Phil's shoulder, noticing Phil's fingers dampening.

Was he was crying?

"God, Phil . . . don't."

"I'm, uh," sighed Phil, wiping his eyes. His nose reddened. "I'm going to recommend Jeff Hyatt. He's the best around, ya know," Phil went on, trying to maintain control.

Sebastian swallowed hard and sat silently, taking all the reality in.

Ta'Rae was trying hard not to show her feelings. She'd become a master at it over the last seventeen years being married to a man like Sebastian. She'd become a professional at doing "fake."

"Doctor York, your wife is here." Sandy, the secretary, buzzed in. Sebastian hadn't heard over the music. Sandy buzzed again.

"I know he's in there," she told Ta'Rae, who waited in irritation.

Sebastian had missed their lunch date. He had been acting strange for a while now, and it was working Ta'Rae's last nerve.

"You know, Sandy, I don't have time for this," Ta'Rae finally said, walking past the woman and into her husband's office.

Seeing Sebastian conducting his invisible orchestra caught Ta'Rae by surprise. Her bursting in apparently caught him off guard as well. He quickly pulled the earphones off his head.

"Sweetie!" he exclaimed.

"Don't sweetie me. You stood me up, Sebby, and I'm wondering what's going on," Ta'Rae began. She swore she wouldn't go off. She told herself she wasn't like her sisters, tough and ghetto. "Sebby?" she inquired again. Sebastian stood staring at her, his mouth hanging open.

"I, uh . . . I forgot," he said, sounding lost and confused, glancing at the wall clock.

"You forgot?" Ta'Rae asked, her tone sounding a little tighter.

Hold it together, girl.

"I forgot. I mean, no biggie," Sebastian said now, pointing the remote toward the stereo system, shutting it off.

"No biggie?" Ta'Rae asked, emphasizing the word *biggie* as if it had been said in another language.

"No biggie," he repeated, grinning at her.

You are pushing my buttons here, Seb.

"Sebastian, I waited in the cafeteria for over an hour."

"Well, it seems like you should have figured out sooner than that that I wasn't coming," Sebastian responded with a chuckle as if the picture of her waiting struck a funny bone.

That's it, Negro! Ta'Rae suddenly felt her neck jerk. "Oh no, you didn't just say that to me," she growled, feeling her hand creep onto her hip.

"Yes, baby . . . Yes, I did say dat." Sebastian went on mocking her, jerking his own neck and then cracking up at his own joke.

"What the hell is wrong with you, boy?" Ta'Rae yelled, losing her cool.

"Boy? Boy? I got cho boy!" He chuckled, digging in deeper.

"Sebastian, stop!"

"Lighten up, gurl. Shoot. It's all good," he said, moving from behind the desk and taking her into his tight embrace. "Gimme some love," he went on in his ethnic charade, planting a sloppy kiss on her lips before swatting her rear. "Isn't that what Terrell says to Rita all the time? Gimme some love," he repeated, lowering his voice and taking on a thuggish tone in imitation of his brother-in-law—Ta'Rae's younger sister's husband. Although Terrell was a lawyer, as it was often said, you can take the boy out of the ghetto but . . .

Ta'Rae pushed Sebastian away from her and looked deep into his eyes. First of all, his acting anything like her sister's husband was inconceivable. Terrell McAlister was crass, and even though he'd become quite a successful lawyer in the last few years, Sebastian and Terrell were nowhere on the same page in Ta'Rae's mind.

Something was wrong with all of this action playing out in front of her. Either that or she was in the wrong office and this man was not her husband.

Standing on a metal chair, Rita hung the streamers. It had been difficult staying in bed for weeks on end, and the minute the doctor released her, she was up and running. As her arms, held above her head, tired, she realized she had overdone it.

"But it doesn't matter. I'll grab a quick nap. This little stuff isn't gonna stop me. I'm getting back to work Monday. Wild horses couldn't keep me away," she told herself, swinging her hips to the rhythm of the song by her favorite group GrooveWave pouring out of the stereo. They were going to be in concert next month, and no matter the cost of the tickets, she was going to go see them. Maybe Terrell would stay home with the kids and she would do the sister thing with Carlotta, Trina, and Rashawn; she thought about maybe even asking Qiana to come along. Qiana had become like family over the years. It was nice having her around; she sort of replaced Ta'Rae, who was always too busy to just hang out with them.

Yeah too busy, Rita thought now with a smirk coming to her face. *Thinks she's too good for us; that's what the problem is. I'm not even gonna ask her stuck-up ass to come over for the party—let her see how it feels to be left out.*

"Naw, Qiana is on bed rest with her baby. She can't go," Rita said aloud.

Qiana and her husband, who was Terrell's law partner, had been trying for years to have a baby, and now it looked as if it was going to finally happen for them. All systems were go.

Qiana had done everything by the book to ensure a good pregnancy for herself—bed rest, the right foods, and according to the family gossip grapevine, she'd not let Nigel near her in months.

"Better safe than sorry," she had reportedly said.

"Po' man, no wonder he's all cranky," Rita said to herself, thinking of Nigel and his uptight attitude lately.

Rita's mind moved quickly through her thoughts about friends and family as she held the strip of tape between her lips, freeing her hands to cut and stick the crepe-paper streamer to the wall above her head. She loved being involved with things like this. Her mother was the same way.

Rita missed her mother. Now with five children, two sets of twin boys and a new baby girl, she wished her mother had been around to meet her children. She'd even named her baby girl after her mother—Zenobia. Her sister Rashawn had already named her son after their father, Reginald, so it only seemed right to pay the same homage. Zenobia Ams had been a fiery woman with a lot of life in her. Rita could only hope that her daughter would turn out the same way. Being close with her sisters, of which there were five—Carlotta, Ta'Rae, Trina, Rashawn, and Shelby—Rita felt they should be together every day, either by phone or in person; she believed in that. But Ta'Rae had become so distant in the last year or so, it troubled Rita. It wasn't how their mother taught them to be.

"But, as Mama used to say, she'll need us before we need—" Rita began saying, right before the small scissors slipped from her grasp.

"T!" she called. "T!" Rita called again louder. "Terrell!"

He came into the living room holding Zenobia in his arms with the toddling twins hanging close around his legs.

"Yeah?" he asked. Rita looked around for a place where Terrell could lay Zenobia down. She then noticed the first-born twins had trashed the living room and were now off into other devilment. The second-born twins, now noticing the mess, let go of Terrell's legs and ran over to finish what the others had started. She could hear them yelling, "Teeeee," in imitation of her.

"Terrell, go get them boys in here to clean up," she requested without thinking of the inconvenient timing of the request.

"Rita, I can't do all that. I've got the new dudes around my legs, little dudette in my arms; I can't go chasing the old dudes," he smacked, showing irritation.

"Can't you see I'm stuck up in this chair?" Rita said, apparently catching the "old" dudes' attention as they ran back into the living room screaming, enjoying a game of tag.

"Mama! Mama!" they wailed.

"Hey, slow it down, y'all," Terrell said.

"That's not gonna work, Terrell," Rita said, agitated at his lack of parenting skills. "You gotta grab 'em. I'll do it," she said, starting down from the chair but tangling herself in the streamer and losing her balance.

Terrell rushed around in circles looking for a safe place to lay the baby. Unable to find one, he ran toward the back of the house to place her in her crib.

Rita, as if he was abandoning her, called out to him in panicked anguish. The four toddling look-alikes screamed and cried upon seeing their mother hurt on the floor covered with colored tissue paper and sticky tape. That is, before the colorful paper became the vehicle to the new game of catch-me-if-you-can.

"Rita, you know you can trust me, right?" Dr. Robbins said, smiling ever so slightly.

"Noooo, no, I don't trust you," Rita whined and pouted, pain surging through her entire leg.

"Stop that," Dr. Robbins said calmly. He'd been the family physician for many years. "Believe me, breaking it will help it to heal faster and cleaner than it will if I leave it the way it is. This is a nasty hairline fracture; it's not going to heal well—"

"Oh my God," Rita exclaimed, her copper-colored eyes wide with both fear and other building emotions.

"It won't be worse than having a baby," he explained.

"Break my ankle? Break my ankle?" Rita was panicking, searching for someone to convince her that this man was talking crazy. But there was no one. Terrell was with the children in the waiting room, and everyone else was busy, too busy to come to the hospital right then and there. It was the middle of the day, the middle of the week. . . .

"Rita, now listen to me," Dr. Robbins began again, trying to speak above her growing volume.

"My God, get my sister. She's a doctor in this hospital. Get Ta'Rae York to do this," Rita yelled; then, with a deep voice as if suddenly possessed by something other than an earthly being, she growled, "I don't know you. . . . Who are you?"

Dr. Robbins threw up his hands in frustration.

"You've lost your mind," he said, heading out of the room.

Ta'Rae got wind that Rita was in the hospital. She had avoided the fourth floor all day hoping not to run into her or her other sisters. First of all, she didn't have any plans on attending Trina's birthday party, and secondly, hearing Rita go on and on over a simple thing as a fractured ankle, well, it would just be too much. With Sebastian acting strange, she really didn't have time for such trivialities as her family. With each year that passed, they became more and more bothersome. There had been some real issues facing her sisters, like Rashawn being stalked by a rapist maniac who turned out to be the father of her child. The incident escalated until she ended up committing manslaughter. It was just by Terrell's talents that she didn't go to prison. Granted, that was a true family crisis, but that was over three years ago now . . . long forgotten. Rashawn had made the necessary changes in her life to ensure her safety and peace of mind. She had moved back into the old neighborhood—near friends and family. She had gotten married to a caring man and had another child to cement the building of a family on a strong foundation.

Rashawn was a strong woman, not one requiring a lot of worry, not like Trina. Trina, on the other hand, was a constant source of stress.

Trina had issues.

First, she had allowed her husband to plagiarize her work and get himself on the Essence Best-seller List using her manuscript as a platform, unbeknownst to anyone—except Trina. By the time she finally told anyone that he had stolen her manuscript, he was in the middle of attempting to steal yet another one. And she'd almost conceded, giving in to her weakness for the ugly freak.

Carlotta, the oldest sister, was another story. She had just practically reinvented herself after having barely survived empty nest syndrome by the skin of her teeth. The mother of five grown children and married to a successful businessman like Scott, Carlotta could have had whatever she wanted as a lifestyle. "So she chose to open a barbecue stand?" Ta'Rae heard herself ask aloud. The reality of her sister, married to such a wealthy man, slinging baby back ribs while wiping sauce on an apron always hit her wrong. But cooking was what Carlotta loved.

She's just like Mama was, Ta'Rae realized, remembering their mother and her love for cooking.

Ta'Rae and Carlotta were a year apart. Well, heck, they were all a year apart, except for Shelby, the baby, who managed to somehow grace the scene after a ten-year break from childbearing.

"My mother, the baby maker," Ta'Rae often said, having had only one child—with no intentions of having another. Even at forty-four, many of Ta'Rae's friends were going out of their way to push the limits of womanhood. One of her girlfriends just had twins the year before. "What's that all about?" Ta'Rae muttered. "Let it go . . . grow up."

Maybe that was Ta'Rae's problem with all the women in her life. She had outgrown them, had no need for them. Her sisters being the worse of the "gaggle" of females she knew.

Always pecking, bickering, carrying on in the most brainless, wasteful ways. I can do better on my own, Ta'Rae thought, shaking her head at the mental picture.

Exiting the elevator on the fifth floor, with plans on taking the stairs to the third floor, thus avoiding the embarrassing parade of family in the fourth-floor waiting room, Ta'Rae ran smack dab into Sebastian coming from the lab. He was rolling down his sleeve, and Ta'Rae couldn't help but see evidence of blood work.

"Hey, Sebby," she purred, coming at him with puckered lips.

Sebastian stood stiff and guilt ridden.

"Hey, baby," Sebastian answered tightly.

Baby? What's up with that? she wondered, cringing slightly yet gracing his cheek with her lips, letting his presence at the lab settle in. She then noticed his arm—again.

"You didn't tell me you were getting lab work done," Ta'Rae stated. Sounding casual and normal, she pulled a stick of gum from her lab coat, then folded it into her mouth. Sebastian's lips tightened. Ta'Rae casually moved her overgrown bangs out of her face.

Her mind drifted while she waited for Sebastian's response to her simple statement.

Nothing.

"Sebastian, you didn't tell me . . ." she began.

His hands flew up in surrender, as if in just those few seconds he'd been challenged and beaten.

"I know, I know, let me think," he said, sounding as if he was sorting through the ordinary lies for a really good one.

She shifted her weight from one leg to the other, her stomach tightening as she began to notice the glistening on his forehead. Sebastian quickly wiped it away, and then looked at his fingertips.

"Is it hot in here?" he asked. Ta'Rae looked around, seeing others coming from the lab. Sebastian's eyes caught hold of the cart of test charts and samples being wheeled past.

"Ta'Rae, I . . ." Sebastian began, just as the overhead page summoned him to the phone.

"Sebastian . . . We need to talk," Ta'Rae began, showing a little more seriousness now. He nodded slowly and walked past her.

"Later," he agreed.

Watching her husband's confident stride as he walked down the hall, draping his jacket over his shoulder, Ta'Rae loved how he ran his fingers through his thick hair. He wore natural waves that he kept perfectly neat. His suit was a designer cut—she'd picked it out. He resembled a model with just a slighter build; actually, now that she noticed, his suit used to fit better. He'd lost a little weight.

Even at forty-five, Sebastian looked good. He'd never known his father, however; his mother told him that he was a Creole man. Sebastian's skin tones were rich and dark; only his hair questioned his ethnicity.

He was strong and powerful, sexy beyond belief— although it had been ages since she'd told him that. Maybe she would—soon. Ta'Rae put the thought of all that mushy verbal nonsense out of her mind, for surely they had a balanced love life, nothing to write home about. Besides, that gooey stuff was only in the movies, right? They would have time for all that junk anyway once they retired. Ta'Rae smiled at the thought of growing old with Sebastian. She could just imagine them making love . . . real slow.

Ta'Rae felt that familiar tingle between her thighs while she was watching him. "Yeah, only in the movies," she mumbled, licking her lips lustfully. There weren't too many minutes of a day she didn't think about "them" and "that." The thought made her giggle a little.

Just then, the phlebotomist came from the lab.

"Oh hello, Dr. York. Did your husband leave?" she asked.

Ta'Rae turned to her. "Yeah, he just left." She pointed in the direction he went.

"Shoot. Dr. Hyatt just called for another test."

"Hyatt?" Ta'Rae asked, having heard the name before. Her mind soared to remember where. She shook her head trying to loosen the memory; it didn't come soon enough, so she quickly pushed the name into the back files of her brain.

"Well, he's gone. I'll let him know when we meet for lunch," Ta'Rae told her.

"That'll be great," she said before disappearing back into the lab.

Ta'Rae pulled Mrs. Blinky's chart from the door and briefly looked it over. Stifling a yawn, she refreshed her memory with the woman and her troubles. Mrs. Blinky had apparently fallen a few months ago, and although her physical injuries had healed, she had yet to get up and going—yet to start living the full life she had enjoyed prior to the accident. True enough, a fall at her age could set her back, but as Ta'Rae flipped the charts, she realized it had been since the death of her husband that Mrs. Blinky seemed to be making more frequent visits to her office.

"It's all in her head," Ta'Rae mumbled, slowly opening the door.

Mrs. Blinky looked up from where she sat on the table. Her heavy limbs hung from under the paper gown. She was a small woman on top, but her legs were thick and heavy looking. Beside her stood one of Mrs. Blinky's daughters; she had three. The woman was rubbing her shoulder almost patronizingly.

"Good morning, Mrs. Blinky," Ta'Rae said, bending

down in an attempt to make eye contact with the down-trodden woman. Her head hung low, and her eyes drooped toward the floor. "What brings you here today?" Ta'Rae asked, sliding the stool up close and placing her cool hands on the woman's leg. Mrs. Blinky flinched and put her hands over Ta'Rae's. Their eyes met.

"It still hurts . . . really bad," she whispered.

"Well . . . ," Ta'Rae began, but then was quickly distracted by the woman's daughter, who was shaking her head vehemently.

"Now, Mother, you know that leg doesn't hurt anymore. See, Doctor, that's what I'm saying; Mother's leg doesn't hurt. She's making it all up; she's just wanting attention. That's why I brought her in today. So that you could tell her she's just wanting attention," the daughter huffed, and then readjusted her purse strap on her shoulder. She seemed antsy and annoyed. Ta'Rae said nothing before giving her attention back to Mrs. Blinky.

"Where does it hurt?" Ta'Rae asked her.

Mrs. Blinky almost smiled, and then with both of her warm rough hands, she lifted Ta'Rae's one hand and placed it on her heart. "Right there. Today it hurts right there."

Ta'Rae swallowed hard and slowly pulled away. "Mrs. Blinky, I think I understand; however, for the sake of this visit, I want to address your knee." Ta'Rae smiled, although for a second her heart hurt, too, for the woman and all she had lost. In just those few moments, Ta'Rae could tell that this woman had suffered more than just a fall on the concrete, more than just a bruise on her hip and hairline fracture to her knee. This woman's life had fallen.

"Yes, Mother, let's address the nonexistent pain in your knee," her daughter remarked sharply.

After the visit with Mrs. Blinky, Ta'Rae was disturbed the rest of the day. The woman's internal pain was great. Ta'Rae could not even begin to relate.

"She needs some therapy," Ta'Rae said under her breath.

"Don't we all," she heard from over her shoulder. She turned to see Chaz Baker, another of the doctors there at the hospital, a colleague. The color of his burgundy shirt showed from under his white coat, and he had on a cartoon-character tie. His blue eyes danced mischievously behind his serious jawline and thick, sandy-blond curls. Simply put, he was gorgeous. It was obvious that he had been a prodigy of some type, as he was younger than most doctors on staff at the hospital. Ta'Rae had heard he breezed his boards, and, basically, his whole career had been coasting along on roller skates.

"You're looking squeaky-clean today. What devilment are you hiding?" she asked teasingly.

"You sound like my mother," he joked back. Ta'Rae wrinkled her nose at the thought of having a son thirty-plus years old.

"Well I'm not," she retorted quickly.

He looked her up and down. Maybe it was unconsciously, but still it happened: he licked his lips and winked ever so covertly. "Nope . . . you're not," was all he said before walking away.

Ta'Rae's face was hot—on fire.

Mrs. Blinky and her problems left her mind immediately.

Ta'Rae entered the house, ignoring the red flashing light that illuminated from the phone. She watched as

Precious bound up the stairs to her room. They had both arrived home at the same time.

Precious was a lovely child. Ta'Rae passed on her mother's copper-colored eyes and a ton of hair to her daughter. When she was a little girl, Ta'Rae always kept her hair in long pigtails that even now, in a long ponytail sitting high on her head, hung around her shoulders, thick and beautiful. She had been blessed with stunning good looks—smooth Godiva chocolate–colored skin, strong jaw, high exotic cheekbones, and narrow hips. *Thank God*, Ta'Rae thought. Having to forever live down the wolf calls and the nickname "ghetto booty" was not what she wanted for her daughter. She herself had barely survived it.

Ta'Rae with her dark skin, full features, thick limbs, and round protruding buttocks—yes, she was sure glad Precious was missing those curses.

How glad she was to have married a man like Sebastian. He was so different from all the other black men she knew. He was so sophisticated. Her father liked him a lot, and though her mother had not had a chance to meet him, Ta'Rae was certain she would have liked him too.

Ta'Rae's father had told her once that Sebastian was almost too good to be true and that she needed to worry about a slick Negro like him, but Ta'Rae had ignored that counsel. Smiling at the memory of her father, Reginald Ams, Ta'Rae remembered how quickly and completely he fell for Sebastian after meeting him.

Ta'Rae's father was a cop, one of the city's finest, gunned down in the line of duty. He would forever be remembered as a good guy. The thought of his smile brought an instant sting to Ta'Rae's eyes.

He was so very stern for the most part; however,

Ta'Rae and her sisters needed his firm hand after their mother died. Without it, who knows what would have happened.

Sebastian had been a good father, too, perfectly loving to Precious. He was attentive and playful, yet stern and responsible.

Ta'Rae remembered Precious's first day of school. Sebastian had taken the day off to be there for her.

Better than me; I had to work and just couldn't get away, Ta'Rae suddenly remembered shamefully. There were many times Sebastian had been there for Precious where she had failed her.

But then, he came from a broken home. He was overcompensating, she reasoned internally.

"Mom," Precious called from the top of the stairs over the banister. Ta'Rae hated when she did that.

Precious was sixteen now. The teen years were in full swing—new car, new friends, and new freedoms. Sometimes Ta'Rae wondered if she was giving Precious a little too much freedom.

"Yes, sweetie," Ta'Rae answered, tapping the phone with her finger as if giving it her attention. She had no intention of listening to those messages. They were probably all from her sisters. Rita needs this. Rita needs that.

"Ugh. She just broke her ankle, not her neck," she groaned in an undertone, almost missing Precious's request.

"Can I?"

"Can you what?"

"I want to go over to my friend's house."

"What friend?"

"My friend," Precious answered, almost with a little tightness in her voice. "I only have one, Mother."

"Fine," Ta'Rae answered, knowing that the "one friend" comment was purely for drama. She then pushed the PLAY button on the answering machine, unable to resist any longer.

"Ta'Rae! If you are not at the hospital, get there right now. Rita has been hurt!" Carlotta yelled excitedly.

"Ta'Rae, this is Rita! They are trying to kill me," Rita cried.

"The surgery went well. We were kinda hoping you would have bought out some time to come down to see us, but I gather you were busy," Rashawn said, almost sounding sarcastic.

"This is Dr. Hyatt. Sebastian, I need you to call my office as soon as you get this message. Catching up with you has been quite the task. Anyway, I have the name of a couple of other doctors I would like you to meet. I think we can help you through all of this."

Ta'Rae was stunned. She repeated the message. "All of what?"

"Yes, dear, you can go over to your 'friend's' house," Ta'Rae answered Precious again, sounding only half-interested. Precious thanked her excitedly. When Precious left, Ta'Rae had missed the fact that Precious had taken her ponytail down and was looking a lot older than her age. . . . And was that lip gloss?

Sebastian drove slowly while listening to his favorite jazz CD. Actually, he'd listened to several, having stopped in at Best Buy. He picked up thirty or forty of them.

"And why the hell not?" he said to the sales clerk who asked curiously if he was sure he wanted them all.

He pulled into his driveway and used the remote door opener to get into the garage. Precious's car was gone, but Ta'Rae's car was parked in its usual spot. The thought of Ta'Rae made him smile. She'd been his best friend for so many years, or maybe he had just imagined that she was. Either way, whatever they were to each other was going to be tested soon. He knew that. He only prayed they could withstand the test.

Listening to his voice mail, he heard Dr. Hyatt, who had apparently finally hunted him down. "Phil musta gave him my number," Sebastian reasoned after hearing the message to get more lab work done as soon as possible.

Sebastian heard the word *chemo* after that, and the rest of the message was a blur.

"And now it begins."

He entered the house through the garage, taking a deep breath, inhaling the familiar aromas of his home. He could faintly smell Ta'Rae's bath salts wafting down the staircase. He called out for Precious, just in case, but there was no answer. Glancing at the phone, he noticed no blinking lights. He smiled at the memory of Ta'Rae's family at the hospital. He knew there had to have been many messages on the machine. *Ta'Rae must have deleted them*, he reasoned, because Ta'Rae's sisters had all but trampled him at the hospital looking for her. They were all in a huff about Rita's ankle and were looking for Ta'Rae. He didn't even lie on Ta'Rae's behalf. "She's probably hiding from y'all," he told them. Everyone blew off the statement like he was kidding, except for Carlotta. She was the only one who knew he was telling the truth. He saw it in her eyes when she looked at him. Ta'Rae had been hiding from them a lot lately.

Sebastian had started thinking it was because Ta'Rae felt that he was all she could ever want for a friend. But lately he was beginning to think something else might be the problem—something dealing with her family relationship. By the look on Carlotta's face when he said she was hiding, he figured Carlotta might have been thinking the same thing.

Sebastian started up the stairs, headed toward their bedroom. Passing it, he glanced in Precious's room; she was nowhere to be found. He went on to their room. Sebastian was right—Ta'Rae was in the bath. He could hear the sounds of the moving water. He took off his jacket, laid it over the winged-back chair, and pulled his shirt from his trousers. The sounds coming from the bathroom were soothing—the moving water, Ta'Rae humming Anita Baker. His body reacted.

Moving to the doorway, he watched her for a moment before she noticed him and smiled, closing her eyes as if taking him in and holding him somewhere in her mind, her heart. He could only hope that was what she was doing. He moved over to the tub, touching her shoulders in a motion of a light massage. She moaned and moved her head from side to side.

"Hey, Sebby," she purred.

"Why don't you ever call me baby?" he whispered in her ear. Her eyes popped open.

Turning to him, Ta'Rae tried to read his face but couldn't. She had never seen this look in his eyes before . . . or had she? Baby. The word itself was starting to really get to her and not altogether in a bad way anymore, as much as she wanted to deny it. Maybe it was just the way Sebastian said it.

She was barely able to voice anything, as she felt her

nipples hardening at just the sound of his voice picking up the chorus where she'd left off.

Standing, Sebastian held her hands so that she was forced to stand too.

"Get out of the tub, baby," he requested, reaching for a towel. She stepped out. He dried her back and arms and then pulled her close to him as he wrapped the towel around her. Kissing her, he let his tongue wander, searching for the familiar, playful kissing that they had long ago abandoned for the common kiss, the everyday kiss. But this was no everyday kiss. Sebastian's hands explored her body—all that had changed over the years, all that had remained the same. She sucked the air through her teeth when he found her sensitive areas and with familiar skills stroked her until her wetness matched that of the hot, soft, oiled water that she had just come from. She called his name over and over again as her head went back in pleasure. He took her breast in his full lips, giving them much-needed attention, as well as her belly, her navel and more. . . .

Holding his shoulders, Ta'Rae was barely breathing. It had been a long time since he'd explored her body this way. He was enjoying it—pleasing her this way, indulging in her sweetness.

Her belly pulled in tight as he sucked gently on her clitoris, and then circled it with his tongue. He almost laughed out loud watching her grope around for something to cling to, the towel falling away completely, as her orgasm nearly took all her control. Ta'Rae was used to having control; maybe she had too much. It was past time she loosened up a little.

"Come on," he instructed, backing her out of the bathroom—naked, exposed, and ready for sex.

Ta'Rae began undressing Sebastian in a fever, hoping that she would not wake up from this dream. He locked the door on the way to the bed, abandoning clothes along the way.

"Where's Precious?" he asked.

"A friend's," Ta'Rae answered quickly, breathlessly, while backing onto the bed with Sebastian strolling toward her, looking dark and mysterious, full of surprises. The color of his eyes deepened with lust.

She was almost overwhelmed and cried out as her body reacted to just the sight of him so aroused. He hadn't even touched her yet. Sitting down on the bed, she pulled his hardness between her lips. She'd not orally pleased her husband in years, but it was like riding a bike, the way he slid in and out of her mouth, his engorgement growing silkier and readier by the second. Faster and faster she took him in until he began long full strokes that she was sure was leading to orgasm.

"You're not getting off that easy," he said, his voice heavy with sexual want.

Moving her into the middle of the bed, Sebastian entered her without further foreplay; his grunts of pleasure were driving her mad. She pulled at his hair and scratched at his back, allowing him the rough sex. It was an itch she needed scratched, and he was not missing any spots.

"Turn it over. I need to hit that ass," he growled, shocking her with his vulgarity, yet exciting her with his power. She could not resist and quickly obeyed, holding on to the headboard, feeling his hardness against her backside. His strong thighs moved her legs apart as she felt tip of his love rod pushing into her. She gasped when he bit the back of her neck, filling his hands with her breasts—tugging at them hard, twisting at her nipples until they were nearly sore. While both on their knees, she reached back, running her hands over his taut thighs and hips, pulling him into her.

Giving way to multiple orgasms, Ta'Rae's mind spun. With his large hand on the back of her neck, Sebastian took what was his, freely and with no request for permission. Long slow thrusts that she could feel in her belly. He was having her tonight—all of her.

Once or twice, Rita had told her about Terrell's prowess, and she had almost envied her. Sometimes she saw Scott lusting for Carlotta, and she once or twice felt a twinge of jealousy in her heart. Sometimes she even saw Chance giving Rashawn a wink and promise of what was to come and she wondered . . .

But tonight, Sebastian made all those fantasies fade. He was all she ever needed in a man.

"Sebastian!" she screamed when he pulled out. She turned to look at him. His chest was heaving heavily.

"What's wrong?" she asked. Her words were loud and wild sounding; she was clearly out of control. "What's wrong?" she asked again, regrouping slowly.

"Do you love me?" he asked her, his voice trembling. She grabbed him quickly, holding him tight against her. His words scared her. The rush was not over yet. Goose bumps covered her. He held on tight.

"Yes . . . yes, of course I do," she answered.

As she pulled him down on top of her, he entered her again. This time he was the Sebastian she knew, slow and deliberate, no fire, no lust. The thug was gone, and now the man she knew remained . . . or was he? Rising up slightly, he gave way to release, before suddenly beginning to weep.

She held him while he cried, heavy sobs that racked his entire body.

"Talk to me, Sebastian." Ta'Rae clasped his head

between her hands, pulling his face to meet hers. His eyes welled with sadness.

Ta'Rae's heart ached instantly.

"Ta'Rae . . . baby." He gasped for air while speaking.

"Sebby, what?" she requested, feeling her body tightening with growing anxiety. "You're scaring me."

"I didn't want to leave you and Precious this way," he mumbled, closing his eyes, squeezing out the last tear.

"What are you talking about, leaving?" Ta'Rae's voice took on firmness now.

"I've got cancer, Rae. It's in my colon. Phil said—"

"What did you just say?" Ta'Rae asked, feeling the heat leaving her body.

"I've got colorectal cancer. When I told you I was away at the seminar a few months back, I was, in fact, having some tests done. I didn't want you to worry," Sebastian answered, his eyes meeting hers and not moving. He waited for her to say more, but she did not. "Phil had found some polyps, so he wanted me to do more tests. Well, the tumors had spread to the regional lymph nodes, and one had penetrated the wall. I'm going to schedule some more tests, but Phil is afraid that one or more have already metastasized and that maybe there's been some movement to other locations . . . like my stomach, which as you know is one of the worst prognostic signs . . ." He paused now, realizing how he sounded. "Bottom line is . . . well, it doesn't look good."

Ta'Rae felt her heart stop.

Sleep had been a miracle for Ta'Rae. She awoke finding Sebastian still sleeping soundly next to her.

They had not dressed during the night and lay naked in each other's arms.

After he told her the news, she had to admit that she wanted it to be some perverse joke or lie and had refused to hear anything more on the subject. Now she looked at him, lying there, sleeping peacefully. She wondered, *How could he have hid all of this from me? How could I have not known what was going on inside of him just from looking? I'm a doctor; surely I could tell if it was true or not.*

She touched his arm softly.

"Good morning," he greeted, smiling at her weakly.

His eyes were tight from crying, and his face looked tired and worn. It wasn't the face she expected to see after a night of bliss. Ta'Rae was apparently silent too long as he raised himself on one elbow and stared at her.

"Rae," he said again, touching her face. She grabbed his hand and stared at it as if belonging to a dream.

"Baby, are you okay?" he asked.

"Are you?" she asked back. Her tone was cool, sterile. As if she was with a patient instead of a lover.

"What kind of question is that?" he asked her.

"I mean, after what you told me last night I just figured . . ." Ta'Rae rose up on both elbows, keeping the blanket covering her.

"I'm sorry I told you that way."

"I bet you haven't even gotten a second opinion," she began.

"I was trying to talk to you last night, but you didn't want to talk about it," he said.

She climbed quickly out of bed and grabbed her robe. "You're damned right I don't want to talk about it, Sebby, because you're gonna get on this phone right

here and call your doctor. You're gonna call Phil and
have him order those tests all over again," she said,
shaking the cordless phone at him. Sebastian shook his
head.

"Rae, I've done all . . . ," he began.

Ta'Rae began to shake her head and then threw the
phone at him, screaming hysterically. "Do what I said
and call your goddamned doctor, Sebastian York!"
Ta'Rae's eyes glowed with the heat of a wickedly hot
fire. Sebastian realized then the shock had worn off,
and she was not taking the news well.

Scrambling to cover himself, he jumped from the
bed and started for her to attempt some kind of reasoning, but Ta'Rae moved quickly to the dresser and began
throwing things—perfume bottles, her brush, novels,
framed pictures.

Fortunately, Sebastian was fast on his feet, and his
response time was right on. He managed to duck most
of the items, reaching her successfully.

"Ta'Rae, stop!" He grabbed her hands.

She jerked against his grip. "No! No," she growled.

He pulled her to him in a tight embrace.

"Baby, don't," he pleaded, holding her close in case
she gave way to tears. "Rae, I'm sorry," he spoke, holding her face up to his to see her sadness, her pain.

However, instead of sadness, he saw what he thought
to be anger. It confused him—that is, until she spoke.

"Sorry? Sorry! How dare you do this?" She pushed
him away.

"What?" he asked, stepping back.

"My life was perfect, Sebastian—our life," she went
on, flailing her arms. "You expect me just to take some
crazy news like this and do nothing. I'm angry! With
you!" Sebastian watched in disbelief as she stomped

around now, picking up the items she had thrown, placing them back on the dresser while going over all the ways his death was negatively affecting her.

She was . . . crazy.

"Rae! Stop speaking right now. Please don't say anything more!" he yelled.

The room went silent except for a shallow knocking at the door. It was Precious.

Breakfast was tense, with Precious eyeing both her parents intently until finally one of them spoke. "So how was your night out with your friends?" Ta'Rae asked.

Precious cleared her throat. "It was fun," she answered.

"So who are these friends?" Sebastian asked.

"Well . . ." Precious began.

"Why are you cornering her as if she's keeping something from *you?*" Ta'Rae interjected. Sebastian huffed, not looking at her but continuing to butter his bread. The comment was intended to stab him and it did.

"I wasn't asking for your sarcasm," Sebastian grumbled.

"I'm not being sarcastic," she said.

"What is up with you guys?" Precious asked, looking at both of her parents. She had heard the argument, at least part of it. Her parents never argued. They always said it was a sign of ignorance and inability to properly communicate.

Sebastian and Ta'Rae stared at each other a long time. It was as if calm came over them, an understanding.

Ta'Rae knew she wasn't really angry with him. She

loved him. But right now, she hurt all over. It was as if someone had hit her from behind with a baseball bat. It was an unfair blow, and she felt disadvantaged.

She hadn't meant to be cruel, and Sebastian's medical condition was of true concern and not for the reasons she had said in the bedroom.

Colon cancer was nothing to play with. This was going to take years of treatments if they were going to fix this. Cure this.

And she was going to have to be by his side, supporting him one hundred percent.

This was her family.

"Nothing, Precious. Mommy is having a bad day," Ta'Rae lied.

"Is it something I did?" she asked, sounding almost guilty, Sebastian noticed. Ta'Rae ran over and hugged her tight around the shoulders.

"No, honey, never think that. Nothing that happens is your fault," Ta'Rae explained.

"But there are things you need to know. You're getting older and—" Sebastian began.

"No, nothing, you need to know nothing," Ta'Rae interrupted.

Sebastian read her face, her eyes.

"You need to know that calling home—checking in—is what you need to do when you stay out late," Sebastian said anyway, defiantly. "I thought we had an understanding." The comment was said to Ta'Rae although directed to Precious.

Ta'Rae sighed loudly.

The unspoken decision to keep the news from their daughter didn't sit well with Sebastian, but after Ta'Rae's performance, he really wasn't up to anything more. If Precious were to lose it, he would just have to call for the check and leave. It had been two days since Ta'Rae had gone off, and still she had not spoken to him beyond the superficial everyday things. She was in denial big time.

This was all getting to be too much.

Today he would go ahead and schedule the resection. The thought of having a colostomy bag, even temporarily, bothered him more than anything. But it was only for a few months and then this whole nightmare would be over.

Dying was not on his mind. He was going to beat this thing.

As a surgeon, choosing from peers was going to be harder than he thought. Would he even get a choice?

"Of course I will," he reasoned, walking into the hospital. "I've been *chosen* before, so people get choices," he said aloud, thinking aloud. The elevator opened, and he stepped in. Glancing around at the others going up to the fifth floor, he wondered how many of these people were dying. What kinds of cancers were taking their lives . . . eating away at them.

"Cancer doesn't always kill," he would say to them during a presurgery consult. But then again, he was a plastic surgeon. What did he know? After years of reconstructing breasts, jaw lines, and other parts of the body mutilated by cancer removal, did he ever really know what happened to those people?

Not really.

"Hello, Sebastian," Dr. Hyatt said, smiling at him. Sebastian sat on the table, allowing his feet to dangle loosely over the side. He dreaded the examination. It was painful, humiliating.

"Phil tells me that you haven't really been handling all this very well," Jeff Hyatt said after the initial exam was complete.

Sebastian, still frowning, left the expression on his face. "What's there to handle well, Jeff?" Sebastian asked gruffly.

"A positive attitude is sometimes what you need to beat this, guy," Jeff answered quickly.

"Don't bullshit me," Sebastian snapped. Jeff's eyebrow rose.

Sebastian knew he was out of character, losing his cool this way. He took a deep breath. "What I mean is—"

"What you mean is I'm giving you bullshit, lying to you. But I'm not," Jeff answered calmly. "From the report, there are several indications that you've had this condition for a while, so you know as well as I do that we have to get very aggressive. If there is no metastasis, then we have to stop this thing, beat it," Jeff assured, sounding confident. Sebastian let the word *if* sink in.

"And if there is metastasis, what then?"

"Sebastian, then we worry about that at that time," Jeff answered flatly.

Apollo Punjab was a respected surgeon. He'd had much success in cancer surgery. He was Sebastian's choice.

Sitting in the cafeteria, Sebastian sipped his coffee while waiting for Ta'Rae to join him. After her silent treatment over the last few days, Sebastian was surprised she had agreed to eat with him today. It was strange to have to ask her. It was what they normally did on Mondays. They had lunch every Monday. It was their routine. Today it was going to be breakfast. "But still, it's Monday," he reasoned.

Sebastian looked around the newly remodeled cafeteria—bright with many more windows than before—and the plants, although fake, looked good against the choice of wallpaper.

Just then, he saw Nigel. He often saw Nigel and Terrell at the hospital. They weren't true ambulance chasers, but they were pretty darn close, in Sebastian's opinion.

Nigel spied him and came over to join him.

"Who you trying to represent?" Sebastian joked.

Nigel shook his head, accepting how it must have looked. "Funny." He laughed. "Qiana had to come in this morning."

"Everything okay?" he asked, regarding Nigel's wife.

"Oh sure. We are just being overly careful this time, you know." Nigel shrugged, trying not to show too much concern. "You don't look dressed for surgery," Nigel observed, noting Sebastian's jeans and polo shirt.

"Oh I'm not. I'm here for some tests," he divulged without thinking or hiding it.

"Tests? You okay?" Nigel asked, showing concern.

"No, actually, I'm not," Sebastian answered. He had told Ta'Rae finally, and so now he would have to tell the family. Nigel was as close to being family as it came, so he would be good practice.

"I have . . ." Sebastian sipped his coffee and sat back in his chair, hoping to look posed and relaxed, confident, smooth. He was trying with all his might to look like himself.

"I have cancer," he said, feeling his eyes burn suddenly.

Nigel's eyes widened, and he gulped air.

"Sebastian . . . that's terrible. I mean, how . . ."

"It's colon cancer. Too much of the good life I guess." Sebastian chuckled. Nigel nervously chuckled too. Just then, Ta'Rae joined the table, her copper eyes glowing and wide. She looked almost crazed.

"Hello, Nigel," she said quickly before picking up Sebastian's cup of coffee, dumping it out in a nearby trashcan. The men watched her as she looked over his tray as if examining his intake of eggs. "You didn't wait for me, Sebby. I would have ordered for us," Ta'Rae said then. Nigel cleared his throat awkwardly. She glared at him.

"Well, Sebastian, I'm going to go check on Qiana. She's probably finished at the lab," he said, standing.

"Is she okay? Of course she's okay. She acts responsibly with her body. She takes good care of herself," Ta'Rae said. Nigel nodded slowly and then looked at Sebastian, hoping to make some type of male contact. He thought maybe he had missed some kind of warning signal from Sebastian, something to explain Ta'Rae's mood.

"What did that mean?" Sebastian asked as soon as Nigel was out of earshot. "And pouring out my coffee isn't going to fix anything except perhaps ruining my morning," Sebastian informed her.

She rolled her eyes. "You know good and well that drinking coffee is now totally taboo. I stopped, too, just today. I figure I can't ask you to do something without support," she said, and then smiled widely, folding her hands together on the table.

Sebastian looked at her and then smiled, realizing what was happening. She was changing hats right here, right now, from wife to mother, right before his eyes.

"I suppose that you will be there for the surgery, too, eh?" he asked, leaning in close and planting a quick kiss on her cheek.

"Of course, Sebby, why wouldn't I be?"

"What about Precious . . . When are we going to tell her?"

"When we need to. Perhaps after the surgery is over. I'm sure then you'll have to do a little chemo, but the cancer will be gone anyway so—"

"The surgery and a little chemo . . ." Sebastian repeated, shaking his head in disbelief at how lightweight she made it all sound. He chuckled.

"What?" she asked.

"Nothing . . . anyway," he began, changing the subject.

"Tonight Susan wants us to come over for dinner."

"Tonight?"

"Yes, Seb, Susan has been wanting us to come over for weeks. I think we should go. She just got that new painting, and I've been dying to see it. She paid a mint for it. Jocelyn said it was overpriced, but I've not seen it, but tonight—"

"I thought maybe we'd get together with the family," Sebastian interrupted.

Ta'Rae blinked slowly. "Whose family?"

"Considering I don't have one outside of you and Precious, I would say yours," he answered.

"You're kidding, right?"

"No. With Rita having gone through the ankle surgery, I figure talking over a good meal would be nice, and then I got to thinking, heck why not just have the whole family involved. Come to think about it, I wish we didn't live so far away from them," he went on.

Ta'Rae shook her head as if hearing a foreign lan-

guage. "I guess we can, uh . . . take something over to
Rita. I hadn't really thought about it," she said after letting his words sink in.

"Well, let's think about it."

"Okay. My, aren't we bossy," she said teasingly.

"Did you ever find out what 'friends' Precious has
been seeing?" Sebastian asked.

"Her friends?"

"Yeah, it just came to me the other night when"—
Sebastian smiled at the pleasant part of the night
they made love and then continued—"when we had a
night alone, that you said she was with friends.
Whose house was she at?" he asked, casual in his use
of grammar.

"Well, I don't know . . ."

"Find out. I mean, this ship needs to get in shape,"
Sebastian ordered, looking at his watch. He had just
enough time to get to his office and see a patient before
his visit with his therapist. He'd been seeing Hilton
Patta for years. She was part of his Monday ritual.
Consultations, therapy, and then lunch with Ta'Rae.
That was his normal Monday, maybe that was why this
encounter with Ta'Rae felt a little out of sync.

"You leaving?" she asked, sounding a little surprised.
She had just started looking over the menu.

"Yes, I have to see Hilton," he answered, standing
now, rattling the keys in his pockets.

"Okay, well this didn't go very well," she said,
standing too. "I guess we don't do well with change."

Sebastian chuckled at her observation.

"See you when you get home, then," she said.

"And then we'll go to Rita's," he reiterated. Ta'Rae
just smiled mischievously. "What is that look about?"

"This isn't some trap to have me there while you

make some type of announcement is it, because if
that's what this is all about . . ."

"I'm not going to say anything about my canc—"
Sebastian began before Ta'Rae's raised hand cut him
off.

"If you want to go, we'll go," she replied before
turning and walking off.

Sebastian watched her saunter off. She was so beautiful, so afraid.

Sitting in the office of his shrink, Sebastian felt far
from comfortable.

"What is your biggest fear, Sebastian?" Hilton asked.

"Actually, I'm not sure. I'm not even sure I'm afraid,"
he answered, crossing his legs in immediate show of
physical contradiction to his verbal response.

Hilton noticed and smiled. "Again, what is your
biggest fear, Sebastian?" she asked.

He smiled. "I'm afraid that I won't have had *peace*."

"Peace?"

"Yes. Peace. You think you have peace and then
something like this happens, and you realize you've
lived a life that was so far from peaceful. Then it hits
you like a brick that you don't even know what peace
is, let alone have had any of it. I've watched my wife
for a couple of days now and my daughter. We just
move around that house like shadows, passing each
other, crossing each other occasionally." He paused,
again reflecting for a moment the night of passion
spent with Ta'Rae. "I worry that I'm going to die, and
they will not know who they are or what real happiness
is or what's going on in the real world."

"And you?"

"Me?"

"What do you want to do before you die?" she asked, as if his demise was certain.

He swallowed hard upon hearing it for the first time from someone else. He'd been negative since hearing the word *cancer* coming from Phil's lips. Actually, no one had told him he was dying, so hearing it now from Hilton this way, it did indeed sound quite ugly. No wonder Ta'Rae had a fit. He was feeling pretty upset, too, just at the sound of it.

"Before I die?" he asked.

"Yes, Sebastian. After your surgery, if the news is not good, what is the first thing you will do?"

"Aside from asking for a recount." Sebastian chuckled, uneasily avoiding the answer. He looked at Hilton. Her blue eyes were piercing. He cleared his throat. "I guess I'll tell Ta'Rae and then her family and then—"

"I'm talking about making peace, Sebastian. How will you find peace?"

Sebastian was silent a long time. He'd not thought about his life in that way. He'd not looked back at all his imperfections and dealings to see if perhaps peace needed to be made. Had he really felt as though he needed no redemption? Had he really viewed his life as perfect?

"I hadn't thought about it," he admitted.

Hilton smiled. "Well, Sebastian, I think you should. You need to find some real peace. You've never been truly happy, not in my personal and professional opinion."

"You're nuts. I'm terribly happy." Sebastian laughed.

"*Terribly* is the word for it all right."

"Anyway." Sebastian snickered, looking at his watch. Their time was up.

"See if you can get Ta'Rae to stop in and see me."

"Yeah, okay, sure." He knew the answer to that request before he even made it of Ta'Rae.

Ta'Rae made a stop at Singers, her favorite eating spot, and picked up her preordered dinner to take to Rita's.

Sebastian didn't actually think I was going to cook for this get-together, did he?

She grinned at the thought of slaving over a hot stove. "That'll be the day," she said aloud, lugging the large bags to the car. "I'm not Carlotta."

About that time, she noticed her car was not where she had parked it. Standing out in front of the deli, she looked around for it. Her first thought was that she had forgotten where she parked it; the next thought was the one she didn't want to face—theft.

"Damn!" she groaned, dropping the bags beside her. She immediately pulled out her cell phone and called her insurance company, who in turn put technology to work, locating the car via an implanted tracking device.

"We've deployed the police, Dr. York; your car has been located," the agent informed her, calling her back within fifteen minutes.

By then, Ta'Rae had gone back into the restaurant. She hesitated calling Sebastian. Why worry him about something she could handle on her own?

She would have to start getting used to handling things on her own.

Her own thoughts caused her to gasp with disbelief. "My God, girl, what did you just say?" she asked herself. "Don't ever think that way again. Sebastian is going to get over this."

"Maybe if you drove a more practical car, nobody would have taken it," Carlotta fussed, looking over the catered food as if it were all poison.

"I drive a practical car."

"I'm just saying, fancy car, expensive food—you were a setup today."

"You can't determine when someone is gonna steal from you," Ta'Rae retorted while setting up the meal in Rita's kitchen.

The day had been a total disaster.

In just the short time it took her to shop for dinner, her Mercedes had been stolen, taken to Oakland, stripped, and prepped at a chop shop. The thieves were pros and had been on a rampage for half the year already. All the cops knew was that they were young, some even high school age. The cars were supplying them with drug money with which these thieves were turning an even bigger profit. They were out of control and quickly becoming a priority for the police.

"But then again, I guess you'll just trot down to the dealership and pick out a new car," Carlotta said, still harping on Ta'Rae's spending habits.

"Yeah, probably," Ta'Rae said, a slight smile curving her lip.

"What's that smile for?"

"I've been thinking about getting a Jag," Ta'Rae admitted, giggling wickedly. "You know, like yours."

"Girl, you are too much." Carlotta scowled. "You guys are living just like, way up there. I know you're both physicians and all that, but money is a tricky thing—

trust me. Beware. That's all I'm gonna say," Carlotta summarized, pulling the plates down from the cabinets.

"Why do you say that?" Ta'Rae asked, wondering if somehow Carlotta knew about Sebastian's illness and the growing medical bills. Maybe she just had never looked before, but Ta'Rae was surprised what their insurance covered and what it did not. At this point in time, the outgoing numbers were far from worrisome, although many would see the amount as staggering.

"You're living like there is no tomorrow," Carlotta went on.

Ta'Rae followed her into the living room that hummed with small talk. "Maybe it's not the time in my life to be practical. Maybe I'm ready to move on past practical to exciting. I could use some excitement. Maybe . . ."

Sebastian heard her and looked up from the conversation he was having with Rita's sons. Sebastian could tell that Ta'Rae had not been in the kitchen telling Carlotta about his cancer, and he'd been in the living room talking about everything under the sun but that topic. Their eyes met for just a second of awkward conspiracy—secret keeping.

"Rae's ready to move onnnn, huh?" Sebastian said, allowing the kids to run off.

"Yeah, like she even knows what moving on means." Carlotta chortled loudly before calling all to eat.

There was only once more that evening where Sebastian caught Ta'Rae's eye, making him think again about her words—twisted and misunderstood as they were, still, the thought of her ever moving on without him had never been a thought before.

* * *

"I know you misunderstood what I said tonight," Ta'Rae said into the mirror to Sebastian, who had climbed into bed.

"No, I didn't," he answered.

"I was talking about a new car," she said anyway.

"I figured that. What else would I think?" he asked, smiling at her.

She stared at his reflection for a long time before her eyes filled with his smile and decided to join him in bed.

He pulled her close to him. "That you were planning to take flying lessons from some foreign guy that you met at Singers named Jag, who works for your insurance company and, by the way, happens to have a new car—blue, your favorite color," Sebastian joked, acting as if he had crossed over into a crazy soap-opera-sounding drama-fest. Ta'Rae laughed, giving him a shove; he grabbed her hand and kissed her palm. She loved when he did that.

"Have you been happy, Rae?" he asked her.

She kissed his cheek. "With you?" she asked.

"No, with the guy with the new car."

"Stop it. Of course I've been"—she held his face firmly—"and I will always be." He closed his eyes, smiling as she felt his body react to her words.

Pulling her closer to him, they kissed until eventually she moved beneath him.

Ta'Rae got comfortable in her seat. It had been a while since she and her friends had done anything together. Life had all but stopped since Sebastian had lowered the boom on her the way he had. Ta'Rae needed this outing. She needed this evening with her close friends.

"So, what does that mean, lowered the boom?" her friend Akai asked, regarding Sebastian.

"Well, we're having some health issues. Nothing serious, just—" Ta'Rae began to explain.

"We? You're sick too?" Sharon asked, sounding panic-stricken while moving her seat slightly from the group. Sharon's body language was speaking volumes.

"No, Sharon, you're not listening," Ta'Rae explained.

"You do look very tired," Deidre added, giving Ta'Rae a closer glance.

"I don't. I look just like I did last time you saw me," Ta'Rae said.

"No, she said Sebastian is very sick. Didn't you hear her?"

"I didn't actually say very sick but—" Ta'Rae interjected.

"Oh well, of course she's tired, then. She's got to care for Sebastian now," Akai explained. Sharon was nodding.

"No, it's not like that."

"Is he still working?"

"Of course he's working. Nothing is—"

"My God, what are you going to do, sell the house?"

"No, I need to do that."

"Didn't you just get that new car? My gosh, all the bills."

"Two incomes down to one. Well, I don't care what you do for a living—you're gonna feel that."

"Well I—"

"What are you going to do?"

"We really don't have to do anything. I am a doc—"

"What about Precious? That poor baby, I'm sure

you're going to take her out of that expensive private school. So she'll probably start regular school in January?"

"No, she's—"

"Oh man, and definitely get rid of her car."

"Of course they will, Sharon," Akai answered.

"Aren't you glad you have family?" Deidre asked, touching Ta'Rae's hand softly.

Ta'Rae pulled back. "You guys, God, listen to you. I didn't think I needed my family. I thought I had my friends."

The women sat quietly, looking around at each other.

"You always need your family," Deidre spoke up.

Ta'Rae, without hearing anything else, knew what that meant. Even without hearing what Sebastian had, Ta'Rae knew her friends could not handle this reality—mortality had touched down too close.

This was not a tummy tuck. This wasn't gossip about an unnamed patient they would never meet. This was Sebastian—Ta'Rae's gorgeous, sexy husband who, even though she hadn't told them, would be losing his hair through chemo and, worse, would be temporarily attached to a colostomy bag.

Ta'Rae was losing her footing within the "perfect life club." But going out easy was not in her plan.

Ta'Rae called Precious.

The number came up. It was her mother. Precious looked around at everyone there: Drake, Tigger, Black, Money, Q, and Rosey.

Drake noticed the little familiar tune and watched her response to it.

"It's ya ma," he said, his words coming long and

drawn out. Precious immediately got into the role—the role she'd been playing a little over a month now. Dime Piece, that's what Drake called her. That was a good thing . . . real close to being a girlfriend, and that's where she was heading. There was no way she wanted him to see her true self, her bourgeois life filled with Barbie-doll dreams and pink canopy beds, matching pillows and comforters coordinated with floral wallpaper and plush white carpet. There was no way Drake could get into all that, and, actually, she was getting somewhat tired of it herself.

Drake was older. He was twenty-two. He was dreamy, with deep green eyes and a milky smooth complexion that spoke of a mixed racial blending. He made her young heart skip a beat. His legs were bowed slightly, and one of his teeth had been capped gold. He would often have his mess of woolly curls tied back by a bandana, which showed off the diamond stud in his left earlobe. His body was built by Bally's or, in his case, the many miles run at full speed, running from the cops—jumping fences and the like. The lion tattoo on his shoulder was darkly colored. He would often let her touch it. Just feeling it released a surge of his power into her.

She was sprung, or a least that's what Rosey had told her. But how could Rosey understand what Drake really meant to her? It went beyond the flesh, beyond his beauty. He was her savior—one kiss from his full delicious lips made life worth living another day.

"Precious," he said now, bringing her back with his voice. She loved his voice. When he said her name, it was like a song. She hoped one day he'd write a song for her, or anything other than the rap he currently wrote, although she'd grown to love every curse word, obscenity, and gross perversion that came from his lips, because she loved him.

"You gone an-sa dat phone? It's ya ma," he repeated. She looked at it in her hand—the connection to her real life, the one that took her away from him.

"Hello," she answered, quickly turning her back on her friends, who for the most part ignored her. They were too busy smoking and drinking while planning the night of fun at the Marina. She'd still not found a way to get out of the house tonight without a lot of explanation . . . but not going was not an option.

"Where are you?" Ta'Rae asked.

"I'm at school," Precious lied.

"Oh, okay, well, tonight we are going to have a family meeting. Daddy and I are planning a new diet, and we want to involve you a little. I mean, not seriously involve, but just, you know, keep you informed with what Daddy and I are doing."

Ta'Rae sounded perky over the phone, her voice, high-pitched and fake. Precious couldn't read past it and so took it at face value—considering her group was making a move and she didn't want to be left behind.

"Yeah, Mom, sounds great," she whispered. "I'll start it with you guys. I could stand to lose a little weight."

"Why are you whispering?"

"Mother, I'm like, in class," Precious said, a little loud.

It caught the attention of Tigger, who imitated her diction. "Like, Motherrrrrr," he taunted.

She covered the mouthpiece and glared at Tigger. He wasn't her favorite person in the group, but he was the closest to Drake, and therefore she had to tolerate him. He had been the youngest among them until she

came along. Tigger was immature, thuggish, a hoodlum with no manners. She didn't like him at all.

"Anyway, Mom—"

"Who is that?"

"Oh, just a guy." She glanced over her shoulder,
catching Drake's eye now. He licked his lips, as was his
unconscious mannerism. Her heart leapt.

"Well, you tell him to get out of your business and
personal conversation!"

"Mother, anyway, I'm gonna let you go," Precious
said, speaking covertly.

"When will you be home?"

"Later," she began, and then figured this was as
good a time as any to plan her evening getaway.

"Later? You know, I'm not sure if this new freedom
thing is gonna work out. I really like knowing where
you are, and you're just not doing your part—you
know, checking in, yada yada—"

"Later, Mom. I was going to spend time with them.
I'll call." She edged close to a lie.

"Precious, who are these friends?"

"Mom, you've met them. I go to school with my
friends. Well, anyway, I already talked to Daddy about
it, and he said just like, actually, like, confirm with you.
So I consider it confirmed, okay? See you later . . . late.
Ciao," she said, taking the step over the edge. She
clicked the END button on the phone.

"Ciao?" Drake whispered in her ear, closing up behind her, rubbing his body against her backside. She
gasped with immediate excitement.

Ta'Rae, on the other hand, sat staring at the phone.
"Late?" she asked herself, wondering if *late* was a
salutation or timeline.

Thinking it over, she decided to call Sebastian; his

number rang and rang until she reached only voice mail.

"Now where is he?"

A visit to the Men's Wearhouse was in order for Sebastian this afternoon. He could have chosen a more upscale store, but this place usually had something he could get quickly without a lot of hassle. He had an off-the-rack kind of build anyway, and besides, "Nothing like shopping to get your mind off ya troubles," he thought out loud, repeating Ta'Rae's mantra for life while looking through the rack.

Gray . . . black . . . brown . . .

"Green . . . yeah, that will work," he said out loud.

"Are you sure?" the woman asked. The familiar voice caused him to spin around. It was her—Stormy Brown. Her badge read S. GUNTHER.

It had been years since he'd seen her, and during that time, he'd managed to get her totally off his mind. And why shouldn't he have? Even then he knew she was just a for-the-moment kind of woman, and he was headed for success.

He clearly remembered the day they met. She was a sales clerk at Nordstrom at the time. Ta'Rae was pregnant with Precious. She'd been cranky and difficult for weeks. They'd not been married long . . . not long enough to accept the changes in his life—marriage and within just a few months, the announcement of a baby on the way. Becoming an intern—working many long, arduous, thankless hours—he needed the break.

To cover his feelings, he doted on Ta'Rae and that day he was buying her a gift. It was pricey, and he knew he probably couldn't afford it, but Ta'Rae was worth it, or maybe he felt he was worth buying it.

He reasoned things so differently back then.

Then he met Stormy. She was young, cute, and bubbly. There was nothing haughty or self-assuming about her; maybe that's what he needed at that time—she was so comfortable. Ta'Rae was such a challenge—every day. He was tired. He remembered that now, being tired.

Maybe it was because he felt the same way today . . . beat.

What got them in bed, him and Stormy, Sebastian couldn't say; however, that's where their chance meeting landed them. Fast and furious was their affair. It only lasted a few days before he came to his senses. He walked away quickly and never looked back . . . until today.

"Sebastian York," the woman exclaimed, the familiar dimple piercing her round cheek. She smiled and then, as if remembering the pain he'd caused, the smile left her face.

"Stormy . . . Stormy Bro—"

"Gunther," she interrupted, pointing at her badge. "I've been married for a long time."

"I see." He smiled, attempting friendliness.

"And you?"

"Still." He paused, wondering if she had ever known he was married. Her widened eyes told him she hadn't known. He hadn't bothered to tell her even that much.

Lustful and young, selfish, and until this very moment, unremorseful, that was Sebastian York back then.

"Oh." She chuckled, as if suddenly getting the answer she had needed for years. She folded her arms across her chest and looked around. An awkward moment was forming.

"I would like to buy you some coffee," he offered on an impulse, thinking about Hilton's words to him, said at their last session.

"Find the peace, Sebastian . . ."

Even if it means finding it for others, he reasoned now, seeing the pain in Stormy's eyes and the bend in her brow. He didn't know if this was the right moment or not, but no better time than the present to jump into the unknown.

Tomorrow belonged to no man.

For the first time in his life, he felt he truly understood that statement.

Maybe he was again being vain, but he felt he was a part of the pain he saw in her eyes. He needed to mend it.

"This is my daughter," he said, showing Stormy the picture of Precious while they sat at the coffee shop across the street from the store. "My wife was pregnant when we met. She was finishing up medical school," Sebastian confessed after they had finished their pie. The conversation was light as they had nothing really to talk about, or so it seemed, despite the information they exchanged.

It was pertinent, and Stormy was very affected. "Oh," was all Stormy could say to his comment about his family—*his wife*. She avoided much revelation regarding herself and how she had spent her life since putting it back together after he disappeared.

"So for you, what have you been up to?" he asked.

She smiled, and nearly blushed, moving a loose

braid behind her ear. "Well, I'm doing good. I'm the manager of the Men's Wearhouse, and—"

"You are? That's nice . . . That's really nice," he interjected, trying not to sound patronizing; however, the frown on her face showed him he had not succeeded.

"I'm sorry I didn't become a doctor like your wife." She sounded sarcastic. Sebastian shook his head and patted her hand to calm her, to keep this conversation civil. "Maybe some of your other trysts turned out better."

"Stormy, I love my wife. I've never cheated on her—not since you, I mean. I—"

"So was I your first or your last?"

"My only," he confessed.

She turned away.

"I was just a kid, Sebastian. I don't know, but I guess I believed in a lot of crazy stuff back then," she said without turning back to face him. She grinned, showing off her dimples full-blown now. Her face always broke into a smile; it was more a habit than a reflection of her true feelings. He realized that now.

"Stuff like what?" he asked.

"Love . . . maybe even love at first sight," she said hesitantly, looking him straight on now.

"You didn't love me." He sat back hard in the seat, unable to keep the stunned look from his face.

She shook her head, staring down at the crumbs on her plate. "I thought I did," she admitted. "And then I met my husband, and he changed my mind on that. I always wondered what I would do when I saw you again. I thought, God help me, I'm gonna scratch his eyes out."

"Woo." He chuckled, trying to keep the moment light, covering his eyes as if protecting them. She laughed and shoved at his arm playfully.

"But people grow up, they change. Now I see my son growing up, and I look at him thinking, one day he's gonna meet somebody, and he's not gonna get it, and she's gonna think—"

"You have a son; chhhheeesus, I never even asked if you had children."

"Yes, I have three. My son, Darrell, and my daughters, Lashay and Shequetta," she answered.

Sebastian let the ethnic names roll around in his head for a moment and then allowed a smile to come to his lips. He remembered the smells of Stormy's small apartment—ethnic smells, fried foods, boiled meats, hair oils, and pressing combs; comfortable smells, familiar. She talked constantly, popping gum and fidgeting with his hair, which she referred to as "good hair." He remembered watching her mouth move, the way he watched it now, although now . . .

His cell phone went off. He glanced at it; it was Ta'Rae.

"It's my wife," he said without hesitation. Stormy cleared her throat and stood quickly.

"No, no, it's not like that," Sebastian said, easing what he felt to be awkwardness.

"Not like what?" she asked.

"Look, I'm dealing with some things right now, and you might be just the person to help me."

Stormy's head cocked to the side. He knew he was being bold in asking, but he had to. "Can I see you again?" he asked.

"No," she answered flatly.

"Why?"

"I don't know what issues you have right now or what you're dealing with, you and your wife, but I'm not the one," she said, shaking her head and heading out of the café. Sebastian laid a bill on the table to cover the coffee and pie and hurried out behind her.

"No, I just have some questions. I'm just trying to get some peace," he called.

She stopped dead in her tracks and spun on her heels.

"Peace! How selfish is that! And you think that you have the right to ask me to help you find it, to come in my life, fuck it all up—again!" she said while storming back to where he stood. "So that you can find happiness? You think that is what I was put on this earth for? My life is perfect—at least that is how I see it, and you have no right to come in here and impose your quest for peace on me. You have no right to come in here and change my perception of perfection for me!" she vented, poking her finger into his chest.

Her vocabulary stunned him. She sounded like a survivor of much counseling, as if her words had been recorded, put in her brain via a tape-recorded message played over and over until she could recite it by rote if the time or need for recital ever came—like now.

"Well . . . that was a mouthful," Sebastian remarked, not meaning to sound as heartless as he had.

"You son of a bitch!" she screamed, slapping him hard across the face. They both stood silent for a moment, feeling the heat their exchange had created. Stormy's chest heaved, and her head lightened. Quickly, she covered her mouth, hiding the remainder of shock still showing on her face. "I'm sorry . . . I—" she began.

He raised his hand to silence her. "I guess I deserved that . . . then. But for now, Stormy, I'm just glad I ran into you, and to be honest, I would just like to see you again," Sebastian continued, speaking with a determined air chasing his words.

"No," she said again, firmer this time and with the same amount of determination.

"I don't want to sleep with you or change your life—"

"It's too late for that, Sebastian. You already did both those things," she said, and then dodging traffic, she hurried back into the store.

Precious was beside herself. How could her father do this to them—to her?

What was with all this not-telling-her stuff?

"What is that all about? I'm not a child. I'm a grown-ass woman," she said out loud, sounding harsh and brash, like Rosey. "And to find out by accident this way. How rude is that? I'm a doctor's daughter. I know how to read a chart. Ugh," she groaned, burying her head in her hands.

"Don't cry, baby, yo man is here," Drake said, sliding up beside her. He sounded lighthearted and full of play. She looked at him, forcing the worry from her brow.

"Your bus musta been early, cuz damn, I just got off the phone wit choo," he noticed, looking at his cell phone, verifying the time. He knew he was closer to the park than she was. Surely she flew on love's wing to meet him. The thought made him grin. He kissed her quickly on the cheek, wanting to see her smile back at him. It was reluctant at first, but then it slowly crept onto her lips.

"What's wrong, baby?" he asked.

Precious thought about all that was on her mind, all the secrets her father had kept from her these last few weeks.

She'd found out about the cancer three days after he

got the diagnosis. He'd left his papers out on his desk. She'd stopped by his office on her way home from school. Getting past his secretary had never been a problem. The woman had always liked her and would allow her into her daddy's office to wait instead of in the lobby with the patients.

That day, she sat at his desk to see how it felt to be in that large leather chair, looking out over the city from the seventh-story window, but instead she saw the report.

She read it over and over again, hoping that it was wrong or maybe just a confidential report for a patient who wanted a consultation, but no. It was his prognosis in that report. Tears could not reach her eyes as fast as the news hit her brain. She slammed the folder closed and just sat staring into space, still seeing the words as if they were floating by her eyes.

When her father came into the office, he'd played it off really well, covering the papers with a stack of patient files. Her stomach tightened, thinking he would say something about the file. But when he didn't, she grew angry. Watching him cover his tracks sickened her—how he immediately decided they should go to lunch at her favorite restaurant, where he spent over fifty bucks. And then he gave her his credit card to use. As furious as she was by then, hell yeah, she hit the mall.

She realized that her father was not going to be truthful and that Drake was the only person on this planet she could trust. She knew Drake would have to be the man in her life now.

Even that night at dinner, she had tried to get the truth out of her father. But there was nothing, just some stupid banter between him and her mother about some new painting they wanted to buy and some dinner parties coming up and where they would go for the summer.

Summer? Colorectal cancer was serious. Would there even be a summer? Precious asked herself before finally shaking the morbid thoughts from her head, realizing that Drake was staring at her. She wrapped her arms around his neck tightly.

"I'm your girl?" she asked.

He snickered shyly and looked around as if wanting privacy before answering. "You know that," he finally answered. "Since the first time I laid eyes on yor fine ass I was like, dayummm." He grinned, kissing her on the lips.

They'd been kissing for a long time, but that was all. She enjoyed kissing Drake. He had been the first to kiss her, and now she felt like a professional. He'd taught her so much and didn't even know it. Drake seemed to be waiting for her to make the first move. Precious was glad in a way, considering she had no clue what that move would be. Sure, she'd read medical books on the subject of sex, but putting the application with the theory just had not all come together yet in her mind.

Coming back to the now, allowing him to explore her mouth with his tongue, engaging hers in playful volley, she felt fever rising inside her. He always had that effect on her. She so enjoyed the little tingle she felt in her lower abdomen. She wanted to kiss him this way forever.

"You got me . . . uhh . . ." He chuckled, causing his dimples to crevice his cheeks while not taking his lips from hers when he spoke. He took her hand and placed it where it had never been before; she felt his hardness through his jeans.

"I do?" She giggled, not taking her lips from his, talking through the kiss.

"Yeah, let's get outta here," he suggested, taking her by the hand.

Speaking covertly to the guy at the door, Drake gained entry to an apartment. Precious looked around at the obvious bachelor pad. Beer cans and smoking paraphernalia lay around, along with big pillows and small car parts. The television was blasting on the Cartoon Network. She looked at the glassy-eyed young man who had opened the door. His hair was wild and his clothes wrinkled and unkempt. He resembled Drake a lot, besides all that negative stuff.

"Precious, this is my brother, Collin," he introduced.

Collin attempted politeness; however, he could only muster a grunt and a nod in the condition he was in.

"What day is it? Are the buses runnin'?" Collin asked.

Drake smacked his lips and scowled at his high brother. "Man, you stay too fucked up all the time . . . shit," Drake fussed, fanning his hand at him while looking in the fridge. He took out two beers and then focused back on Precious. She smiled nervously.

Strolling toward her, he stopped in the hallway and then with a toss of his head, he motioned for her to join him in the bedroom. She noticed Collin putting on his jacket, and extended her hand. He looked at it and then at Drake.

"It was nice meeting you, Collin," she said. Collin smiled crookedly and then shook her hand, grunting a good-bye to the two of them.

"Collin? That's a nice name," she said, easing past Drake into the bedroom.

"Yeah, my mom watched a lot of soaps and sooo . . . But then you know I'm changing my name to Theory, right?" he answered, noticing then her distraction with the posters on the wall and the trinkets all around on the desk, along with the notepads, doodles, and what looked like poetry. She reached for a pad only to have him spin her around to face him, pulling her into a one-armed embrace.

"So you wanna beer?" he asked.

"Yeah," she answered quickly—too quickly. He sat the beers on the thick futon mattress that lay on the floor without a frame.

Flopping down, he pulled her with him. He playfully wrestled her free from her shoes, and he kicked off his own.

"Oh it's like that, huh?" she flirted, removing his beanie and tossing it across the room. He frowned and pushed the bottles of beer from her reach.

"You can forget having my brewsky, messing with my hat like that," he said, kidding around.

"No, I need a drink," she insisted, reaching for the bottle. He pulled her back. She laughed and playfully tussled with him for a moment only to find herself pinned under him, breathing heavily. He, too, was a little winded from the play. The residual of their laughter was all that was heard against the backdrop of cartoon slapstick coming from the television in the other room. Their gaze locked, and again she felt his hardness pressing against her. She audibly gulped, as she anticipated what would come next.

Gaining advantage, she climbed on top of him, straddling him. His eyes covered her like a heated blanket as he reached under her blouse and unhooked her bra, slid his hands to her front, and cupped her small perky breasts.

His touch was fire, and she seethed instantly, sucking air through her teeth. Her nipples hardened.

He slowly removed her sweatshirt over her head, watching her long hair fall over her pretty face. He'd never seen anyone so beautiful before, so perfect.

"Precious," he heard himself say, "you wanna do this?" She said nothing; only her eyes answered, taking him in.

His erection pushed hard against the thick fabric of his jeans. He could tell she felt it as she glanced down at that area. He pushed her off of him and removed his pants. Drake undressed completely while Precious watched, sitting now in the corner of the mattress, covering her breasts with her knees pulled up to her. She looked scared.

"Ready?" he asked. She said nothing, her eyes wide, doelike. He pulled back the comforter and slid under, hoping she would join him. Finally, he opened the corner of it, inviting her. She quickly got under, sliding into his waiting embrace.

"Do you love me?" he asked her. She said nothing, only nodding against his chest. "You know I would never hurt you," he said, stroking her hair, her shoulders, her waist, and then the top of her jeans. "Take these off," he whispered in her ear.

She moved slowly under the blankets while removing the rest of her clothing.

He wanted so badly to see her naked body, yet he knew he had to be patient. He sensed her need for time.

"You okay?" he asked her after giving her a moment to accept her nakedness.

In the meantime, Drake tried to think back to his first time. It had been fast and furious. He was awkward—she was a whore.

This was going to be different. He wanted it to be different, special.

Prying her frozen hands from her breasts, he moved them away and kissed them before placing them at her sides. Slowly he kissed her on her neck while fondling her mounds, before he started to kiss them, taking them between his full lips. She responded by moaning loudly as if what she felt was the best thing ever.

He didn't know what she was thinking, but for him, the thought of being the best thing ever for someone made him smile.

Her eyes were closed when he looked at her, and he kissed her again before moving down on her body, enjoying it thoroughly as she moaned with each area he touched with hands or lips. He reached her thighs and attempted to part them slightly. She at first resisted, clamping them together tightly and then, upon his whispered request, she complied.

"I'm not gonna hurt you," he repeated. Kissing her between her firm slender thighs, stroking her lightly until she again gave way to sounds of pleasure, he enjoyed the fresh sweetness and sensations she gave him as he orally pleased her—her body rising and falling, urging him to explore her further, completely.

Physically she was more than ready for him, but he had to be sure she was mentally at one with him. He would not lose her love over this act. He would not allow her to regret a moment spent with him. This could wait if he had any thoughts that it would ruin what they had been developing together over this last month.

She was what he wanted deep inside. Never had a female affected him the way she had.

"Baby, I'ma do this . . . I can't wait no longer," he whispered in her ear. She nodded, opening her mouth and eyes to take him in one more time before it was confirmed—locked in stone. No turning back.

"It's gonna hurt a little," he guaranteed her. Being truthful would save him a lot of drama in the end. "And then it's gonna be nothing but good," he assured, tearing open the package that was on the dresser and rolling on the condom.

Her eyes widened as she watched, and then her eyes rolled back as he pushed against her virginity. When he pierced her thick wall of innocence, she cried out in a high-pitched shrill that would stay in his ears forever. He kissed her and apologized, stroking her hair, feeling her body fighting, reluctant to give away what it had held on to for so long.

"I love you, girl," he told her. "God, I love you," he whispered, barely able to speak as the pleasure of her uncharted womanhood filled him to near capacity.

She scratched his back as he took what she freely gave him, working with him in a new rhythm—awkward at first and then settling into a pattern, one he hoped would be theirs forever.

Her cries soon eased into sounds of pleasure, the song of true love being written, love in the making. This was no longer just sex. Drake knew that. They were making love. It was like what he'd often heard about in the songs playing on the radio. This was no gangsta sorta love; this was innocent. This was pure. This was some Lutha kinda shit.

Suddenly she began to jerk and speak in tongues as

she orgasmed for the first time in her life. "What's happening to me?" she cried out breathlessly.

"Let it come, baby, let it come." He joined her in full voice, releasing his passion into the sheath that separated them. She was shaking. He wanted to laugh at her, with her, but he knew she was scared.

Pulling away from her, he was careful to keep the condom intact. A mess up right now would ruin the whole thing. "It's okay," he said, comforting her. After tossing the condom, he covered her with the blanket and held her close to him.

"It's so cold," she said, her teeth chattering. He chuckled slightly. "What?" she asked him, grinning broadly.

That was what he was waiting for—her smile. He kissed her.

"Well, you bringing all that wind with that jumping around you was doin'."

"Stop." She giggled, slapping his chest.

"Thank you," he whispered in her ear.

"For what?" she asked, looking innocent.

He kissed the palm of her hand. Precious was affected. She had seen her father do the same to her mother, and now she felt she understood why. She blushed, moving her hair out of her face. Her watch caught her attention.

"You got some place to be?" he asked. Her mouth opened.

Precious knew she needed to call home to check in. Since the night they went to the Marina, she'd tried to keep her end of the communication deal, calling every few hours. Her mother would be getting home right about now. But the more she thought about what had just happened, the less she wanted to be at home. In fact, she never wanted to leave Drake's arms again.

"No, I don't have to be anywhere but here," she answered, pushing the thought of home completely out of her mind.

Drake reached over and grabbed the earlier discarded beers.

"I'm thirsty as hell," he said, still basking in the glow, chuckling to himself, satisfied.

"Drake . . ."

He turned to her.

"Was it . . . good for you?" she asked.

His head went back in laughter.

At dinner, Ta'Rae and Sebastian sat silently assessing their week, ciphering what they would share and what they would not.

"I didn't get a chance to tell you that I made my appointment for the resection," Sebastian said, leading the charge.

Ta'Rae sat down her spoon and folded her hands, tucking them neatly under her chin, trying to hide the fact that her appetite had just flown out the window at the mere mention of the upcoming procedure.

"I'll be out of commission for about a week, but I spoke to Bender, and I can have the time. He can handle my patients with no problem. It's not like I've taken any personals recently," he meandered, finishing his vegetables with vigor.

The meal had all the markings of a hospital dinner menu for the weak and infirm. However, Sebastian wasn't about to complain. He knew he was in good hands. Ta'Rae would take good care of him, if this meal was any indication.

"Okay . . . ," she replied after a heavy sigh, sounding as if she was bucking up for the changes to come.

"The rush is on I guess, because they are proceeding next Friday," he said, pretending not to notice Ta'Rae's loud gasp.

"So are we telling Precious?"

"By the way, where is Precious?" he asked.

"She's with her friends again." Ta'Rae immediately got back on point. "So soon?" she asked.

"Yes, Hyatt wants to get this behind us so we can get to the issue of possible chemo," Sebastian continued, sounding brave and almost nonchalant about the whole thing.

"Good idea," Ta'Rae interjected, their conversation taking on the tone of a consultation between colleagues.

"I called you today. Where were you?" Ta'Rae asked.

Sebastian froze for a second before answering. He looked at the carrot and then bit it softly. He'd made another trip to the Men's Wearhouse. Stormy hadn't been there.

"Went looking for a suit," he answered.

She smiled and shrugged. "You always look good in a new suit," Ta'Rae flirted. Sebastian's eyes caught hers. He thought about the past—how hurt she would be if she knew how lightly he had taken his vow when they first married. How would he fix it? Back then, he had no idea how much he would love her now.

"Ta'Rae," he began, "if things don't go well—"

"Sebastian," she interrupted.

He raised his hand. "Let me say this. If things don't go well, I want you to know that I've always loved you.

No matter what comes with all of this, please just remember that I love you," he repeated.

Ta'Rae nodded, swallowing hard. Her expression said she truly understood what he was saying.

"What will come?" she asked.

"I have no idea," he answered with a worried chuckle.

Ta'Rae felt her stomach tighten.

"You do realize that without this surgery, I could just take my chances that the tumors won't grow—"

"And with it, the cancer will be *bothered* and therefore will grow faster than before," she interjected.

"If they are malignant, I'll be dead within two years," he said.

"God, Sebby." Ta'Rae turned her head, holding her fist to her mouth to keep from crying out. She turned back. "How could you have ignored your symptoms so long?"

"Well, I didn't, not really. I was kind of wondering, when the discomfort and slight bleeding started about a year ago—"

"A year ago? Why didn't you tell me?" she blurted.

"I didn't want to bother you with it. I just figured it was maybe like hemorrhoids or something," Sebastian admitted.

"And what, you're too cool to tell me about hemorrhoids?" Ta'Rae fussed.

"What does that mean?"

"Look at you," Ta'Rae exclaimed. "Mr. Perfect. Heaven forbid you have a hair out of place let alone a little thing like a hemorrhoid or bleeding from the rectum," she screeched.

"And what about you, missy? I haven't seen you sharing too many of your bathroom issues with me.

When's the last time you had a bowel movement, oh, or passed some gas? When was it, Rae? During dinner here, did you let out a little toot or two?" Sebastian jeered, growing more animated. Ta'Rae's discomfort showed.

She fanned him on. "Stop it, Sebastian. You're just being gross now," she snipped angrily.

"Ta'Rae, you know as well as I do what can happen. I can go bald from the chemo. And our sex life . . ." He dug deeper.

"Stop, Sebby."

Sebastian got up and moved slowly over to her side of the table while still speaking in graphic generalities about what could be in store for them.

"Sebastian, stop! I can't handle this right now. This isn't intimacy. This is abusive."

"Get used to it, baby, because I've got colon cancer, and if you can't get intimate with me now, you never will be able to. It's not going to be pretty at all, Ta'Rae." He glowered, standing over her. "And I'm not a patient. I'm your husband. This is in our face, your face."

Just then, Precious walked in.

"What's going on here?" she asked, seeing her parents at each other's throats.

Ta'Rae pushed Sebastian back and jumped to her feet. "Nothing. Daddy was being rude," Ta'Rae excused.

"Yeah, I was talking about my bathroom habits, comparing them with your mother's. Hey, by the way, did you have a bowel movement today?" he asked Precious, who immediately frowned.

"Dad, you are getting so gross." She giggled.

"See, honey, I can talk to Precious here about it," Sebastian said, his tone lightening up.

Ta'Rae, who had yet to recover from the verbal

abuses, smiled tightly, then said, "Well, that's because she deals with gross people all day."

"I do not," Precious blurted, louder than intended, gaining both her parents' attention. They both looked at her.

"Okaaay," Ta'Rae remarked, sounding relieved to take her mind off the conversation with Sebastian and put it elsewhere.

"Seriously, Mom, why would you say that? My friends are very cool," Precious insisted, pouting her full lips.

"Cool? You kids don't know cool."

"Oh paaalease," Precious retorted. Ta'Rae jerked her neck tauntingly, yet with a playful intention behind it. Sebastian watched his two favorite girls horsing around. It warmed his heart.

"Why don't you have your friends over, then?" Sebastian asked. "We don't rate cool?"

Precious, pulling her hair down from the ponytail and shaking it loose, just rolled her eyes. "Don't even, Dad."

Sebastian noticed her with her hair down. How much older she looked than her age. With her smooth face and physical development, she was definitely a Nubian beauty. But then, in his opinion, with a mother like Ta'Rae, how could Precious be less? Often Sebastian felt that Ta'Rae was embarrassed about her size, her height, her thick limbs and heavy hips. She dieted constantly, hoping to appear petite or Twiggyish—which was never going to happen. She was solid, and that was that.

The thought of her body made Sebastian smile. She was a beautiful woman. He felt blessed to have her.

The thought of another man taking his place one day—any day—was something he could not handle right now.

He made a mental note to address that issue with Hilton on his next visit—along with the new situation. Stormy Brown-Gunther.

Terrell made it to the office today. Maybe having a nanny was going to work out.

After Rita got home from the hospital, it had been decided as necessary; even though Terrell didn't want some strange, weird, flaky-teenage-looking freak up in his house around his kids, the girl, Kenita, had moved in.

"And don't think I'm not gonna run a background check on her," Terrell said. Nigel just smiled, making a mental note to make sure Qiana never stood on any chairs. This whole situation with Rita had gone completely beyond logic. Terrell was about to lose his mind, or maybe responsibilities were to blame for his irritability.

"Okay, well, we have an appointment with this woman today—another mother wanting us to represent her *oh so innocent* hoodlum son," Nigel informed, looking tired of the same ol' thing.

"What? Another kid that didn't do anything wrong?"

"Exactly. This one didn't jack a car and assault a gas station attendant."

"Are we just about tired of all these kinds of clients or what?" Terrell sighed. "Lawd, is anybody paying fa all this?" Terrell asked.

"Actually, yes, I was quite surprised—a healthy little retainer too. Hard-working single parent. It's sad to have her waste her money this way."

Terrell's attention returned to the intake file that Nigel had put together on the potential client. He had to admit that since taking on their new partner, a female attorney/former district attorney, their client list had darkened; yet, oddly enough, revenue had increased.

Around noon they arrived, mother with son practically in tow. The boy was over eighteen, yet his mother still yielded a heavy hand.

He had been arrested on assault and grand theft auto charges.

"Look how little he is. Now you tell me how in the world he is supposed to have beat that man up like that," his mother protested. "I want a private investigator involved and, like, whoever else you need to get this matter resolved and prove my boy innocent. Oh, and that car thang, he was not alone in that. We 'bouta name some names," the mother fussed on. She was a black woman with pretty, small features that probably once belonged on a pretty, small body, gauging by the small size of the boy, but now after years of bad choices and compulsive eating, those features now lay on a large frame. She huffed heavily, settling her eyes on her son who shifted uncomfortably in the seat.

"Is this what you want, Tiger? You want us to work for you?" Nigel asked the boy, who looked at him with a scowl.

"It's Tigger, and hell yeah that's what I want, foo'," he said between clenched teeth.

"Well, you're not gonna get it if you don't act like a man and get some respect jumpin' off in his joint," Nigel quickly replied, losing all hint of professionalism.

The mother snickered to herself and then glanced at Terrell, who was also in the middle of his own private laughter. Nigel was cracking them both up with his attempt at getting on the same level with the boy Tigger.

Tigger almost went off. But he was already in trouble for his temper. *Yeah, I beat the hell outta that guy. He was all up in my bizness. What of it? And that car? It was just sitting there in front of that fancy restaurant—easy pickings, askin' to be stole as far as I'm concerned.*

He looked around the small office at the pictures sitting all around—blacks and whites mingled through the family portraits.

"Oh I get it now," he mumbled under his breath, understanding suddenly why the white guy thought he was down like that.

His eyes continued to glance over the pictures while his mother spoke with the attorneys on his behalf. Just then, he caught sight of a familiar face.

"Who is that?" he asked, interrupting the conversation between his mother and the attorneys.

Terrell looked at him and then at the picture. "Somebody you will never meet," Terrell said flatly.

"Funny, guy. Hell, I already know her."

"Please, everybody's got a twin, and you musta met hers, because there is no way in the world you've met my niece—unless of course you stole her car or something. She wouldn't be running in your circles, young man," Terrell explained.

"Whatever," Tigger said with an ugly smirk coming onto his face. "You guys always think you know stuff. Y'all don't know nut-n from nut-n."

The week flew by. Precious managed to get to Drake only once more before Friday. She had needed to see him before her father's surgery date. She needed to feel him close to her before her life changed forever.

Their lovemaking was more passionate than the first time—wilder, and she less inhibited. She had so much on her mind, and Drake could take her so far from her realities. She would give him whatever he wanted just to go with him.

"Damn them," she cursed her parents, realizing that they still had not even alluded to the fact that her father was going under the knife in less than twenty-four hours. She had found out by snooping around again.

"And what if he dies?" she growled, angry and hurt, realizing her parents' lack of appreciation for her maturity and her need to know. "What if he dies tomorrow?" she asked herself again.

She was in her father's home library. She'd been reading up on the cancer he had, reading with full understanding of the treatments and procedures. Figuring out on her own what stage of cancer her father might be in.

"Since nobody is telling me nothing," she spat.

"Chemo . . . Oh my God, he's gonna need chemo," she said while reading, feeling her eyes burning. She slammed the book closed.

Her cell phone vibrated on her hip.

Drake.

"No, I don't even want to go here with him. He can't possibly understand what I'm going through," she reasoned, thinking about his carefree lifestyle. How could he relate to something so serious as this?

Drake was her getaway from all this real stuff. It would ruin everything they had developed to drag him into her world right now. He knew nothing about her life as the daughter of two successful doctors, as a debutant whose parents belonged to an elite social club and hobnobbed with the rich and famous. Drake had no clue about any of her life as Precious York.

"Thank God," Precious mumbled, noticing her father's carafe of brandy sitting on the large cherrywood desk. She moved over to it, looking around as if the walls now had eyes.

She poured herself a drink. The liquid burned going down. It was a good burn though, a soothing burn. While she felt it, good thoughts ran through her mind. *Drake and his kisses, his love . . . her favorite class . . . her favorite color.* Taking another drink, she felt the room darkening, closing in. She needed to breathe.

She took the carafe and left the house.

Mrs. Blinky was waiting when Ta'Rae came through the front desk area. She looked through the divider at her.

"Mrs. Blinky, what are you doing here? Did you have an appointment?" she asked. Mrs. Blinky looked around nervously, and then suddenly her daughter came into the waiting room. Mrs. Blinky's daughter carried with her a cane.

"Here, Mother," she said, sounding ill-humored and impatient. Ta'Rae read disappointment on Mrs. Blinky's face. She had sent her daughter to get the cane, hoping to have a moment of Ta'Rae's time before she got back, and had failed.

"Are you having some problems?" Ta'Rae asked, thinking of her own life.

Tomorrow Sebastian would have surgery on his colon. They would remove the polyps and assess the cancer's progress. Remove it. Cure him.

After tomorrow, things would get back to normal.

She wanted so badly to believe that. Ta'Rae wanted to get back to minding Precious. She'd seemed distracted lately. Perhaps it was just the mood of the house—off-kilter.

"Yes, I uh, hurt," Mrs. Blinky said unconvincingly. Her daughter twisted her lips and glanced heavenward.

"Can you be a bit more vague, Mother? Sheesh," she remarked rudely. Ta'Rae read Mrs. Blinky's eyes and then the eyes of her daughter. The tension was there, the resentment felt, the anger. Ta'Rae could see the denial in her daughter's eyes, the lack of acceptance of her mother's pain—although it was mostly emotional pain, something still hurt.

"It's okay; I can see your mother. My last patient has stood me up, so I'm free." Ta'Rae smiled, tapping the front desk receptionist on the shoulder and shaking her head slightly, instructing that Mrs. Blinky not be put on the schedule as an add on so that she would not be billed. The receptionist caught on immediately and went back to her computerized solitaire game.

Opening the door, Ta'Rae led Mrs. Blinky into an empty examining room, instructing her daughter to wait in the lobby. The woman huffed and left the office completely. "Call my cell phone when she's done," she called over her shoulder.

The room was dark, but Ta'Rae knew Sebastian wasn't asleep. She craved his body but didn't want to push things. He was having surgery in the morning. She knew he needed all of his strength.

For days she wanted to touch him, feel him close to her, be one with her. Their years together meant so much to her, and she had never given a thought of life without him, but this week, she felt the winds of change blowing into their bedroom window. She felt a strong sense of invasion coming over her mind and heart. At first it scared her, but then, over the last couple of days, a strange feeling began to comfort her. It felt like her mother's arms around her, encasing her, protecting her.

"How silly is that?" she asked herself.

That night, Ta'Rae fed Sebastian well, and the evening was a quiet one. Ta'Rae's friends had canceled dinner plans using the lamest of excuses. Ta'Rae didn't mind, nor did she fight it. She knew a brush-off when she got one. She'd been doing that to her family for months. For years every first Sunday of the month Carlotta cooked for the family, yet Ta'Rae had become pretty creative at finding ways not to attend the gathering.

Sebastian hated missing the dinners, but after a while he seemed to accept that she just didn't want to go anymore and left it at that. He never asked her why she didn't want to go, and actually she really didn't know why. She didn't know why she was feeling many of the feelings she had lately toward her sisters.

While Ta'Rae's mind drifted back to the first time she got out of the standing invitation to Carlotta's, from under the comforter, Sebastian's hands began to wander. She turned to him and kissed him lightly on the lips, running her fingers through his soft hair. He returned the affection, touching her face, her lips and hair.

"I want you," he whispered, kissing her again.

"You should rest," she suggested.

Instead, he moved atop her. "I've got plenty of time for resting, Rae. We've got to love each other as much as we can before—"

She shushed him and held him tight.

"Do you know yet about the sexual side effects of the chemo treatment?" Ta'Rae asked.

"I didn't even want to ask," Sebastian admitted, stroking her legs gently, easing himself into her.

She closed her eyes, moving with him in the rhythm that had been theirs for a lifetime—slow, deliberate. He came before she did and moved off her quickly, without lingering.

"I'm sorry."

"No . . . no, don't be."

"I've just had so much on my mind, and it's all catching up to me."

"I can only imagine."

They lay silent next to each other; it was obvious they both had secret thoughts—thoughts too deep to share.

Finally, Sebastian spoke up. "Have you ever stopped to think that you might be punished for thinking too highly of yourself?" he asked.

"What?" Ta'Rae asked, rising up on her elbow.

"Have you ever really honestly looked at your life and thought, 'I'm a haughty jackass, and now I'm gonna pay for it'?" he asked.

Ta'Rae laughed. "No."

"Well, I've been thinking about it a lot lately," he admitted.

"Then stop it. You're perfect, Sebastian."

"No . . . no, I'm not," he said, shushing her with his hand over her mouth. She pulled it away.

"Yes, you are. You're the perfect husband, faithful, true," she went on. Sebastian groaned loudly. "A perfect father, attentive and—"

Just then, they heard a bumbling noise coming from

outside the door. It was a sound different from what should have been Precious coming home. Sebastian jumped up, adjusting his pajama pants and pulling on his robe. Ta'Rae followed close behind him, tightening her robe.

Bravely Sebastian jerked open the bedroom door. It was Precious. She had come up the staircase and stumbled on her way to her bedroom, dropping her purse through the rails on the banister. It had fallen down to the tile foyer below, emptying its contents.

"Shit," she groaned, sliding down onto the cool wood floor. Her hair was all over her head, and it was obvious she was intoxicated—the smell was a giveaway if nothing else.

"What the hell is going on here?" Sebastian yelled, clicking on the light. Precious, on the floor, rolled over on her back to look at him, shielding her face from the light shining brightly in her eyes.

"Daaaaaamn," she moaned, and then attempted to get to her feet.

Ta'Rae couldn't speak. Everything from way back in her roots was rushing forward, fueled by the same temper and lack of tolerance for breaking the rules she remembered her mother having. There was no time for formalities or anything else cultured, prim, or proper— Zenobia Ams was filling her, and Precious was about to catch hell.

If anyone from the country club had been passing by, surely the Yorks would have lost their membership because within seconds, Ta'Rae lost it completely.

Ta'Rae was on Precious like the proverbial white on rice, grabbing her to her feet with almost superhuman speed and strength.

"I'm gonna beat your ass," she said, shaking Precious like a rag doll. Sebastian attempted to pull her off. But it was of no use; Ta'Rae was beyond reason and control.

Precious began howling like a wounded animal. Fear and inebriation were clouding her senses, but she admitted to nothing.

"Ta'Rae, let her go," Sebastian said.

"Let me gooo," Precious whined.

"With all that's going on, you have the nerve to do this?" Ta'Rae yelled.

"What's going on?" Precious asked, trying to sound cognizant.

"Nothing, Precious, nothing," Sebastian interjected, finally managing to pull her free from Ta'Rae.

"Go to your room," he instructed forcefully, spinning her around in the direction of her room.

Precious heaved once and let go of her stomach's contents.

"Shit!" Ta'Rae hollered.

Precious dropped to her knees with pain-filled groans.

"I'm calling somebody's parents right now! Who were you drinking with? Who bought the liquor?" Ta'Rae asked with her voice still loud. Precious started crying pitifully, leaning against the banister, hoping to maybe support herself or get to her feet somehow.

"Nobody . . . I was drinking alone," she cried.

"Don't lie, Precious. You best tell me who!" Ta'Rae yelled in her face, up close and personal. She then grabbed her shoulders and began shaking her again.

"I'm upset, Mama . . . I'm . . ." She glanced at her father. There was something in Precious's eyes that spoke to Sebastian. At just that second, he felt he understood completely what she meant.

"Rae, let it go. We'll figure it out tomorrow. Let it go," Sebastian suggested strongly, helping Precious to her feet, careful to avoid the mess she had made on the hardwood floor.

"I love you, Daddy," she simpered, leaning against him. "I love you so much," she whispered, grabbing him tight around his waist.

Sebastian caught Ta'Rae's eyes. She was glaring angrily at the both of them.

"Daddy loves you too, baby," Sebastian told Precious.

The surgery went quickly as Dr. Apollo Punjab opened Sebastian up and then closed without much else to be done. There would be no need for a lot of prying around. The cancerous cells were spreading too quickly to stop them.

Gasping for air, Precious's lungs burned and the tears poured down her cheeks. Drake pulled back. He'd filled her mouth with smoke from his hit.

He'd called it a *supercharge*.

It was the first time they had gotten high together. It wasn't like he'd suggested it since she'd never asked. It seemed that every time they had all gotten together for that purpose, Precious had refused. But not tonight. Tonight Precious had hung in, actually sitting in with them at Tigger's place, smoking.

The laughter was heavy and the music loud, yet Drake noticed Precious's lack of involvement in the merriment. Her tears were more than just from the smoke. They were from emotion.

"What's wrong, baby?" he asked her, rubbing her thighs. She smiled and shook her head, fanning him closer, wanting another hit from him. He obliged her and then looked at her responding the same way as the first time—gasping and coughing. She knew so little about things. It was hard for him to believe she was twenty-two years old. Actually, he figured she wasn't really that old.

Precious had not cried when her mother told her the truth—the whole truth about her father's condition.

Finally.

"So how long?" Precious asked her concerning her father's fate.

"With chemo we can fight this thing," Ta'Rae answered yet not answered, while smiling tightly.

"Fight it?" Precious asked Drake, sounding high and confused. Drake had no clue what she was talking about. "How can you fight the inevitable?" Precious went on to explain, gesturing emphatically.

"You can't," he answered, kissing her. She offered him a sloppy one, unable to control herself now. He laughed at her awkwardness. He had to admit he was a little high too.

Collin copped some good shit this time.

He looked around at the others who had moved on to something stronger. Tigger caught his eye and offered the pipe to him. Drake declined, pulling Precious tighter into his lap. She was nodding against his chest, giggling in between saddened whimpers.

"But if somebody is gonna die . . . I mean . . . ," she began, raising her head to see Drake's face. He shushed her quickly.

"Nobody is gonna die," he said.

"Oh yeah, he's gonna die," she insisted, holding up her fingers—two and then one and then three. "Hell, I don't know when, but he's gonna die," she said, releasing more tears now.

Rosey and Money had started making out, giving in to their inhibitions as if no one was around. Tigger looked at Drake and Precious.

Drake noticed his eyes on her ass. Was he lusting after her? Was his best friend after his woman?

"What you lookin' at, Tigger?"

"I'm lookin' at her," he admitted freely.

"Well stop it," Drake barked, catching the attention of Collin, who grinned wickedly, settling on a little self-stimulation.

"Yeah, stop lookin' at her ass; that's Drake's department." He laughed stupidly. "He's been lookin' at it enough for everybody lately." He cackled.

"Shuddap," Drake fussed, realizing that although Precious was dozing against him, she might easily hear their crude remarks.

Precious was special. There was no way he was sharing her with Tigger and Collin—no way. He was younger when Rosey had been "their" girl. Those days of communal sex were over, besides, the way Rosey had been going at it with Money lately, apparently she felt the same way.

"Yeah, I need to tell you something about yo gurl," Tigger said, sounding slightly insidious.

Drake nudged Precious, making sure she was asleep. She did not respond.

"There's nothing you can tell me, Tig. Just stop, aiight? No drama zone," Drake added, fanning the area around himself and Precious. Tigger smacked his lips and went back to the pipe.

"Punk," Tigger grumbled.

"What?" Drake asked.

"Nothing," Tigger lied.

Sebastian came home after a few days. His recovery from the surgery was quick, and within a week he was back on his feet, milling around the house and calling his office.

"Being nosy," Sandy, his secretary, called it.

They'd not talked about the cancer as a family, although Sebastian had called Hilton for an appointment as soon as he could get in. His visit with Hilton again gave him food for thought, information for action—positive action.

Sebastian suggested Ta'Rae get in to see her as soon as her schedule allowed for it.

"I'm not seeing a shrink, Sebby. You know how I've always felt about that," she fussed.

"I just think she's needed right now."

"No, you can see her. I have my friends in my corner," Ta'Rae explained, slightly and unconsciously wringing her hands. Sebastian knew then that Ta'Rae was not sure about whom she had in her corner of the ring.

Ta'Rae went to visit Carlotta. She knew she was unexpected because Carlotta actually did a double take when she heard the door jingle upon her entrance.

"I know you are not gracing my establishment," she said. Ta'Rae looked around anxiously and then sat. She was uneasy with this meeting, wanting to pretend it was like any other visit to her sister's place. But it had been nearly a year since she'd been to Carlotta's restaurant, and she hoped Carlotta wouldn't bring that up.

"Yes, and I'm hungry," she said as the aromas brought back a long-lost appetite.

"What can I get my baby sister?" Carlotta asked, stepping behind the counter, playfully shoving her waitress out of the way. "I got this. This here is royalty," she kidded.

"Carlotta, stop." Ta'Rae sighed.

"Trina had her party; oh, and Rita is doing okay too. They got a nanny to help T with the kids. She's weird, and I don't like her," Carlotta began to ramble quickly, Ta'Rae only catching half of what she was saying but nodding all the same.

Ta'Rae enjoyed hearing her sister's voice; it was soothing and needed like a cool glass of water on a hot day. Ta'Rae's urge to be around her sisters was strong lately, and it was getting harder to fight it—but she was trying.

The food came without her needing to order. Carlotta knew what she liked and just the way she liked it.

Chewing slowly, Ta'Rae continued to listen to Carlotta going on about her life. She talked about how she was dealing with the kids being gone and keeping her weight off through increased sex. Carlotta also filled Ta'Rae in on Rita and the kids. "Lawd, she don't need no mo'. Oh, and Trina has lost like forty pounds now, after finally listening to me," Carlotta said. Ta'Rae listened.

"And about Rashawn, did you know she is trying to actually be dean of that hellhole of a college she works at? They need to tear that place down and put up a Wal-

Mart; more people would want to go there." Carlotta chuckled before sipping her tea with her pinky up.

Ta'Rae snickered.

"And now you . . . What is up with you?" Carlotta finally asked.

Ta'Rae wiped the corner of her mouth with the napkin and thought, *My husband is dying of cancer. He could go any year, any day, any minute. We don't know yet because he's got to try the chemo that will take his hair, his looks, his strength . . . his virility.* But Ta'Rae answered, "Nothing."

Carlotta looked at her.

"You're lying," she said, pointing at her with an accusative finger.

"Carlotta, I'm not lying," Ta'Rae said timidly, in that way that said clearly, *Oh yes, I am and in a big way too.*

"Whatever, Ta'Rae. As Mama used to say—"

"Funny you should mention Mama," Ta'Rae interrupted, although Carlotta was already headed to the kitchen mumbling euphemisms their mother used to say.

"You coming to dinner this weekend?" Carlotta asked upon her return to the counter. She had two small bowls of pineapple sherbet—Ta'Rae's favorite.

Ta'Rae thought about Sebastian. He was up and about, and the outing would do him good; and as much as she didn't want to admit it, her too.

"Of course," she answered without delaying further. Carlotta grinned, licking the back of her spoon before filling it again with the sherbet.

ANGER

"You're looking kinda tired, Sebastian," Scott said, noticing Sebastian's hesitance before taking his swing at the ball. Their golf game had moved at a snail's pace.

"Got a lot on my mind I guess," Sebastian excused.

"Like what?"

"Real estate," Sebastian lied.

Scott owned one of the most prestigious real estate broker firms in the Bay Area. He was a self-made millionaire by the time he was forty; he was sixty now.

"Where?" Scott asked, taking his turn.

"The Palemos," Sebastian said, stunning Scott into temporary silence.

"You're kidding, right? You thinking of buying in the hood?" he asked, jesting about the neighborhood where Carlotta, Ta'Rae, and the others were from.

Sitting off from the more progressive neighborhoods, the Palemos had many families that still lived in this neighborhood of tract homes since its inception in the seventies. Misnamed after the mispronounced Palomino horse, the Palemos was a small community that had become a town unto itself.

With no more than three to six city blocks of houses and a narrow strip mall, the houses were all quaint and of equal size—about fifteen hundred square feet, with fenced yards and overgrown mature trees. Some buyers in the late eighties attempting to upgrade some of the homes caused only a strange mishmash—two-story glamour palaces next to cracker boxes. The neighborhood was a mess. It was a ghetto that had missed much funding and repairs, although it had not missed the increase in crime.

But the area lent itself to a homey feel, and it was where Rita still lived in their parents' house, and Rashawn, returning to the neighborhood, bought a place up the street from her two years ago. Even Qiana and Nigel were inhabitants of that small community. It was close living but comfortable for those who enjoyed that sort of thing. Ta'Rae had said many times it was not her preference.

Sebastian, growing up as a latch-key kid in the heart of San Francisco, always liked the Palemos, and for all the reasons Ta'Rae didn't—block parties, open barbeques, and even the smallest of holidays celebrated with gusto, loud music filling the air and the sound of children playing in the streets.

"I'll see what's on the market," Scott agreed as they loaded up his SUV. He looked again at Sebastian. Hearing Sebastian talk with such affection about the Palemos, Scott knew he was serious about wanting to buy there. But there was more to this; Scott could feel it. "You sure you feeling okay?" he asked.

Sebastian smiled. It had been a month since the surgery and the start of the chemo treatments. Ta'Rae had not spoken about it much, not to their friends, not even to him, but the time for all this denial was over. It was time to get real with this thing. He knew he would not be able to keep all this to himself any longer.

"I feel like shit," he told Scott, whose mouth hung open after hearing the news of Sebastian's condition for the first time. They stood by the car while Sebastian told him, Scott's hand gripping the door handle, frozen, unable to move an inch while he listened to all Sebastian had been through over the last few months, all he'd been dealing with without the support of their family to help him.

"And that's partly why I want to buy a house in the old neighborhood."

"Well . . . Damn, uh, are you working?" Scott asked awkwardly, rubbing his sweaty hands together. He'd grown tense while listening.

"Yeah, I'm seeing patients—consults mostly. To tell you the truth, those people are starting to make me sick—pardon the irony—with all their bitching about their noses and asses," Sebastian fussed, sounding nothing like his normal smooth and mild-mannered self. Scott chuckled at his comment, however. "Well, does anyone in your family know?" Scott asked, referring to any relatives of Sebastian's; although, in all the years that he and Ta'Rae had been married, no one had ever met any of Sebastian's relatives.

Sebastian smiled slowly. "You are my family, Scott."

Scott patted Sebastian on the shoulder and then pulled him into a tight manly hug—it was comforting for both of them.

"And so we were supposed to find out when . . . ?"

Scott asked after they released from each other and climbed into the car.

"I know what you're sayin', Scott, and to tell you the truth, I'm so tired of going round and round with Ta'Rae on this. She has insisted on dealing with this"—Sebastian made quotation marks in the air from where he sat in the passenger seat—"privately. I'm about to lose my mind," he confessed.

"I had a feeling something was going on though. Something in the way Ta'Rae looked the last time we were all together. The way she seemed to be guarding your conversation. You guys were acting like newlyweds . . . in a bad way."

Sebastian burst into laughter, nodding emphatically. "Let me know as soon as you find a house available and not totally falling apart," Sebastian said, climbing out of the car. They had reached the restaurant where they had met for breakfast prior to hitting the green. "I'm serious about wanting to buy there. I think it will be good for Ta'Rae to be around her sisters instead of way out where we are now, and Precious really needs some . . . something," he added, sounding a little concerned about Precious as well.

"You gonna sell the one you live in?"

"No, I think the move is just temporary. I wouldn't ask Ta'Rae to do that. She loves that house."

"I feel you. I've owned my house since I was in my thirties; I've put my life into it. There is no way I'm selling that place for anything . . . less," Scott explained. Houses in the Palemos were nowhere near the value of either man's home.

"I hear ya. I guess you could say I put my life into my house too." Sebastian chuckled. "And my job . . . and all sorts of things that will mean nothing in the end. So it's time to start putting my life into Ta'Rae and Precious and their future."

Sebastian looked at his watch. He had another doctor's appointment. Ta'Rae was going to meet him there. She'd been just short of motherly the last few weeks. Lately she was less of a wife and more of a caregiver. He wasn't sure if he liked it or not. No, the more he thought about it, the more he realized he hated it.

When he looked at Scott, he seemed caught up in deep thought.

"You okay?" Sebastian asked him.

"Yeah . . . I'm okay," he answered, smiling warmly.

Jeff Hyatt, Ta'Rae, and Sebastian looked over the X-rays, which showed the spread of the cancer, and then reviewed the latest progress reports since the beginning of the chemotherapy.

"I'm thinking that maybe . . . maybe we can do something else," Sebastian suggested. Ta'Rae all but pushed him out of the seat, punching him so hard.

"What he means, Jeff, is he's not been dealing well with the chemo. The vomiting has started," Ta'Rae interjected. "Oh, and the pain, what can we do about the discomfort he's begun to experience? I was thinking about—"

Sebastian ran his hand over his dry mouth and then over his thinning hair. "No, I'm saying I don't want to do this anymore. None of it! I'm sick of being sick," Sebastian fussed, raising his voice a little.

"Sebastian, don't be absurd. Of course you will continue the chemo; we just have to try to work with this—"

"We . . . no, I . . . I don't want to work with it," Sebastian blurted.

Jeff watched the both of them in silence as they bickered. Finally, after a few more heated exchanges, he interrupted. "Sebastian, I have a new medication for you to try that will help with the vomiting; however, it's going to have a new set of possible side effects that we need to explore. As far as the pain, well, morphine is always an option, but I'd like to hold off until—"

"You know, if the cancer doesn't kill me, these treatments sure as hell will," Sebastian said, chuckling sardonically. Jeff ignored him.

"Sebby, you promised you would not get like this," Ta'Rae bit.

He glared at her. "My name is Sebastian Conrad York, not Sebby, not Seb. It's Sebastian, Ta'Rae," he voiced, making himself crystal clear.

"Excuse the hell outta me," Ta'Rae huffed, slapping her thighs hard before jumping to her feet.

Jeff continued his explanation of the medicines and what Sebastian could, and should, expect with the passing of time.

"See you next week," Jeff said after finishing, handing Sebastian the prescription and walking out of the examination room.

Sebastian sat in silence while Ta'Rae began to gather Sebastian's clothes from the chair.

"Ta'Rae . . . honey," he blurted. She froze for a second and then continued to assist him. "I'm not an invalid," he went on, his volume lower now.

"I didn't say you were," she answered, holding out his shirt for him to put his arms in the sleeves. He sighed heavily.

"I don't want to argue with you," he admitted while obediently sliding into the shirt.

"But you have been," she informed him.

"I can't help it," he confessed.

"Yes . . . yes, you can," she went on, growing more emotional by the second.

Sebastian began to get angry again. "Ta'Rae! I'm trying to apologize here," he began, sounding far from sorry for his outburst earlier.

"Well, you're doing a piss-poor job of it," she said, with a newfound calmness in her voice, before heading for the door. "Meet me in two hours; I'm going to stop in on a patient and then meet you in the first-floor coffee shop," she instructed.

Sebastian slid from the chair and stared at his clothes as they hung on his frame. The trousers didn't fit right anymore, and that made him angry. The shirt was rumpled and wrinkled. His life was coming apart at the seams.

A man's gauge of togetherness is in his look; it is in how he dresses. Sebastian believed that.

"I look like shit; therefore, my life can't be far behind."

He looked around for the prescription and realized immediately that Ta'Rae had taken it, no doubt to fill it. She knew him well. He would have thrown it away. He was angry with Ta'Rae; no, he was just plain ol' angry.

Precious took a long drag from the cigarette only to instantly begin hacking and gagging, bent over with burning eyes and in pain. Rosey quickly took the cigarette from her fingers and patted her back.

"I thought you smoked."

"I do," Precious lied. Rosey took a long drag and stared at her with arms folded.

"No, you don't. Why you lyin'?" she asked. Precious, finally regaining composure, looked up at her before standing. She wiped away her remaining tears.

"I'm just . . . ," Precious began, "upset."

"Why? Did Drake do something?"

"No, nothing," Precious assured. Drake had done nothing, not in days. Not even a kiss. Although she'd seen him every day, it was almost as if he'd figured something out about her. He seemed frightened almost, leery even.

"Yeah, I bet he's been a perfect angel," Rosey laughed.

"What do you mean?"

"As if you didn't know."

"I don't have a clue what you're referring to," Precious said before catching her uppity diction.

"You don't have a clue," Rosey said with an I gotcha air, mimicking Precious but adding a British accent to the words. Rosy then flicked the cigarette butt high in the air, letting the wind take it away.

The season was changing, and the bay was blowing cool air over the city. Spring was definitely here.

"Rosey, what is going on? For the last coupla weeks, everyone has been tripping toward me . . . even Tigger of all people. He had the nerve to be acting like he's better than me."

"You can watch ya self Ms. High Society, judgin' folks. Sure Tigger's got his issues, but still he's one of us. He and Drake were best friends—before you came along."

"What is up with you? And what does that mean, before I came along? You don't consider me one of you, and hey, what do you mean, high society?"

"You, Ms. Liar." Rosey's tone was sharp and intimidating, but Precious stood her ground.

"Liar?" she asked.

"Yeah, liar. You're a minor and one with a rich mama and daddy and a lawyer for an uncle, which makes you a liar from hell."

"What?" Precious asked, her voice taking on shock and dismay at the thought of being discovered. Rosey looked at her without smiling, without friendliness.

"Yeah, you said you were from the East Side—Palemos. And you're not. You're not even from around here. You're just a rich kid out slumming. Now how rude is that?" Rosey took on a mocking tone again.

"What are you talking about?"

"Tigger found out some things. And not only did he find out you didn't live in the Palemos, he fount out you just some bougee sixteen-year-old girl out slummin' like I had said," Rosey went on.

"No, that's not true," Precious explained, growing a bit antsy with this third degree she was getting.

"Yes, it is, Precious, and you 'bout to get Drake in some deep shit. He told Money that you two been going at it like rabbits, and that is not cool."

Precious knew immediately that Drake was one to kiss and tell, she was mortified.

"He . . . he did?"

"You are so stupid . . . yeah, you sixteen. Damn, I knew a lot more than you at sixteen even. I already had my son at sixteen," Rosey began, and then stopped herself short. "I thought I was your gurl, Precious. You didn't even tell me about the shit," Rosey went on, showing the true direction of her annoyance.

"You have a son?"

"Anyway, Precious," Rosey growled, saying her name

like a curse word, holding up a hand to silence her, "that's not what we're talking about here. Drake has goals and dreams, and you could ruin all that fa him lyin' 'bout cho age like this," Rosey fussed.

"So do you think Tig is going to tell him what he knows? How did he find out?"

"I told Tigger that it was for you to tell him. All Tigger told him was that he knew something bad about you and that he needed to cool things for a minute, maybe ask you his-self what was going on with you. They nearly got in a fight over that statement alone. Drake's got his nose wide open now, not liss-nin to nothin'. So I guess we all just waitin' for you to tell him."

"I can't tell him," Precious answered, her voice barely hiding panic.

"You better, or Tigger is going to, and that is not going to be good for you, Ms. Thang. Cuz you playin' his bouy, and it ain't right."

"I didn't . . . I'm not," Precious attempted to explain as her mind ran through everything going on. Her needs right now, her home life and the mess that it was in, and now her personal life—it was all too much.

About then, Tigger and Money strolled up. Tigger moved consciously to make eye contact with her. She avoided him, moving about suspiciously and then shoving her hands deep into the pockets of her jacket.

"Hey, Trick," Tigger called to her. He had come to calling her by that name when Drake wasn't around. "How's the money?"

"You got something to say to me, just spit it out," Precious said, deciding to get this confrontation over with, standing tall, fearless.

"No. I don't have a damn thing to say to ya lyin' ass."

"Are you sure?"

"Yeah, I'm sure. I'm sure about alotta stuff," he said, cocking his head to the side and slamming his fist into his hand, biting his bottom lip. Precious took a defiant stance. She could see that Tigger, too, was ready to get this out in the open. Tigger was jealous and didn't wear it well. Precious had come in and taken his friend away, and he had been hellbent on breaking them up, and now he'd found a way. Precious felt stupid for allowing him the window of opportunity.

"What the fuck do you think you know?" she challenged. She didn't really care anymore what he had to say. What difference would it make anyway? Her life was shattered. She'd only come here tonight to say good-bye, or maybe, *Hello, I'm here to stay*. But now Tigger had raised doubt in Drake's heart and mind. What if Drake, after hearing the truth, rejected her? She couldn't take it if he rejected her.

"Why you playin' my bouy Theory?" he said, using Drake's rap name.

"I'm not playing your boy," she replied, sounding fresh out of parochial school. Apparently, the jig was up, so there was no longer a need for the pretense. She was angry at being exposed this way and wanted to lash out. She looked at Rosey who seemed to be sensing her building explosion. She'd backed up just a little, hoping maybe to miss the spark. But not Tigger; he closed in on her. They were nearly toe-to-toe.

"What is your problem with me and Drake being together, Tigger?" she asked, sharing his air, smelling his cologne.

Tigger's dark eyes burrowed through her. How she

wanted to share her pain with him. Maybe even cause him a little for his attempt to come between her and Drake.

"I think you're a fuckin' trick, slumming for the hell of it. I think you think we're just bottom dwellers, and you're just here for the thrill of the catch," he sneered. She could see Money nodding in agreement out of the corner of her eye.

"You feel that way, Rosey?" asked Precious, turning to the one she thought was her friend. Rosey just looked away.

"I think you're trying to get our bouy all sprung, and then maybe when you're all done, you'll let your daddy put him in jail—or your uncle find some charges to put on him," Tigger went on.

"Jail? Why would I do that?" she yelled.

"Maybe fa thrills . . . But looka hear, bitch." He bumped up against her. He was getting loud and maybe a little bit crazy. "I'll break you in half, and nobody will find your skank-ass pieces if you—"

"Wait, Tig, don't take it there," Rosey intervened, stepping forward now.

"No, Rosey, it's okay," Precious braved to say. "Go ahead, Tig, call me a bitch, threaten me. I don't care, because you don't even know what I'm feeling. You don't even know what I'm dealing with." She flailed her arms and hands in his face.

Tigger bit his bottom lip again. He was angry and wanted to slap her, but he knew Drake wouldn't allow that, and if he found out, it would be a mess. There was no way he was going to let this little girl from the rich side of town come between him and his best friend. They had enough issues yet to deal with, like the stolen cars. Beating his heffa's tail would not be adding anything good to the mix.

"I swear, if you let my bouy get locked down behind yo ass, I'ma . . . I'ma hurt you." He gritted his teeth, growling.

"She wouldn't do that, Tig," Rosey assured. "You don't have to hurt nobody."

"Why would I do that? Why would I send him to jail?"

"Yeah, Tig, why would mah girl do that?" Drake asked, coming up behind Precious, wrapping her in his strong arms. "Why? Because falling in love with her should be a crime," he snickered, not realizing how true his words were. She smiled, turned, and kissed him passionately.

"Get me outta here," she begged.

"Bus ain't running for forty-five minutes. We got time. So what's goin' on with my bouy, Tig? Whaddap?" he asked, slapping Money's hands and giving dap. He leaned to do the same to Tig, but he simply shoved his hands in his pockets and shook his head, saying nothing.

"Yor gurl, dawg, she's a fuckin'—" he began, and then decided against it, throwing up his hand.

"My theory is this—me thinks my dawg gots a green eye," Drake said, using the trademark poetic language that usually drove the others nuts. He had that way about him that just didn't fit his outward appearance sometimes—at least in Tigger's opinion. Tigger was the one who started calling Drake "Theory," as he was always justifying facts to fix his own reasoning on matters.

In Tigger's opinion, Drake's thoughts on most issues were bent, like this one. And maybe he needed to get *put straight* on this matter concerning Precious. Because this little girl, Precious, was the niece of an attorney and the daughter of a doctor. She lived in the most expensive town in all America, from where Tigger sat. There was no way in hell that her parents were gonna sit back and allow her to lay up unda some po' no-educated-ex-juvie-convict-goin'-nowhere-fass-nig like Drake Hamilton, aka Theory. No way in hell. All the fancy words in the world weren't gonna save his ass on Judgment Day.

"Take me outta here, Drake," she insisted again, pressing her car keys into his palm. He looked at them and then at her and then at everyone around them there at the park. He looked out toward the street; there were several cars lining the curb, none of which looked like one a girl like her could afford.

"What is this? You steal a car?" he asked, chuckling nervously. The thought of going back to jail scared him shitless. But he hid it well. It was bad enough he was in this mess with Tigger and Collin and their penchant for jacking cars, but he would deal with that when the time came.

"Let's just go," she pleaded, pulling his sleeve, urging him to follow.

"Just go with her, Drake," Rosey spoke up.

Down the street and around the corner, parked out of view, sat Precious's car, bright, shiny, and loaded with many expensive gadgets. It was instantly clear to him how she always made it to the park so fast after he would call her to meet him.

Drake had never driven a Porsche before, never even stolen one. He was nearly scared to turn the key. When he did, the doors locked and the sounds of contemporary pop poured out of the Bose twelve-inch speakers.

The car was loaded. He looked at her. She had laid her head back against the passenger seat and closed her eyes as if the comfort of the car, the music, and the plush leather seats were what she was used to. He looked in the rearview mirror to make sure the police weren't on his tail.

"Where we going, baby?" he asked.

"Just drive," she whispered, putting her cell phone up to her ear, making a call to her mother.

"My parents aren't home; they won't be there for a couple of hours. Take me to my house."

He patted her leg, bringing a smile to her pretty face, and obeyed.

Precious gave him directions that took him on the freeway—headed toward the North Bay and Sausalito. Her house.

She pulled down the visor and pushed the garage door button as they neared the house. Drake said nothing. He simply gripped the wheel as if allowing himself to be taken into a dream.

Getting out of the car, she took the keys from him, opened the door, and walked in the house through the garage as if . . .

. . . well hell, as if she lived here!

Drake dragged behind her, entering the house and looking around.

The oil paintings, the antiques, the sweet aroma of money filled his senses. "Who lives here?" he asked finally after she clicked on a small lamp in the living room and flopped down on an Ethan Allen piece. Even he knew Ethan Allen when he saw it. And this piece came right out of the window display.

"Who lives here?" he asked again.

"I do, Drake," she confessed.

He wasn't sure if his knees buckled or if he was just reacting to the shock, but he sat hard on the chair that was waiting to catch him.

"Tigger was trying to tell you," she began, rubbing hard at the tears that were coming before she was ready.

"I don't understand," he stammered.

She moved quickly to the floor between his strong legs. Before saying anymore, she took him in, studying his features, his broad nose and full lips, his eyes. She touched his face.

He took her hand and kissed her palm, sucking lightly on one of her fingers. He closed his eyes, remembering their time together.

What he had taken that afternoon in his room, it was more than her virginity. He knew that. He had taken her heart. He was no fool.

Or was he?

Opening his eyes, he caught sight of a family portrait on the wall above the mantel. He saw Precious smiling between a distinguished-looking man and a beautiful woman whose eyes looked like hers.

"Your folks?" he asked.

She nodded, looking over her shoulder in the direction of the picture, the pictorial confession of her status—the two people in the picture, who, without her permission, had changed her life. Looking at her father in the picture, her eyes burned with anger.

"How dare he," she mumbled.

"What?"

"Nothing," she said, looking back at Drake and then glancing at her watch again, making sure they had enough time to talk.

"What's going on, Precious?"

"Drake, I have to tell you something . . . about me. But kiss me first," she begged, moving up on him, covering his mouth with hers.

He was hesitant, but she was hard to resist.

Even though she fought him to keep the kiss going, he finally pulled her off him. "Talk," he said, bringing her back to earth. "What the hell is going on?"

"This is where I live," she said.

"I got that much."

"Those are my parents . . . Drs. Sebastian and Ta'Rae York."

"Doctors with an *S?*"

"Yes. And I didn't go to Richmond High. I . . . um . . . I go to—"

"Go to," Drake interrupted, grabbing her by the arm. "You better be meaning vocational training."

She shook her head. "I love you, Drake, and you have to believe that. I know Tigger thinks I'm just playing with your feelings but I'm not. I—"

"Believe you? You better start talking straight here, girl, or—"

"Drake, don't get mad," she whined, seeing his emerald-colored eyes blazing with growing emotion. She burst into tears.

"Mad! Do you know what I did with you?" he spat, grabbing her arm harder. "You're telling me that you are a minor, and your folks are doctors? Do you realize what they are going to do to me? Are you stupid?"

"No, Drake, no . . . See, that's what I'm saying. I love you, and it's not what you did; it's what we did."

"Fuck that, Precious. Ain't that much love in the world for people like you."

"People like me? Don't say that," she cried.

"My bouy Tig was trying to tell me? Been trying to

tell me for weeks." Drake shook his head, biting his bottom lip in growing frustration.

Precious was beside herself now. She was crying nearly hysterically. The thought of Drake siding with the crew, returning to Tigger instead of staying with her was nearly too much for her to handle.

His face was angry. He sucked his teeth and shook his head as if the thought rolled through his brain again, restarting a fire there.

"So what are you saying to me, Precious, just spell it out to me like I'm stupid. Tell me what the fuck you've gotten me into. What game you got going with the dunce named Drake."

"You're not a dunce. You're my man. Drake Hamilton. You're smart and talented and—"

"And you're what? Fourteen, fifteen?" he yelled, looking around for grade school awards, the kind proud parents like she no doubt had would put up on the walls.

"Drake, you don't understand. Listen to me."

Precious was shaking her head vehemently when, suddenly, the door opened. "Well, Sebastian, what did you expect Hyatt to say? He is the doctor this time . . . and you . . . You are the damn patient!"

"You know what, your attitude is not helping me any!"

"Thaaat's right, this is all about you!"

"As a matter of fact, damnit, it is!"

"Who the hell are you?" Ta'Rae screamed upon seeing Drake sitting in her favorite chair and Precious practically in his lap.

Drake jumped to his feet, nearly knocking Precious to the floor.

"Daddy! This is—" Precious began.

Sebastian eyed the obviously streetwise young man

up and down. He recognized the type right off. Mentally he paced off his steps, in case his .45 became needed.

Drake stepped away from Precious. His eyes were wide with desperation. He'd faced this type of thing before—he had his theories on this too. He was looking at a trip downtown.

Tonight he wasn't about to get locked up, not over a misunderstanding.

"Look, ba—Precious—" Drake began, claiming Precious yet, with just that correction in his words, letting her know he would protect himself first in this situation.

"Drake, these are my parents," Precious interjected quickly, stepping up.

Ta'Rae, watching yet another piece of her perfect existence fall away, just sighed heavily.

"Damn, damn, damn, Precious, I just don't believe this!" she cried out, almost sounding wounded by what she imagined to be going on between her baby girl and this . . . this man. "Look at him! He's got a beard and everything. Oh my God," she moaned, pointing at the hair outlining Drake's face.

Sebastian still said nothing. By now, he and Drake had locked eyes and the manly stare down had commenced.

"You do realize she's only sixteen?" Sebastian asked, coolly cutting through all the mess.

Drake blinked only once. "No, sir, I did not realize that," Drake answered.

"You do realize that if there have been improprieties and liberties taken with my daughter—"

"Pardon?" Drake interrupted, blinking quickly, trying to get the gist of what Sebastian was saying. He wasn't stupid, true, but other than his own flashy vocabulary, he wasn't really used to hearing all these fancy words coming at him all at once—and with so much authority behind them.

Sebastian swallowed hard before continuing. He was trying somehow to separate the words from the realities of whom they applied to.

"Sex!" Sebastian blurted finally. Ta'Rae groaned even louder and dropped onto the small upholstered wooden bench, the one built into the wall for holding umbrellas, taking off winter boots.

"Daddy!" Precious screeched, grabbing Drake's arm. It was as if she saw him tense.

"Your silence troubles me, young man—emphasis on the word *man*," Sebastian spoke through gritted teeth.

Drake's jaw line tensed, and his full lips tightened along with Sebastian's stomach.

"Did she tell you her father is dying? Did she? Did she tell you that?" Ta'Rae cried out, bursting into hot tears. She was hoping her words carried the weight they were intended to. She wanted death to make this boy run, to disappear.

"Mom!" Precious exclaimed.

Both females' volumes were high pitched, clashing acerbically against the low roar of the men.

"I think you need be ax-n yo dawda 'bout that," Drake smarted off, speaking only to Sebastian's question. His pride had been touched.

"No, I'm ax-n you," Sebastian smarted back. "Nigga, that's my daughter . . . my little girl! Don't even think about crackin' slick with me in my own house! I'll bust yo' ass," Sebastian threatened. Both women silenced immediately and turned their attention to him. They had never heard him angry like this.

This was not Sebastian York the sophisticate. This was Sebastian York, who spent his teen years hustling on the streets and now was the man who needed to protect his family.

"Daddy," Precious interjected, literally jumping between the two men whose physical presence had closed in tight. The heat between them was intense. She had her hand on both of their chests at this point. "Daddy, talk to him. Please, Drake, talk!" she begged, noting the widening of Drake's nostrils.

"He don't want to talk to me. Can't you see that?" Drake told her.

"You got that right!" Sebastian agreed.

"This is some shit, Precious. Look, you my number one, but you gonna have to do this one wit out me. I don't need this drama. You and me—"

"There's no you and her," Sebastian interrupted. "Get out of my damn house."

"Daddy!"

"Boy, did you hear me? I said get the fuck out!" Sebastian exploded.

"No problem," Drake growled, moving past Precious and slamming out the front door.

"Drake! Drake!" Precious started to run after him. Ta'Rae stopped her. "Daddy, how could you?" she cried now, pulling away from Ta'Rae's grip and running up the stairs to her room. Ta'Rae and Sebastian both heard the heavy door slam.

"God, Sebastian, what are we going to do?" Ta'Rae asked.

Sebastian sighed heavily. "I don't want to talk about it, Rae."

"We have to. We have to," she insisted.

Sebastian looked around for escape. He could not

address his emotions, his pain, his fear . . . his failures. "I can't," he said, his voice lowered. He spied the door, the same door that had just let the boy, the man who was now a part of his last memories—Drake—out.

Sebastian walked out. He could hear Ta'Rae calling his name, even with the windows of his car rolled up.

What would the neighbors think? What did they think already? he wondered to himself.

"The Yorks are falling apart. That's what they'll think. But to hell with them," Sebastian said aloud. "To hell with everybody!"

Precious refused to open the door. After screaming, pleading, begging, and bargaining, Ta'Rae was left smoldering with arms folded and jaw tight.

Finally, for lack of any other ideas, she called Carlotta.

"I give up," she admitted after reluctantly divulging what had happened.

"Oh no, you don't give up. You get to the bottom of that mess. See, that's the problem with you modern mothers, always giving up."

"Carlotta, I don't have a problem being a mother," Ta'Rae told her, commenting on the remark quickly.

"Whatever. I'ma be there in a minute," Carlotta said, hanging up before Ta'Rae could say anything further.

Within minutes it seemed, the lights of Carlotta's Jaguar were seen pulling into the driveway.

Ta'Rae barely got the door opened before Carlotta brushed by her and stormed up the steps toward Precious's room.

"Open this damn door!" she screamed while approaching.

Ta'Rae cringed at the volume and language. At this

time of the evening, everyone was home and no doubt noting all the action at the Yorks' place.

"Precious, do you hear me?" she called again.

"Go away, Aunt Lotty," Precious called from behind the door.

"Oh, you done lost your mind!" Carlotta said, lifting her foot and putting it to the door with a force Ta'Rae only remembered their mother having. She jumped in a start, at the memory, as well as the noise. She had for years worked at temper. Even now she regretted having lost it the night Precious came home drunk. That was never a way to work through an issue—screaming, yelling. That was never the way, right?

The door cracked but did not open. However, the show of force must have scared Precious, as she quickly opened the door.

Carlotta went inside.

"I'ma beat your ass if you don't start talking really fast. You are a child, sixteen years old."

Precious opened her mouth to talk.

"Do you know how close you are to getting your ass beat?!" Carlotta went on before Precious could even speak.

"Let me explain."

"Shut yo mouf," Carlotta snapped, not caring that she had just told the girl to talk.

Ta'Rae slowly entered the room and stood in amazement at everything she was witnessing.

This is all so against the books on childrearing. Yet, it's effective, she thought.

Precious started crying again.

"Carlotta, I can take it from here," Ta'Rae lied. She actually didn't know what to do at this point. She feared she might shake Precious's brains out of her head if left alone with her or just the opposite—do nothing at all for fear of losing control.

"No, I know what to do from here—beat her little fass tail." Carlotta turned back to Precious. "You out there tryin' ta be grown, you gonna get your fass self in trouble. You think it's cute to be called nasty names like 'slut' and 'whore'?" Carlotta went on.

Precious began to cry hysterically. "I love him."

"Carlotta, stop," Ta'Rae said, attempting to intervene.

"You don't know what love is," Carlotta said, her voice softening just a hair.

Ta'Rae felt instantly sick inside. Did Precious really love this boy—man? And what if she did? Had she gone all the way?

"Precious, have you slept—" Ta'Rae began before Carlotta held out her arm to silence her, without looking at her.

"Precious, Ams women don't go cheap," Carlotta now said, her volume coming down a lot more.

"But I'm not an Ams. I'm a York," Precious corrected.

Carlotta looked at Ta'Rae. "What the hell does that mean?"

"Carlotta, thank you for getting Precious out of the room, but truly, I can take it from here," Ta'Rae quickly said, almost as if rushing her out of the room with her words.

"What the hell does that mean?"

"Nothing. She's upset. We have a crisis here," Ta'Rae explained.

"I guess you're not an Ams, either. You're a York," Carlotta said with a sneer, making the word *York* sound evil.

"Carlotta, stop it. You're being childish," Ta'Rae said, answering Carlotta's remark with that comment.

"No. I'm angry. I came over here in the middle of the night—"

"It's not the middle of the night," Ta'Rae interjected.

"Anyway, it's the middle of my night. I thought there was something really big going on. I get here and it's just Precious showing her ass, and now I'm getting told that she's not my blood, she's a York. Well, I want to know what the hell that means?" Carlotta fussed, her hand slamming on her hip. "Is that why you didn't come to Trina's birthday party, or to the hospital when Rita almost broke her neck?"

"She didn't almost break her neck, and can we talk about all this another time? My family is having a crisis right now," Ta'Rae attempted to explain, keeping one eye on Precious, making sure she didn't ease her way out of the bedroom and into another hiding place.

"Your family? And what am I? What are we?" Carlotta asked, regarding Ta'Rae's attitude toward her other sisters. Ta'Rae smacked her lips and said nothing more. This was not a good time to go into all of it.

Deep inside, Ta'Rae wanted to shout out the truth, to tell Carlotta about Sebastian. But then again, what did Sebastian's condition have to do with Precious and her bad behavior?

What did anything have to do with Sebastian's condition?

Sebastian watched from the coffee shop. She was locking the door to the store, looking around cautiously, or maybe she was waiting for someone. Her normal exit was out the back door, but tonight she was dropping off the merchant bag at the next-door bank. She hated making the night's deposits by herself.

He moved quickly, hoping to get across the street before she saw him and took off.

"Stormy," he called.

Her expression lightened and then suddenly, as if again remembering her rehearsed thoughts, she scowled and kept walking to the bank. With Sebastian hot on her heels.

"What did I tell you, man?" she asked, sounding abrupt. He waited while she dropped in the small bag into the merchant drop.

"You told me we couldn't see each other again," he answered.

"And so . . . ?" she asked with her arms out wide as if to say, *And so what is this?*

"I'm just out taking a walk, and, umm, ended up here. Besides, I still need a suit," he ribbed. She stared at him and then as if she could not resist, she burst into laughter.

"You are so crazy." She chuckled.

"I know, and I'm even crazier tonight," he added.

"Uh-oh."

"My daughter," he divulged.

"Oh my God, don't even go there." She looked around as if her words could raise some horrible sleeping beast. They slowly strolled back toward the store.

"Did I hit a nerve?"

"My son, no, all my kids—I just wanna kill 'em." She chuckled. "I swear, I'm like crack to them damn kids," she went on, explaining how intrusive her children were. "All up in my stuff all the time. I tell my husband, Jerry, put a lock on the damn door, but no, he thinks that it's abusive to lock your kids out of your room. It's like telling them you're not approachable—some bull-shit like that." She glowered. Sebastian felt his head nod as if Jerry's parenting concept was foreign.

"So, Jerry, he's your husband?"

"I just said that, Sebastian," Stormy answered sar-castically, yet with play in her tone.

"My daughter is having sex," he told her, spitting the words out quickly. Stormy said nothing. She just stared at him blankly. He couldn't read her face.

"I'm sorry," he said.

"No, no, I mean . . . Did you just find out or some-thing?"

"Tonight," Sebastian answered, seeing Drake's face, his tightened, angry jaw line, in his mind. His anger raised the bile in his throat. "Drake," he said.

"Drake?"

"Little bastard's name is Drake. Sounds like the name of a soap opera actor. Even an actor would have been better than a damn thug," Sebastian said, continu-ing to curse.

Stormy laughed. "You don't know he's a thug. You don't know anything about him, do you?"

"I know he's all up on my daughter," Sebastian growled.

"Umm, sorry, baby, but kids are doing the do all over the place. Where you been?"

"Stormy, I've been raising my daughter to be a lady. I've been—"

"Shit." Stormy laughed again, heartier this time. "And it really worked, I see."

"You know what—"

"What did your wife say when she found out?"

"My wife"—Sebastian paused, thinking of all Ta'Rae was dealing with right now—"she has a ton of stuff to deal with right now. I'm hoping to take this off her shoulders," he said, taking on more of a serious tone.

"So she doesn't know?"

"Oh, she knows, but—"

"But you are trying to save her from this?"

"Yeah, something like that."

"So where is she?"

"Home."

"Where is your daughter?"

"Home."

"Sorry, Sebastian. Again, you are in the wrong place at the wrong time where your wife is concerned— maybe your daughter, too," Stormy said frankly.

Her words rang true. Again, he had chosen Stormy over his wife and daughter when they both needed him the most.

"Girl, you are saving my life," he said, smiling broadly. "I told you. I knew it would be you to teach me a few things about myself."

"That's me, always the one to bring out the worst in folks." She chuckled.

His smile was warm, and Stormy was instantly affected. It was not sexual what she felt, yet she was moved from deep inside. His eyes went through her, touched her.

"Mom!" she suddenly heard.

It was Darrell.

Stormy looked at Sebastian and then at her son. Panic flashed instantly across her face.

"Dad parked behind the store. What are you doing out here?" he asked while looking Sebastian up and down.

Before speaking to him. Darrell outstretched his hand. "I'm Darrell," he introduced politely.

"I'm Sebastian York," Sebastian said.

"Doctor York," Stormy added, trying to think on her feet.

"Doctor? You sick?"

"No, I'm a plastic surgeon." Sebastian chuckled, without realizing he had not told Stormy his field of practice.

She stared at him.

"Plastic? Yeah, plastic. I'm thinking of having my, umm, my lips done," Stormy lied, badly.

She had perfect lips.

Both Sebastian and Darrell now looked at her as if her words were gibberish. "Your lips?" they both asked.

"Well, you know . . . something. I mean, everybody is fixing something these days. I was just like asking about prices and stuff. Right, Dr. York?" she asked, boldly putting him on the spot.

"Uh, yeah, I'm pretty pricey—about four thousand for just this area here," he said, lightly touching her top lip area.

His hands were softer than she remembered.

"Well, Mom, you can get your lips and your grass done for all I care, but another time, okay? Dad was, like, busting a gut when you didn't come out the back. So I specks we besta get goin'," Darrell teased, sounding parental.

Sebastian stared at him for a moment longer.

Tall, smooth, and handsome—his hair, tresses of soft waves that dangled over his forehead. He was slightly bowlegged, with large hands—the hands of a surgeon.

"Please, Mrs. Gunther, stop by my office anytime for a consult," Sebastian said now.

"Can I have your card?" Stormy asked with sincerity and concern showing through her façade.

Sebastian quickly retrieved one and handed it to her before watching her and Darrell walk away. From behind, watching the young man walking beside her, Sebastian was hit with an instant feeling of déjà vu.

Drake was heated. It had taken him hours to get home from the Yorks' house—or should he say, mansion.

How could Precious have lied to him this way, deceived him?

"Put me in this position?" he asked himself, wrestling with the key. Anger again became the only emotion he felt.

There was no way he could pull himself together.

Slamming his way into his brother's apartment, Drake looked around at the mess—the remainders of Collin's last drug binge. It was obvious there had been others here. The place was tossed even worse than normal. Collin was sprawled out on the sofa. He'd soiled himself and had the whole room smelling foul.

"Clean this shit up!" Drake yelled, kicking Collin in the leg, hoping to raise him. Collin didn't move. Drake yelled at him again, only this time he got closer—that's when he saw the blood.

The paramedics laughed and talked while waiting for the coroner and police to come.

Drake couldn't think. He just stood against the wall and watched. His heart was beating like a jackhammer in his chest.

"So you found him like this?" the police officer

asked. Drake nodded, quickly catching the tear that fell from his eye.

"Where were you?"

"I was at mah gurl's . . . I was visiting a friend," he corrected, thinking now about Precious and the changes there would be in their relationship.

"Her name?" the officer asked.

Drake took a deep breath and then let out a cleansing sigh. "York. Precious York," he answered.

"Precious York?" the officer asked, smiling at the sound of it. Even Drake had to admit that he'd never said it all together that way.

"Yeah, she lives in Sausalito. It took me a while to get back without a car," Drake explained.

"I can imagine," the officer said, finishing the report before signaling the men to remove Collin's body from the apartment. Both Drake's and the officer's eyes followed the gurney out of the apartment and past the rubberneckers in the hall.

"Well, don't leave town. We have some questions, but this looks kinda open and shut," the officer said, looking around outside the dirty apartment complex.

"Open and shut? My brother was mur—"

"You live here, right?" the officer asked, avoiding Drake's growing emotions.

"Yeah," Drake answered, "but I've got to get outta here. I can't be here tonight." The officer nodded in understanding. He seemed to feel a little of Drake's pain.

Murder . . .

Drake could barely formulate the thought. He needed to see his friend. He needed to talk to Tigger.

He called him.

* * *

The city was renovating some of the old neighborhoods near the Palemos. Many young folks were hanging out there now since security was made up more of rent-a-cops than real ones. Drugs flowed freely, and it was a convenient place to just hang out undisturbed. Tigger met Drake near one of the heaps of concrete, wood, and metal that would soon be an out-of-place, overpriced high-rise in a low-valued neighborhood. Tigger was higher than a kite; Drake could tell. As he approached, Tigger looked at him, his eyes glassy; however, he seemed to have his wits about him . . . enough.

"Yo, s'up man?" Tigger asked.

"I can't believe this night, man," Drake exploded, still staving off his tears. He hadn't even called his and Collin's mother. How would she take the news? It would kill her. Collin was her pet, Drake always knew that.

Call their father? Didn't have one.

Together Drake and Tigger went into the large building under construction. It was a shell, held up by scaffolding. They climbed to what would be the third floor. They had found that spot to smoke. It was high enough to be out of the sights of the weak security there.

"Yeah, man . . . daaamn . . . That's some fucked up shit, man . . . yup . . . das fucked up 'bout ya brotha, mannn," Tigger began, sounding heavy-hearted and regretful.

"What do you mean?" Drake asked, surprised by his comment.

"You just said—" Tigger stammered.

"I didn't say fuck about Collin. I didn't even say his name. What do you know?" Drake yelled, grabbing Tigger's collar. Tigger pulled off, staggering slightly.

"I don't know shit," he growled. "I just figured you were all tor' up about Collin. He got in some mess with a car—didn't deliver the money from the parts, or some-n." Tigger sniffed loudly and then laughed out loud "Or maybe it's that trick Precious. Maybe she's the one what's got yo head fucked up, got you cryin' and shit," Tigger added, laughing louder.

"Cuz, umm, Rosey said that Precious called her and that you two broke up, that you got busted by pops. Bitch musta really be tryin' ta get your ass sent uptown . . . had you all up in the house and shit." Tigger continued to chortle, wiping the run from his nose.

Drake sucked air through his teeth and ran his fingers through his woolly hair. He then glared at Tigger, noticing the scratches on his face.

"What car? What parts?" Drake asked. Tigger shrugged.

"What happened to your face?" Drake asked, pointing at him. Tigger rolled his eyes upward as if he could see his own forehead.

"What the fuck happened to my head?" he asked as if just realizing he had been hurt, and then stupidly burst again into laughter.

"You're wasted, man," Drake said with a disgusted sigh. "My brother was killed tonight, man, and . . . and you are acting like a damn fool," Drake added, still holding back growing emotion.

"I'm going to court in a coupla days, man. I got matters of importance affecting my own ass," Tigger yelled, getting up in Drake's face, trying to speak articulately.

Drake pushed him back. "Tigger, did you not hear me? My brother died tonight! This is the bigger issue here—my brother. He's dead."

"I know that. I knew before you," Tigger yelled.

"What are you saying?" Drake yelled back, the two of their voices raised high above the sounds of the night—the distant traffic, sirens, and other noises of the inner city.

"I was there, mannn; I was there with Collin when it happened. I told you he was in some shit with—" Tigger began confessing.

"Who killed my brother? What happened?" Drake interrupted, again grabbing Tigger by the collar. Tigger pulled away from him.

"Oh, now you wanna know. No, uh, uh . . . no," Tigger slurred, and then looked around as if maybe looking for the remainder of a drink. "It was his own damn fault," Tigger went on, wandering around on the third-floor platform in the darkened shell of the building.

"What are you talking about?" Drake asked, watching him.

Tigger was meandering. "You know Collin; he can never keep his mouf shut," Tigger explained, and then looked at Drake with his head cocked to the side slightly. "That's what he depends on you for, Drake," he said, as if informing Drake of something he didn't already know.

"What happened to my brother, man?"

Tigger rubbed at his eyes as if trying to see things a little clearer. "He got shot," Tigger answered with an eerie calm chasing his word into the night air.

Silence momentarily came over the area where they stood.

"What did you just say?" Drake stepped forward.

"No, man, don't." Tigger's voice cracked before he went abruptly silent. "I'll take you out just like—" His tone was insidious.

"What did you just say?"

"Don't get up in my face."

"You shot my brother? For what? Why?" Drake asked, still moving in on Tigger.

"I—" Tigger's words were cut short by Drake's fist in his mouth.

"You killed my brother?" Drake asked again, his voice strained and high pitched.

The air around them filled with the heated musk of growing hatred—a scent that had never passed between them before. It caused insanity to immediately follow.

Sniggering perversely and sounding twisted and deranged, Tigger wiped the blood from his lip and then fanned Drake on tauntingly. "You don't even know what happened. You wasn't there—you was too busy getting played by that trick," he said.

"You sonofva . . . ," Drake growled.

Tigger began to laugh smugly. It was too bad the coolness of the night hid the heat of Drake's building rage—perhaps Tigger would have stood a chance of escape.

Drake attacked.

Tigger stumbled back, shoving his hand in his pocket, pulling out something.

Drake didn't care about anything except for the rage he felt.

The next few seconds ran like a movie in slow motion.

Drake heard the loud noise and felt the burn as the bullet grazed his arm before he heard Tigger's screams. The fabric of Tigger's jersey ripped as it tore on a large nail that had attempted to catch his fall. He toppled from the open wall and onto the wet concrete of a foundation slab three stories below.

For a second Drake stood in shock before running to the edge and seeing the remainder of Tigger as he sank deep into the wet concrete that would become his tomb for the next ten years.

Ta'Rae was beat. She watched Carlotta drive off with Precious in the car with her. A week or two away would be what they all needed right now. At least it would be what Ta'Rae needed right now. After Carlotta calmed down and they talked about her misunderstanding of Precious's expression about being a York, Precious made a couple of phone calls and got herself ready to leave.

"Lord, why me?" she pleaded with a heavenward glance. The answer didn't come, so she fixed herself a drink instead.

Glancing at her watch, she wondered where Sebastian was and why he hadn't called. It had been over two hours since the fiasco with Precious and that . . . that . . .

"Drake person," Ta'Rae groaned, moving from the wet bar to the living room divan. She moved slowly, with no intentional aim, picked up the family photo album, and began to thumb through it. The pictures of Precious made her eyes burn. She looked so sweet, so innocent. The pictures of Sebastian had Ta'Rae rubbing her eyes, catching the tears before they came. She looked at her watch again.

"Where is he?" she asked, right before the door opened. She quickly set down the photo album, hurrying to the door.

She could tell Sebastian had been drinking and grew immediately angry.

"Where were you, Sebastian? You're drunk!" she yelled.

He held out his hand. "I'm not drunk, woman," he scolded. Moving her out of his way, he started for the stairs.

She ran behind him. "We need to talk."

He spun around on his heels. "Now we need to talk? It's too late, Rae. This family is falling apart, and there is nothing to talk about," he said, turning back to the stairs.

"What about your medicine? You've been drinking. What about your appointment in the morning?"

"I'm not taking that stuff, and I'm not going in the morning." He jerked his neck side to side mockingly. "As a matter of fact, get up here. I'm ready to go to bed," he ordered, fanning Ta'Rae in the direction of their bedroom. Ta'Rae simply smirked and put her hands on her hips in defiance of his ridiculous demand.

"I'm not going anywhere with you, silly man," she told him, "especially into the bedroom."

He frowned and stepped back off the steps. "What did I tell you?"

"You don't *tell* me anything," Ta'Rae said, trying to fight the urge to jerk her neck, too, but failing.

His face was angry. But Ta'Rae stood her ground until their chests met.

"Oh, you just gonna stand up in my face like you a man, huh?" His voice rumbled low and threateningly.

"I guess one of us has to be," Ta'Rae answered the challenge.

Sebastian's lips broke into a crooked smile. "Yeah, I can see you're trying to take over my job, but you better get busy growing you some serious balls if you want to fill my shoes."

Ta'Rae's eyes burned as she fought back angry tears. Never had Sebastian spoken so crudely to her before.

"You're losing your mind," she said in a low voice.

"I got your crazy," he said in her ear, touching her neck.

His large hand ran down from her earlobe to her shoulder, falling off as if he suddenly lost interest in the game of intimidation he had been playing. He backed away from her, his eyes at half-mast now, and licked his full lips.

"Come to bed with me," he said again, a little less gruff but still with no true love behind the words. They were still filled with vulgarity and a cheapness that she wanted no part of. "You better catch this. It might be the last one you get!" he added, moving his hand along his crotch area, indicating a growing erection. He'd not had one for weeks.

"You haven't even asked about Precious," Ta'Rae said, hoping to snap him out of this craziness. "Carlotta came and got her."

"Of course Carlotta had to come get her. She had to take her away as if saving her from this . . . this abuse!" He yelled the word *abuse* at the top of his lungs.

"Don't start getting loud, Sebastian," Ta'Rae said, moving away from him as if instantly embarrassed. She hated loud talking.

"Why?" he asked, keeping the same volume. "We're alone. I can say anything I want. We're alone, or are you afraid the neighbors will hear? Cuz, see, I don't care what they hear, and I'll say what I want."

"Lower your voice—please," Ta'Rae pleaded now. It

was what the neighbors would hear that Ta'Rae was trying to avoid; it was what he might say next that she wanted to defuse.

"We can talk about anything we want. Hey, let's talk about Precious and her new boyfriend," he said, snapping his fingers as if the thought had just jumped into his head. Ta'Rae immediately refused, continuing on her way up the stairs.

"Let's talk about my cancer—the cancer that I have!" He yelled at full voice again. "No, let's talk about how our marriage is falling apart because I can't give it to you anymore. Because that *is* what this is about, isn't it? See, I find it funny how we can transfer our frustration to other things. I've been watching you, Rae. You got things on your mind that you want to get off."

Now she turned to him. "Is this how you want to play this, Sebastian—down and dirty? Is this how you want to do this?"

"I want some-n, Rae!" he screamed at her with arms wide as if wanting an embrace. Ta'Rae stood still for a moment, and then slowly she began to descend the staircase, her entire countenance changing right before his eyes.

"Okay, Sebastian," she began, walking past him and to the telephone. She dialed Rita's number. "You want things off my mind, you got it."

It took almost a half hour before Carlotta, Rashawn, Trina, Rita, and their families gathered at the house. Ta'Rae let them all in while Sebastian sat on the sofa watching her, not believing she would go through with all of this. She'd even made some quick hors d'oeuvres and opened a bottle of wine as if it was a social gathering instead of the emergency she claimed it was.

It was nearly midnight now, and everyone sat around wondering what was going on, until Ta'Rae called all of them to attention. They sat around as if about to be a part of a seminar. Ta'Rae even brought in a flip chart and pointer from the garage. Sebastian closed his eyes and rubbed his temples while she set it up.

"Okay," Ta'Rae finally began. Everyone stared at her in a quandary. "I've called you all here to make an announcement followed immediately by a Q and A session that I hope you find informative and helpful in assimilating the information I'm about to impart," she began, and then smoothed back her hair, still avoiding Sebastian's eyes completely.

"First, Sebastian"—she pointed the stick at him as if he was a cadaver on a slab—"he is dying," she said coolly.

There were gasps. Terrell even stood and started to go over to him, but Ta'Rae quickly slapped the coffee table with the stick. "There will be time for all that later," she stated matter-of-factly, clearing her throat after catching Rita's glare and Rashawn's puzzled expression. Ta'Rae knew she must appear mad, but in a way, she felt she was. What other emotion was left?

Carlotta said nothing; no doubt Scott had already told her, or perhaps Precious had cried the blues on the way to her house. None of it mattered to Ta'Rae at this moment. She was barely holding on to sanity.

"It's colon cancer," she continued. "I would have had pictures, but this is so impromptu that the best I can do is draw a picture if need be," she suggested, looking around for response; only dumbfounded expressions came back in return.

"Okay, the prognosis is not good, not good at all." She then gave everyone a quick down-and-dirty overview of the disease, watching everyone's eyes darting back and forth between the flip-chart diagrams that she sketched and Sebastian, who simply sat in silence with his hands folded, his thumb pressed against the bridge of his nose, smoldering in his humiliation. "Now, with that said, I'm sure you're all just wondering, Well my God, when the hell is he gonna die? Hmm, good question. Sebastian," she then said, tossing the stick to him, which he allowed to hit the wall close to his head without even a meager attempt to dodge it. "That sounds like your cue," she said snidely before turning on her heels and storming up the stairs to their bedroom, slamming the door.

"I can't believe she did that," Rita said, releasing a loud sigh before gulping down the burning liquid from Sebastian's stash. He and the men had migrated into the library, and the women gathered purposely in Ta'Rae's kitchen, pondering their next move.

"Well now, Rita, you have to understand," Rashawn began, only to have Carlotta speak up.

"Understand nothing. She was wrong for leaving us in the dark—trying to anyway," Carlotta barked. "I knew something was wrong. I felt it in my gut. When Scott told me, man, it floored me."

Trina said nothing; she just kept looking over her shoulder toward the living room hoping Ta'Rae would walk in. "I'm worried about her," she said.

Carlotta smacked her lips. "She's not going to come out. She's stubborn. She's . . ." Carlotta could think of no more words to describe her.

"Scandalous," Rita yelled, emptying her tumbler again, rattling the ice around while staring off into space with a scowl covering her face.

"Rita, come on," Rashawn interjected. "I understand how she is feeling. She wasn't trying to hurt us. She was trying to protect us."

"Protect us? What about Precious and Sebastian? That man and that child need family. They need support at a time like this," Rita went on, setting the glass down firmly on the counter and gathering up her crutches, preparing herself to take the staircase. The alcohol had emboldened her.

"Damn, Rita, it's not that serious," Trina chimed in.

"Yes, it is. She has been pulling away from this family for way too long. And now this! To drag us out in the middle of the damn night to talk to us like we're what? Some strangers on a bus tour. I'm pissed," Rita vented, still trying to work her way toward the stairs. "And her ass needs to know it."

About that time, the men came from the library where they had been talking, drinking, laughing, sharing a manly moment of commiseration. Terrell noticed Rita.

"What are you doing?"

"I'm going to talk to my sister. No, I'm going to go choke my sister's ciddity neck," Rita fussed.

"Stop, stop," Terrell said calmly, reaching out for her.

"Ta'Rae is hurting," Sebastian said.

Rita looked at him and burst into sudden tears.

"Ta'Rae needs you, but not to be mad at her," Sebastian explained, wrapping himself around Rita's shoulders. Rashawn moved past the two of them and up the stairs.

"I can't handle this," Carlotta burst, walking out the sliding door onto the deck.

Scott patted Sebastian's shoulder; he nodded in full understanding of Carlotta's reaction.

"Look, look, I know this was shocking and an awful way to let everyone know. I should have been more up front and just told everyone myself, but it's been very difficult," Sebastian said now, speaking to everyone within earshot. "But we are gonna get through this—together as a family," he added, making sure everyone was listening, except for Rashawn who had reached the bedroom door.

Rashawn could hear Ta'Rae moving around in the room. She knocked.

"Ta'Rae, honey, it's me," she called, her mouth close to the door.

"I can't talk, Shawnie. I just can't," Ta'Rae answered.

"You can talk. Come on," Rashawn begged.

"This was bad. This is bad," Ta'Rae explained. "I'm so glad Precious wasn't here to witness this."

Rashawn twisted at the knob.

"It's not that bad," Rashawn explained.

There was silence, and then the door cracked. Rashawn slipped in.

Rashawn had never seen Ta'Rae's room in such disarray. She had to wonder how long it had been this way. Now that she thought about it, never had she seen Ta'Rae looking so rough. Her nails needed a touch up. Her perm was growing out. And Sebastian . . . His hair was kind of looking scruffy, and even his clothes weren't as crisp as they normally were. They had been struggling for a while it seemed, trying to hold this secret in. It was tearing them apart, and they probably didn't even realize it.

Rashawn moved a pile of clothes off a large winged-backed chair and sat down. Ta'Rae looked around as if for the first time in weeks. She chuckled uneasily. "It's a mess in here." Rashawn nodded and smiled weakly. Ta'Rae then sat on the bed, burying her face in her hands. Rashawn waited while she gathered herself together before speaking.

"You know tonight was just . . . just plain ol' bad," Rashawn finally said.

Ta'Rae took a deep cleansing breath and then nodded. "Bad to the bone," she concurred, trying to make light of the awful situation she had created. *No! Sebastian had created this—let's not get it twisted.* "I can't do this. I thought I could, but I can't," Ta'Rae admitted.

"Yes, you can. What are you talking about?" Rashawn asked, sounding casual.

Ta'Rae shook her head. "No, I can't. Just what I didn't want to happen has happened now."

"And what is that?"

"Everybody's involved. It was going to be hard enough to deal with Precious and her issues."

"Which are?"

"Oh my God, I thought for sure you knew. Precious is having sex," Ta'Rae announced.

Rashawn barely raised an eyebrow. "Okay."

"Okay?" Ta'Rae's face twisted.

Rashawn spread out her arms in a relaxed manner. "Okay," she repeated.

"She's sixteen for goodness sake."

"And you were?" Rashawn asked.

Ta'Rae's mouth dropped open. "It's different," she argued.

Rashawn fanned her hand, silencing her. "How so?"

Ta'Rae thought about it and then just curled her lips in defeat. "Anyway . . . And I was seventeen, and the boy was not some old man."

"Precious had sex with an old man?" Rashawn asked, not having heard the story quite like that. Carlotta had been quick to call her as soon as she found out.

"He has hair on his face, chile," Ta'Rae said, slipping into her casual language, which Rashawn hadn't heard in a long time.

Rashawn burst into laughter. "Come on, Ta'Rae. Now, I'm not minimizing it, but twenty-something is not an old man," she reasoned.

"Oh, so you do know all about this?" Ta'Rae asked.

"Just found out tonight; Carlotta told me. It really hasn't sunk in, but yeah, I know."

"But Sebastian's news has you pretty speechless, huh? That one still gotcha, huh?" Ta'Rae added sarcastically.

"Yes, Ta'Rae. You surprised us all with that. But you know what would have been worse?"

"What?"

"If he had died before you told us," Rashawn said, standing now, readying herself to leave.

"Where are you going?"

"Back downstairs," Rashawn answered, waiting for a second to see if Ta'Rae would at least apologize for her comment.

"Oh okay, fine. Just go," Ta'Rae responded angrily.

"That's all, just go? I'm dismissed?"

"Yeah." Ta'Rae nodded. "You're dismissed."

"You know what, Ta'Rae? Rita was right. You've lost your mind. But I ain't mad at cha, because you know what? Like Mama used to say, You'll need me before I need you," Rashawn said before walking out. Ta'Rae had to realize how often she was hearing that lately.

Rashawn wanted to believe that she heard Ta'Rae crying from behind the door, but in all honesty, she didn't think she did.

Downstairs everyone was readying to leave. It appeared as though Scott and Sebastian had been in a deep discussion because Scott was making an appointment to meet and discuss something with Sebastian the next day. Rashawn made a special note to find out what that was all about.

Precious eased her way into the library where her father sat in the dark, staring out toward the streetlights of their cul-de-sac. This house had been where she lived her whole life.

This room, smelling of deep pine oils and well-kept books, was one the maid came into every week and kept in tip-top shape.

Would they keep the maid after he died? Could they afford the maid? Precious had no clue about their finances. Why would she have concerned herself with such matters? Why was she concerning herself now? It just seemed normal to wonder about the possible changes yet to come. "Daddy," she whispered. He said nothing. "Daddy," she called again. He jumped slightly as if just now hearing her. She'd been gone a couple of days staying with Carlotta, but to her it seemed he jumped as if she'd been gone from the house for months.

"Oh hey, Precious," he said, smiling at her, holding out his large hand for her to take. She hesitated at first, thinking about how much she had hurt him, about how much he had hurt her. Finally, she took his hand and followed it around to face him. She then squatted at his knees, leaning on them for support. He looked so tired—aged. It was amazing that she hadn't noticed all this earlier.

"Mama really did it up, huh? Everybody is still so mad her," she said.

Sebastian just smiled weakly and said nothing.

"I guess I did too," Precious admitted while thinking about all that had come out over the last few days. "Is everyone still mad at me?"

Sebastian stroked her hair. "So, his name is Drake, and he's what, twenty-one or two or five, and you think you love him?" Sebastian told and asked at the same time.

Precious didn't know what to say. He had pretty much all the facts now. She didn't know how to feel. "Yes," she replied.

Sebastian nodded as if his worst fears had been confirmed with just that one word; however, he knew in his heart he had prepared himself to hear it.

"Well, that young man is a criminal—a thief."

"Daddy—" Precious started.

Sebastian shushed her. "No, no, now listen. He came into my world and stole what was still mine," Sebastian said in a low voice.

"I know," Precious said, accepting his words painfully.

"You know sending him to jail is what I need to do, right?" Sebastian asked her.

Precious's eyes grew wide with fear and then regret as she shook her head. "Daddy, no. Please, no. I would never forgive you," she said, tears rolling down her smooth cheeks.

"Never?" he asked, smiling an eerie smile.

Precious broke down crying on his knee, realizing they no longer had *never*.

"Daddy, don't do this, please," she cried.

"He's not good enough for you," he told her. "I want you to know that. I want you to know what you're worth, Precious, so that when I'm gone, you don't make life hard on yourself," he explained. "Or on your mother."

"Daddy, you're not going anywhere," Precious cried.

"The time of denying this thing is over, honey. Daddy is dying," Sebastian said now, flat out and in full voice.

"Stop it, Daddy. Stop." Precious cried inconsolably now.

"So you have to start accepting some things, since you think you're all grown up," he added.

Precious looked up at him, her face drenched with tears. "What are you saying to me?"

"Since you think you are a woman now, you're gonna have to accept some womanly things. One, I'm not going to tolerate a bunch of bullshit," he said firmly. "I don't have the time or the energy for it," Sebastian added. He was exhausted, had been for days.

"You will stop seeing that man and—"

"Daddy, I can't promise you that," Precious interjected firmly.

"Then you can get out. If not my house, then out of my face," he said flatly. "Because if you insist on breaking the rules as well as the law, well, I'm just not gonna stand for it. You must think I'm a fool."

Precious stood. "Daddy, I can't believe you said that."

"I did say it, and it goes for your mama too. I've

worked too damn hard just to be disrespected the way I have been disrespected here in my own house," he stated.

Precious, taken aback, was left speechless when her father stood and walked out of the library.

Soon, Precious heard her mother's yelling and ran to see what was going on. Looking up toward the stairs, she only caught the tail end, but it was obvious her father was leaving the house—with no intention of coming back, at least not tonight.

The next two weeks seemed endless for Precious and Ta'Rae.

Precious could not find Drake anywhere. She'd gone to his apartment only to find it taped off with the yellow tape normally found at a crime scene. Drake's number was disconnected as was Rosey's. She had no one to talk to about it, no one to ask for suggestions on what to do when the police came to ask if Drake had been with her during the time his brother was shot.

Precious was mortified when, after the police left, her mother, in horrid silence, sealed her feelings about Drake in stone. He had caused the police to come to the York house for all in the neighborhood to see. "He is a no-good troublemaker, and he better not ever come near this house again," she said after the police left.

She was panic-stricken, thinking that possibly Drake had ended up in jail. What if her father was right and he was just an ordinary criminal?

Feeling a chill, Precious realized that although the summer months were quickly approaching, it was nothing but cold and lonely in her world.

Ta'Rae, too, found herself in a bad place. Too much

pride prevented her from asking her family about Sebastian—where he might be hiding out; she figured they had to know. She was even tempted to stop by his office to see if he was there. The two of them needed to talk. How dare he just walk out on her this way. He had started the argument. "You can dish it out but you can't handle it, eh?" she asked his picture.

"Can you?" she heard behind her.

The woman's voice was so very familiar, but when she spun around to see who had come into her home, there was no one there.

Mrs. Blinky was moving slowly today. It was obvious she was feeling poorly. Ta'Rae took her vitals and found nothing overtly wrong with her.

"It's my husband's birthday," she told Ta'Rae.

"Oh, I see," Ta'Rae responded, trying not to think about Sebastian not making it to his next birthday.

"He was always so sweet to me on those days," she reminisced. "He would buy me a present. I would tell him, 'Peter, this is your day,' but then he would simply kiss me," she continued, sighing with the memory of his kiss. "And he would say, 'Mother, you are my present.'"

"Mrs. Blinky, from what I can gather, your health has done some changing since his death. Have you ever thought that maybe you are allowing his death to rule over you too much? Have you ever stopped to think that perhaps you should let him go?" Ta'Rae explained, trying to use tactful language.

Mrs. Blinky looked at her strangely. "I don't understand."

"Oh, I think you do," Ta'Rae said.

Mrs. Blinky smiled. "If I let go, who would catch me?" she asked before she continued to talk about her husband as if he were still alive and the two of them still blissfully wed.

Sebastian hesitated before entering the Men's Wearhouse. He wanted to see Stormy, but for the first time felt a little guilty about his feelings. Perhaps it was because he didn't understand them. It was the first time he was seeing Stormy with no real purpose other than the pleasure of her company. This was the first time he would be seeing Stormy with hopes that she would linger on his mind—in a good place. He was also hoping to see Darrell again; there was something about that boy that Sebastian could not get out of his head . . . or his heart.

"Sebastian, what are you doing here?" Stormy asked, sounding shocked yet holding on to her professional voice level.

"I came to see you," he answered honestly and without hesitation.

Stormy seemed almost surprised by his quick answer. "Well I don't want to see you," she insisted, whispering low so that nosy customers would not hear her.

"We need to talk about your lips," he said with unplanned flirtation coming through. She looked at him with a twisted brow, and then, remembering her own lie, she chuckled.

"You crazy, man," she responded, playfully touching his arm. He so needed the touch, a hug, some kind of affection. Ta'Rae rushed to his mind.

He fought the thought of her.

"I want to talk to you," he said, sounding insistent.

She looked at her watch and then around at the customers.

"Okay. Let me tell my head clerk that I'm leaving for the night and that he has to close," she explained, and then went over to a lanky young man who looked up at Sebastian, smiled, and then nodded.

When she came back, Sebastian asked her why the boy smiled. "Oh, I told him you were my brother," Stormy said. Sebastian smiled and then on an impulse pulled her into a tight embrace. She pushed away from him quickly.

"What are you doing?"

"Hugging my sister," Sebastian teased.

Stormy looked around and then at him. "Don't ever touch me again," she said through gritted teeth. Sebastian, feeling better now, just nodded and led the way to the coffee shop across the street.

"I'm hungry. I wonder if they have food here other than just pastries," he asked as soon as they entered.

"You not eating at home?"

"No, I'm not," he answered, trying to keep his words indistinguishable and without any inflection that might tell of his marital state.

Stormy was too astute for that trick. "Ah . . . you got put out." She giggled. "So what was your crime? You forget to set the TiVo?" She ragged on him as if frivolities were the extent of what was important in his marriage.

"No. As a matter of fact, I didn't get put out—I left," Sebastian smarted off.

Stormy swallowed hard, nearly audibly gulping. "You left?"

"Yes, but that's not what I came to talk about, actually," Sebastian went on, looking over the pastries

under the glass, disappointed. "Maybe my sister-in-law
will cook for me tonight. She likes me pretty well," he
mumbled, thinking about Rita and the offers she'd been
making for him to stop by anytime.

Since he'd left Ta'Rae and Precious, he'd had nothing but offers to come eat, sleep comfortably, and be a
part of a family unit, but he'd declined, settling for a
hotel room instead.

"You look tired," Stormy told him after they settled
into the booth.

"I am," he confessed, rubbing his eyes.

"Maybe you should go home . . . I mean . . . or wher-
ever," she suggested.

They stared at each other for a moment before he
spoke. "No, I needed to see you. I'm on a mission."

"Oh yeah, for peace," she said, smirking at the memory of their first encounter.

"Yes. I wasn't lying to you."

"What put you on this quest?"

Sebastian hesitated and then realized it would not be
fair to put her through this, knowing the truth. Of what
good would it do her? Them? What if she felt sorry for
him and wanted to take him to bed?

His mind wandered.

"Sebastian . . . hello," Stormy called, snapping her
fingers in his face.

"Oh yeah," he stammered.

"You went to la-la land really quick," she noticed.

"Yeah, my quest . . . Yeah well, I have a question,
and I'm just gonna spit it out," he began.

She sipped her coffee and nodded. "Shoot, but
before you ask, no, I'm not hiring right now," she
joked.

"Funny lady. No, seriously." He paused and then

with eyes closed he blurted, "Is Darrell my son?" He then looked at her straight on.

Stormy's eyes froze on his, unmoving. She would not show her hand. Her face was that of a professional poker player.

"No," she said flatly, and then sipped her coffee again.

"You're lying," he retorted.

"How dare you call me a liar. You're the one walking around with the dreaded LBMS."

"What the hell is that?"

"Lyin' black man syndrome. You've heard about it; one out of every one black man has it," she clarified.

"Please, you have never met a more truthful man than me," Sebastian boasted.

"Hmmph, then I guess you told your wife about me."

Sebastian was stymied by the statement and was shocked into silence.

"Just like I thought, and your case of LBMS is old—probably in progressed stages." She laughed out loud.

"You're the only lie I've ever not told my wife," Sebastian assured, sounding serious. Stormy again grew quiet and looked deep into his eyes. Falling for him again would be so easy if she wasn't careful. He was a beautiful man physically, and as far as his power over her heart, well, she just wouldn't allow him to get that close. It wasn't that she didn't love Jerry. It was more that she had always loved Sebastian.

"No, Darrell is not your son," Stormy reiterated.

Sebastian smiled, looking self-assured, and then he took a bite from his scone. He looked at the sweet bread and frowned. "This is not going to work, not at all. Will you go to dinner with me?" he asked.

Stormy again looked at her watch. "I can't. My husband is coming to pick me up in a half hour."

"Will Darrell be with him again?"

"I don't know. He might have one of my girls. Sebastian, please, don't start this quest for peace thing with Darrell. I've allowed you my time for . . . for whatever reason," Stormy began to plead, even reaching over and taking his hand. She squeezed it tight. "Don't bring my son into this. Don't make me have to get ugly with you."

"I don't want any drama," Sebastian assured.

"Then don't ask me any more about Darrell," Stormy requested strongly. Sebastian nodded, sliding from the seat. Suddenly he felt weak and nauseous. His head spun. He could hear Stormy's voice but could not speak to her. The pain in his gut was intense, and he felt something give way internally.

Ta'Rae jerked awake at the sound of the phone ringing. She'd forced herself to go to sleep early. What else was there to do without Sebastian to talk to? It wasn't as if she and Precious had spoken since the night he'd walked out. Ta'Rae reached for the phone.

"Mrs. York?" The voice sounded soft and timid. It wasn't a patient; of this Ta'Rae was sure, due to the way she had been addressed. With one eye open, she glanced at the clock. It was nearly eleven P.M.

"Yes, this is Mrs. York," she answered. There was a long silence, and then the sounds of the woman catching her breath.

Is she crying?

"It's your husband. He's in the hospital. Providence on the East Side," the woman said before hanging up, saying nothing more.

Ta'Rae jumped up from the bed and quickly began scrambling to dress. Without thinking, she ran into Precious's room, shaking her awake.

"It's your father," she yelled. Precious, too, ran around the room dressing quickly before even hearing anything further by way of explanation.

"God, please let my man be all right," Ta'Rae prayed aloud as she raced to her car with Precious right on her heels. "God, please!" she screamed.

She could hear Precious on her cell phone. She was calling Carlotta.

"Please come, Aunt Lotty. Please, I think my daddy is dying," Precious shrieked.

The lobby filled with family within the hour. Ta'Rae could barely breathe and paced the halls until finally Phil showed up.

"Phil, what's happening?" Ta'Rae charged. "They wouldn't let me in there!"

"Ta'Rae, you know that's impossible."

"I'm a doctor for crying out loud, Phil!"

"Not tonight, Ta'Rae. Tonight you are just an ordinary wife . . . a wife whose husband is very ill," he said, sounding solemn.

"Oh, Phil . . . is he . . . ?"

"No, not tonight; he got here just in time. He's just out of surgery. That's all I can tell you. We got the situation under control, but, Ta'Rae, it's all a temporary fix. You know that."

"Where was he? How did he get here?" Ta'Rae

asked, trying not to hear what Phil was saying. It was more than she wanted to wrap her mind around.

Phil just shrugged. "You'll have to ask him that in the morning." Phil smiled, his statement sounding hopeful that indeed Sebastian would make it to morning. He patted her shoulder.

"I need to see him—right now. I need to see him."

"You can't, Ta'Rae . . . not until morning," Phil said again, firmer this time, before he walked away.

When Ta'Rae turned around, all eyes were on her. She opened her mouth but could say nothing.

"What would you do if I died, Lotty?" Scott asked as they climbed into the bed. It was well after three A.M. by the time they got home from the hospital.

"Shut up, Scott," Carlotta barked.

"I'm serious, Lotty. I'm sixty years old. Damned if I know how I've lived this long," he admitted.

Carlotta stared at him as if she hadn't thought about his age in a while. She then pulled him into a passionate kiss. "You die on me and I'll kill you."

"You are crazy, woman." Scott laughed, knowing deep inside she was serious. She had not thought about a moment without him; however, Sebastian's impending death had made him think. Scott could only hope it was making everyone think.

"I love you too, Lotty," Scott said to her, returning her affection and then turning off the light.

Qiana and Nigel sat up on the bed holding their newborn—their perfect gift. They had brought him home today.

A new turn in the circle of life.

He would live and Sebastian would die.

As if both thinking the same thing, Nigel kissed Qiana's forehead.

Ta'Rae did not leave the hospital that night. She slept in the uncomfortable seats of the lobby.

It was odd not moving about the place as a doctor. She didn't even know where the cafeteria was. She had to wonder how this hospital was the closest to where he was tonight. Where had he been? Providence was clear in the city. After all her questions, all Ta'Rae had found out was that "someone" brought him in.

Who?

A woman?

Couldn't be.

Sebastian had become nearly impotent over the last few weeks due to the chemo treatments. An affair was highly unlikely.

Ta'Rae shook the negative, hateful thoughts free from her head. All she wanted was for Sebastian to be all right, and in a few hours, she was going to see him, whether they let her or not.

By daybreak, Ta'Rae had made it to Sebastian's side. She'd managed to get into the ICU and stay until Sebastian stabilized. He was then moved onto the second floor and into a private room where he continued to rest comfortably with a morphine drip for the pain. Ta'Rae's mind ran across many things while she waited for his condition to turn. She at first was scared, and then she grew angry and then ashamed . . . So much shame came with her thoughts. *How can I worry about such trivialities while my man lies here fighting for his life?* she asked herself.

However, the issue of the woman and the phone call sat on her mind in a strong first-place position. It would have to be addressed. One day, she would have to find out who that woman was.

Around noon the following day, Rashawn showed up. She had brought with her a change of clothes for Ta'Rae.

"I figured you would want to change," Rashawn said, setting the clothes on the foot of Sebastian's bed. He was still sleeping and had been for hours. Once he had opened his eyes and smiled at Ta'Rae, but that was all. That was enough, as far as Ta'Rae was concerned.

"Change?" Ta'Rae asked, smoothing back her hair, realizing suddenly how she must look. It hit her, all the people she had spoken with in the last twelve hours, colleagues and strangers. How she must have looked. The thought of being so untogether made her chuckle.

"What's so funny?" Rashawn asked, glancing over at Sebastian. Her face showed concern, worry.

"Nothing, just thinking about how crunchy I must look." Ta'Rae laughed, picking up the clothes. "I wonder where their intern's showers are. Maybe they'll let me use one," she said before easing out of her chair and heading out of the room and down the hall with the clothes in her arms.

Rashawn sat where Ta'Rae had been sitting.

Suddenly Sebastian's eyes opened, and he turned and looked at her.

"You're awake. I thought you were asleep," Rashawn said, jumping to her feet and coming to his bedside. He reached for her hand. She took it.

"How do you feel?" he asked her. Rashawn sighed, not catching the tear before it dropped from her eye. She quickly wiped it away.

"Sebastian, I can't believe you are asking me that," Rashawn began before falling upon his neck and kissing him tenderly. "The doctors say you are going to be all right. It was a crisis, but you came through like a champ. You didn't even need any blood," she told him.

He simply nodded, closing his eyes and settling his head against the pillow.

"I'm surprised you got all that information," he said.

"Oh . . . Well, you know us Ams women. We get the 411—you can cash that check," Rashawn said, snapping her fingers. Sebastian smiled but held back the painful laughter.

"Where is Ta'Rae?"

"She went to find a shower," Rashawn answered.

"Rashawn, I need to talk to you about something before she comes back."

"What is it, Seb? You know I'm here for you."

"I need you to be there for Ta'Rae." As Sebastian squeezed her hand tighter, Rashawn felt the tightening of her stomach. This was more than just a casual comment.

"I know that, Seb, but she's gonna be all right. She'll see that we're here for her—"

"No, there's more."

"What is it, Seb?"

"Another woman," he began.

Ta'Rae followed the arrows until she found the doctor's lounge. She entered.

"Can I help you?" one of the young interns asked immediately.

"Yes, I'm—"

"This is Ta'Rae York, one of the leading physicians at Alexian Brothers. What are you doing over here at Providence? You slumming?" It was Chaz Baker, Ta'Rae's colleague.

"What are you doing here?" she asked, unconsciously smoothing back her hair again. She noticed the tight lips of the young female intern who apparently picked up on Chaz's flirtatious tone.

"I'm not as specialized as you are. I go where I'm called. I know you just have your patients airlifted back to—"

"Stop, Chaz," Ta'Rae said, abruptly ending the exchange. She realized suddenly how tired she was, and this nonsense talk was just not meeting any of her needs right now.

He stopped speaking quickly and sipped his coffee.

"I need to take a shower. I've been here all night with my husband," she explained.

"Your husband?" Chaz asked, now growing serious. "I've been here all night myself. I didn't know."

"Yes, he came in ambulatory. It was pretty serious," Ta'Rae went on, hoping to avoid a full explanation, because she didn't have one. It was embarrassing enough to not have been the one to come in with him. Chaz put his finger to his head in deep thought.

"Yes, of course, Sebastian York . . . came in around ten last night. His sister brought him in. Gosh yes, he was in such bad shape. How is he?" Chaz asked now.

"His sister?" Ta'Rae asked, nearly dropping the clothes in her instant disappointment. She could not hide it.

"Yes. I was thinking it odd at the time that you weren't with him, but then you know, a night of crazy ER and well, it slipped my mind to ask her where you were," Chaz admitted now, showing his lack of sleep as well.

Ta'Rae was speechless. She couldn't even form the words to say that Sebastian had no sister. She simply pointed toward the shower room, and Chaz moved out of her way.

The water felt good in many ways. It washed away the night. The stress. The tears.

When she came out, Chaz was still there. He had waited. He looked apologetic.

"Ta'Rae. Did I say something wrong?" he asked.

"No," she answered fretfully.

"Gosh, I'm realizing what I said after I said it. Your husband is here. What's wrong with him?"

Ta'Rae took a deep breath before she spoke. She didn't know where to start.

"He's got cancer."

"Cancer? What stage? I mean, he looked fine the last time I saw him."

"Apollo says it's involved the small liver nodules now, and he's afraid it's going to progress to his lungs before this is all over. There's some metastasis and—"

"God." Chaz gasped, assessing his own mortality.

"He's got about two years at the most and that's with aggressive—"

Chaz stopped her from speaking by touching her arm. It was as if he could feel her pain coming through her practiced words.

She was so controlled while she spoke, so strong. He had always admired Ta'Rae York, and now, at this very moment, he felt so much more.

As she glanced at her watch, Chaz could tell she needed to be with her husband.

"You've got to go to him," he said. It sounded almost like a question.

"Yes."

"Ta'Rae, you know that I've always . . ." Chaz paused, still holding her arm slightly, stopping her from leaving. She looked at him. Her exotic eyes stirred him like never before; he felt drunk. "Call me if you need to talk," was all he could say. She smiled warmly and left.

Stormy had been feeling low and altogether disjointed the day he walked into the store. He was tall and beautiful, and she caught herself staring. Her colleague Janie caught her staring, too, and nudged her, urging her to approach him before anyone else did.

He bought the most expensive chain in the case, and she got a hefty commission on it. He was just good luck all the way around, she thought.

When he came back the next day, he asked her to join him for coffee. She'd never been asked to go out for coffee before. The fools she hung with only knew about getting high and drinking forties. This man was different, way different, and she was eager to see how far it would go.

It never occurred to her that he was already taken. For some reason she fantasized that he had just dropped from heaven and was hers for the taking . . . for the keeping.

The first time they went to bed together, he seemed rushed and mentally disturbed, guilty—if she wanted to take her mind there, which she didn't. He had reached a place in her mind, touched her body in ways no man had ever done before, and therefore she wasn't about to even broach the idea that he couldn't stay with her forever.

Sebastian York. Even his name was unusual to her; she'd never met anyone named that before, and she called him Sebastian. It tasted sweet in her mouth. She would say it over and over again while they made love.

They'd been together about a week. She didn't even have his phone number, but he had hers and called it every day—and that's all that mattered to her. She'd called her mother to tell her about the man she'd met and how wonderful he had been to her. Even her mother agreed that falling for him was a good thing and that she needed to hang on to this one.

Saturday night he was supposed to come by. It was the week anniversary of their meeting, and she was going to tell him that she loved him. She'd even bought a new outfit for the occasion; it made her look sophisticated and classy. She could tell being with Sebastian was going to mean a change to the urbane, chic, and well put together, as he spoke about his dreams of being a doctor one day, and that would mean a totally different life from the one she had known. But she waited for Sebastian; she waited until late.

He never came.

"Until he needed me again," Stormy said in an undertone, slapping the bubbles in the tub, buckling her lip. Her eyes burned. "And here you are right there for him . . . again. Why are you being so stupid, Stormy? Why are you even giving him the time of day?"

Just then there was a knock on the door. "Mom, are ya gonna be in there all night? I mean, dang, do I need to hit the gas station just to go to the bathroom?" It was Darrell.

Stormy burst into tears realizing the answer to her question stood on the other side of the door.

"Maybe you should go home and get some rest," Sebastian suggested after tapping Ta'Rae on the leg, waking her up. She smiled, stretched, and glanced at her watch.

"Perhaps," she agreed, although reluctantly. She'd been by his side for three days straight and was actually getting used to that chair.

"I don't like Precious being at the house by herself overnight," Sebastian added.

"She's been there? I thought she was at Carlotta's."

"No. I spoke with Scott earlier; he called while you were in the cafeteria, and he said that Precious insisted on going home."

"I hope—"

"No, Ta'Rae, I know Precious would never have anyone at the house."

"She did before."

"Well, that was different. She was acting out, I'm certain of it. I can't even fathom that my child would do something like that right now, under these circumstances."

"You'd be surprised what people would do under duress," Ta'Rae said.

Sebastian stared at her, wondering why she said what she said—wondering if she knew about Stormy.

"Have you spoken to Rashawn?"

"No," Ta'Rae answered, smoothing the blankets on the bed before checking his pulse and reading his vitals.

"Ta'Rae, stop now. We're paying for this service.

Let the doctors do their jobs," Sebastian insisted, pulling his arm away.

"I'm sorry. I'm just trying to show you I care."

"You can do better than that," he said.

His words slapped her. Perhaps he hadn't meant them to, but they had.

"What do you want from me?"

"If I have to tell you," he answered.

"I love you, Sebastian, you know that."

"Yes, I do."

Stormy had not been able to function all week. Her mind was on Sebastian from the moment she awoke until she made it to the hospital and, once getting home, until the moment she went to sleep.

Jerry noticed her distraction.

"Stormy, what's happening?" he asked, watching her tug at her braids while in front of the mirror. She quickly tied up them up in a rag and brushed by him on her way to bed.

"Nothing," she lied.

Jerry watched her jump in the bed, pulling the covers up over her shoulders as if that act would convince him she was truly asleep. He climbed in next to her and decided on the surefire test—he nibbled on her neck.

"Oh, Jerry, I don't feel well tonight. I think I'm catchy," she lied, faking a hearty sneeze.

"Stormy, what's going on?" he asked.

Stormy slowly sat up in the bed.

"I won't get mad, baby, just tell me," Jerry pleaded. "You've been bugged for days now, and you need to just tell your man. It's gonna be all right," Jerry assured.

"You sure? Because . . . ," she began.

He kissed her.

"Yes, I'm sure," he promised, making eye contact with her. "I love—"

"I've been seeing him," she blurted.

Jerry froze, his lips still parted in speech. "Him?" Jerry asked. The question came out squeaky, as his voice was nearly lost.

"Him, Jerry . . . *him*." She groaned, covering her face.

"By 'him' you mean, him?" Jerry slid quickly from the bed. Stormy nodded into her hands, giving way to tears.

"I've been seeing him nearly every day. We talk and well—"

"Shit," Jerry's words came out with a heavy sigh. He ran his hands through his wild afro. The silence between them was only interrupted by her sobs.

"Did you sleep with him?" Jerry asked after giving her a minute with her own thoughts.

"Ohhh, Jerry, no. I would never do that to you. Baby, I love you," Stormy explained, looking up with tears staining her face, shaking her head vehemently.

"Well that's good to know," Jerry said, sounding only half-convinced, shoving his hands deep into the pockets of his sweatpants. "So how long has this been going on?"

"Not very long. He came by the store, and then he came back and we . . . we had coffee and then . . . and then he started asking me about Darrell and—"

"Oh hell nah. He can't be askin' about Darrell! Nigga is pushing it now!" Jerry exploded. "Shit nah!"

Stormy immediately shushed him. "I already told him that, Jerry. Listen . . . listen," Stormy pleaded, climbing quickly out of the bed and running to Jerry's arms.

"What's there to hear, Stormy? What? What?" Jerry asked, fuming.

"He's dying!" Stormy blurted, and then after hearing the words in the air, she said them again. "He's dying."

"What?"

"The other night, he had to be rushed to the hospital. That's why I was late getting in. I went with him. I thought he was dying right then. I was so scared. I'm still scared. I've been going by the hospital every night. I'm so . . ." Stormy paused, waiting for Jerry's response.

"You've been lyin' to me to be with him."

"I had to," Stormy said, defending herself. "Jerry, I can't expect you to understand what I'm about to say, but listen. That man came to me to find some peace before he leaves this world and—"

"So you just found out he was dying?"

"Yes."

"So until now what was it all about?"

"I don't know," Stormy admitted. "I guess maybe I was looking for some peace myself."

"Have you spoken with Rashawn?" Sebastian asked after a particularly rough day. He could even see Ta'Rae flinching during the initial morning exam by Dr. Punjab. It had been more tiring and painful than he could have ever imagined.

He had been in the hospital over a week now. But it was finally coming to an end. Both he and Ta'Rae were worn out.

"I'll be glad when they let you come home," she commented, mindlessly looking through a magazine.

"I asked if you've spoken to Rashawn?" he repeated.

Ta'Rae looked at him. "No. Why?"

"Nothing," he answered, sounding disappointed.

About that time, Precious bounced into the room and ran to his bedside, throwing herself over him. "Daaaaddy, you're awake," she squealed.

"Yes, Precious, Daddy is awake," Ta'Rae said, joining Precious in her joy.

"When are you coming home?" Precious asked.

"I was thinking the very same thing. Phil hasn't said a word," Ta'Rae said.

"Glad you two are both asking me, and I know it's kind of an awkward time to say this, but I'm not coming home," Sebastian announced without much hesitation.

Ta'Rae slapped the magazine shut in her instant irritation. "Stop it, Sebastian. Now everyone is over all that happened."

"Everyone?" he asked, looking at her out of the corner of his eye, his focus still mainly on Precious.

"Sebastian," Ta'Rae began. Her entire mood had changed. She looked serious. "Who brought you to the hospital that night?"

"Does it matter, Mom? No, it doesn't matter," Precious answered quickly.

Ta'Rae glared at her, wondering what she knew. "Oh yes, it matters. Sebastian, what is the real reason you're not coming home?"

"Peace, Ta'Rae. I'm still looking for it."

"Damnit, Sebastian! What do you want from me?" Ta'Rae asked, her words sounding pained and tired.

"I want you to be my wife, not this . . . this plastic, fake whatever you've been."

"What are you talking about? I've been nothing but supportive since this whole thing started. And what have I gotten in return—disloyalty, Sebastian?" Ta'Rae asked with accusation in her voice.

"What are you saying, Ta'Rae?"

"Stop! Both of you stop it," Precious pleaded. "Can't you see you're killing him?"

"Is that what you think, Precious, that I'm killing him?" Ta'Rae gasped, shocked at the comment.

"No, she didn't mean that. Now listen, Ta'Rae," Sebastian intervened, trying to take Ta'Rae's hand.

She pulled it away. "You think I'm killing you . . . killing us?" Ta'Rae asked.

"I bought a house in the Palemos. Scott has been handling it while I've been in here. I'm going to move in there when I get out. You and Precious are more than welcome to live there with me," Sebastian finished explaining his reasons for not returning to Sausalito. "That's what I mean by not coming home—I should have clarified, the house." Ta'Rae just stood stunned, with her arms folded over her chest. She hadn't heard him, as she was still trying to figure out how she had become the bad guy in all of this.

"I'm sorry for what I said, Mama," Precious began, knowing her father's words were devastating to her mother. Ta'Rae refused her affections too.

Precious and Sebastian looked at each other and then back at Ta'Rae, who backed toward the door and then quickly darted from the room. Precious went out after her.

Just then, the phone rang.

It was Stormy.

* * *

Ta'Rae felt Precious following her, but she didn't want to talk to her, so she slipped into the doctor's lounge again, taking solace behind the door, out of sight.

After a moment or two of making sure she had avoided Precious, Ta'Rae paced the lounge, thinking about the scene that had just played out in Sebastian's room.

How could he just say he bought a house and he's gonna live in it with or without me—just like that!

"What the heck does that mean?" Ta'Rae asked Carlotta, who apparently knew about Sebastian's plans. Ta'Rae had decided to call her. It was a knee-jerk reaction.

"It means he's bought a house, Ta'Rae," Carlotta simplified.

"Why would he not want to stay with me? Why do something so crazy at a time like this?" Ta'Rae asked Rita after ending the call with Carlotta.

"Ta'Rae, perhaps it's time you faced the facts. Life as you know it has not been what you think it's been. Sebastian is angry," Rita answered frankly.

"When . . . When did all this happen?" Ta'Rae asked Rashawn after ending her phone call with Rita.

"Ta'Rae, I can't tell you about your own life. I can't tell you anything about anybody's life except my own," Rashawn answered cautiously. "I just know you need to talk to Sebastian . . . really talk to him, and listen more than anything."

"What did she mean by that?" Ta'Rae asked Shelby.

She'd not spoken to her baby sister in over a year. Ta'Rae didn't realize it until now. Hearing her voice brought inexplicable comfort. Shelby was sounding more and more like her mother over the phone—that soft voice with just a hint of an accent. It was almost as if Shelby, despite how young she was when their mother died, remembered the strong African dialect she had. Shelby took on this accent, even going as far as learning the language in order to keep her mother fresh in her memory.

Shelby and her husband, Bishop, both had played pro ball for many years—until the baby came. Now Bishop was a life coach for athletes who were about to retire. He helped them segue back into the mainstream, and depending on whom he worked with and how long it took, Shelby and the baby followed him from town to town every few months.

"Rashawn meant that sometimes you start believing the fantasy that you made for others to see," Shelby explained.

"Fantasy?"

"Do you think my life is good?"

"I think it's perfect, Shelby. You have the most perfect marriage and exciting life—"

"Ta'Rae, Bishop and I do not have a perfect life. Do you think I enjoy flying all over the place with a small child, moving my life on the whim of some whiny ex-athlete? Well, I don't. I want a home and more children and a man willing to give me those things," Shelby admitted.

"Shelby, honey, I had no idea," Ta'Rae responded.

"Well, now you do. I feel terrible that Sebastian is sick. I wish I was there to hug him, but I can't be. I've got my husband and family to care for and deal with. We're way the hell across the country, and I can't even be there for my brother-in-law." Shelby paused for emotion. "So, Ta'Rae, since I'm not there for Sebastian, you need to be—because we can't always have what we want," Shelby said flatly, and then abruptly ended the conversation.

Ta'Rae hung up the phone slowly, a little taken aback by Shelby's wisdom. When had she grown up?

Hearing someone clearing their throat behind her, she turned around. It was Chaz. "Oh, thought you had gone home by now," she said, hiding her disconcertment. He smiled and moved closer to her, taking her in his arms and hugging her tight.

"There," he said after releasing her. "You looked like you needed that really bad," he explained. She smiled, wanting to deny it but unable to. She needed that and more. However, it was the *more* part that had her confused. What was it she needed to put her life back together?

"And maybe some coffee? Dinner?" he offered now.

"No, actually I need to get back to my husband," Ta'Rae began, reaching for the door.

Chaz stopped her. "Actually, I just ran into the floor nurse, and she informed me that your husband has been given his nightly meds and is"—Chaz looked at his watch—"probably calling the hogs right about now." He chuckled.

Ta'Rae looked at her watch. It was no doubt true; this was the time that Sebastian usually dozed off. She was feeling a growing appetite, despite her disturbance with everything and everyone close to her.

Chaz's eyes lit up with the repeated offer for dinner. Maybe she would be able to unload on him. He was male; surely he would understand why Sebastian was taking her through this hell. Maybe he could shed some light on all of this.

* * *

Sebastian watched the slow drip from the IV. Tomorrow they would remove it. He couldn't wait. And then after another day of watchful eyes, he would be going home.

Sleep was not coming.

Suddenly the door cracked. He hoped it was Ta'Rae, coming back to talk about things . . . to work things out.

"Hi, York," Stormy said, smiling shyly. Sebastian's heart expanded. Just seeing her made him feel good—perhaps not the way he would have felt seeing Ta'Rae, but good all the same.

The laughter helped. Chaz was a funny and entertaining young man with a strong, attentive ear for listening. He was a master in the kitchen too. Before she realized it, the time had run away from them. It was way after midnight.

"Oh my goodness, I have to be going," she explained, grabbing her jacket. He took it from her quickly and pulled her into an embrace, kissing her lightly. She was too stunned to move.

Her first reaction was to pull away; however, this all felt so needed—a man's arms around her, the kiss. How she missed Sebastian's affection. She had taken so much for granted.

"Chaz, thank you for listening to me tonight, but this . . . this isn't going to work," she began before he stopped her words with another kiss, this one coming with a playful tongue looking for a mate—but finding none. She pushed away now.

"What's wrong, Ta'Rae? You need this. I know you

do. I know what Sebastian's condition is putting you through, and it's not his fault but—"

Ta'Rae raised her hand to stop him from saying more. She pulled on her jacket and slipped into her shoes.

"I can't be angry with you; of course you would think that's what I wanted tonight." She chuckled, shaking her head at the sad scene she must have played out for him—sick, impotent husband who has, of all things, had the nerve to walk out at a time when their family needs him the most. *Yeah, I must seem pretty pathetic in his eyes,* she thought. "But, Chaz, I'm not thinking straight, and this would not help me at all," she assured. His eyes defied her comment, and he shook his head, adding to his position on the matter.

"There are so many changes ahead, too many for a woman who has never been alone before. I know. And trust me, I'm not just trying to get into your pants, Ta'Rae. I so admire you. I have for a long time. I'm not just some young punk wanting only one thing," he protested.

"Chaz, you want sex, and only sex," Ta'Rae told him. "You're young and attractive and probably having a dry spell of some kind and I'm vulnerable. I admit it," Ta'Rae went on.

She thought about Precious.

"My God, my daughter is, too, and has fallen into the arms of the wrong person for comfort." She thought about Shelby's comments aloud. "I wasn't there to hold her and so . . . she held someone else."

"Wrong person?" Chaz asked, sounding a little put out and insulted.

"I'm sorry, Chaz. I've got to go," Ta'Rae said, reacting to her gut instincts and her need to be with her daughter. She rushed out of his house.

She heard him call after her, but she didn't turn around.

Drake stood staring at the slab of dried concrete, smoothed over as if it had never been disturbed. The answer to so many questions buried within. He shuddered at the thought that haunted his dreams the last few nights—the visions of Tigger, having been buried alive in that concrete.

"He had to have died when he fell," Drake mumbled, hoping that by hearing the words he could find peace. "He killed Collin. He all but admitted it," Drake went on, still wondering what really happened at the apartment.

"That gun." Drake sighed. His arm throbbed under the bandages. There was no way he was going to the hospital.

Just then, he heard his name.

Turning, he saw Precious rushing toward him. She'd found him. He wanted to run but couldn't. Her beauty held him captive. Her tears called out to his heart with each that dropped from her cheeks.

When she reached him, she held him tight. It took a minute before he finally wrapped his good arm around her, his other arm held still by keeping his hand in his pocket. Rosey had tended to the wound, but still his arm ached terribly. Precious pulled away from the weak embrace.

"Drake, where have you been?"

"I been around."

"The police, they came to my house looking for you.

I told them you had been with me when Collin was killed. He was killed? I was so scared," she blurted. His eyes widened just a little at the realization that he *indeed* needed an alibi. He was glad she had given him one. Tigger was wrong; Precious loved him. She really did—he knew that now.

"Yeah, well," he replied.

"Drake, we need to talk about what's happened. What's going on?"

"Precious, let's not," he answered.

"What happened at your place? What's going on? Where is Rosey and Tigger?" she asked, firing questions left and right.

"Be quiet," he whispered before covering her mouth hungrily with his. She gave in to the affection with the same appetite—maybe more.

He knew he could go no further, despite his body's reaction to hers, so close, so hot. He pulled away from her.

"Don't, Drake. I need you. Please, I need you so much," she begged.

"Precious, go home to your family," he insisted.

"Or what? You're going to tell me to forget about you? Is that your next line? To leave you when you're obviously in trouble? Well, it's bullshit, Drake—it's a bullshit line," she cried, spitting the words angrily.

"Look, Precious. You were fun, okay. And we had some laughs. I mean, you got a sweet ass, okay? But it's, like, over. You gon' have me doin' time behind that and well, my theory on the matter is that it just ain't worth it," Drake explained coldly.

Before accepting how much his life had changed with Collin and Tigger's deaths, he'd actually pondered a different theory on this situation. On his way home from Precious's house, he had let it cross his mind that he would buck up the nerve and speak with her father—explain how he felt about Precious. He was going to maybe beg him if he had to, to let them stay together because he loved her. He would do whatever it took, but none of that could happen now. He had to leave. This whole mess with Tigger and Collin and the gun, the cars—all of it had him developing a new theory on the subject of his life.

"What?" she asked, her mind spinning on his words.

"You heard me."

"Is there someone else?" she asked, sounding naïve, but what else could she ask?

"Yeah, there's always someone else," he answered, straight-faced and convincing.

Precious knew her face was distorted. She could feel it stretching as pain and agony traveled from her brain downward. "You bastard," she exploded. The pain passed heavily from her lips and headed downward toward her heart. She backed away.

"Well bastard this, here. Get on home and don't look for me anymore. You might not like what you find," he told her.

Looking around, he found a small pebble. He threw it at her, knowing it would miss—barely. She ducked and then looked at him with hurt, more hurt than he could handle, on her face. He threw another one, this one hitting her on the arm.

"Drake," she screamed, backing away still. "Don't . . . please don't," she cried.

"Get on nah, little girl," he taunted, finally picking up a rock that would surely hurt if he hit her. "Don't make me really hurt you," he threatened.

She turned and ran, crying loudly, pitifully. Drake's

eyes burned. His head throbbed as he watched her, still holding the rock high above his head as if poised to throw it. Soon he heard her car screech away. He dropped the rock and wiped the tear away.

Ta'Rae heard Precious's sobs as she crept past her door. A sigh of relief came in the fact that at least Precious was home and not out with Drake ruining her life. She was hurt. Ta'Rae knew that, but it was nothing compared to the pain being with a man like Drake would bring. Entering Precious's room, Ta'Rae sat on her bed. Precious threw her arms around her and held on tight. Ta'Rae knew this night was not a fix to all that ailed them but a truce, a much-needed moment of re-grouping.

BARGAINING

Sebastian's release from the hospital brought mixed emotions. Everyone was excited, even Ta'Rae; however, no one else was left out of the celebrating except Ta'Rae. As promised, Sebastian did not make arrangements to convalesce at home. He'd moved into Rashawn's condo with her and her family until the house he bought cleared escrow.

"He actually bought a house in my old neighborhood," Ta'Rae told Chaz.

They had decided on lunch together. Ta'Rae felt they needed to talk about the kiss—what it meant and what it didn't mean.

"What's wrong with that? It's therapeutic, I'm sure, for him to be *home*," Chaz explained, licking the flavor of his burger from his fingertips; then, noticing her glare, he grabbed a napkin quickly.

"It's not his home, it's mine. Hell, it's not even mine. It's my old neighborhood. It's where I grew up and, thank God, left," Ta'Rae said.

"The Palemos, right?" Chaz asked. He'd done his research.

"Yes."

"That neighborhood has some good property prices. I once thought about buying over there, near there anyway, in the Sandiville tract."

"We don't need the *good* pricing, Chaz. We live in Sausalito."

"Maybe he's thinking of the future, Rae," Chaz said now, taking a liberty with her name reserved only for Sebastian.

She shook her head. "Don't ever call me that," she said, fanning her hand, clearing the air of his voice.

"What?" he asked while mindlessly tearing into his burger again.

"Rae. That's not my name. It's Ta'Rae or better yet, Travonya; that's my birth name."

"Travonya? That's very unique."

"My mother was from Kenya. She got to name half of us and my father the other half. She named me and my sister Rashawn and Shelby. She saw the name Shelby in a movie once and fell in love with it." Ta'Rae giggled.

"I love your laugh," Chaz said now, ending the mood and causing a new one to come up.

"Chaz, let's not start all that again," Ta'Rae requested, shifting uneasily in her seat.

"I'm not trying to embarrass you. I'm just trying to state some facts, and I don't see what's wrong with that."

"Would you say that kind of thing in front of my husband?" Ta'Rae asked him.

Chaz sat silent for a moment, and then, dusting his hands, he leaned back in his seat. "Would you be with me, talking like this if your husband was here?" he asked.

Ta'Rae looked around, anywhere but into his dancing blue eyes.

"Yes," she lied. "Sebastian and I were a very social couple before he got sick."

"Yeah, right," Chaz said, laughing sarcastically, and then went back to his lunch without saying more on the subject.

"I never told Ta'Rae what you told me, Sebastian," Rashawn told him while helping him into bed. Qiana had stopped in to assist with his medical attention. The incision was very tender.

"Thank you," he answered, sounding a little embarrassed.

"You don't have to thank me." Qiana smiled. "Although, hearing that from a doctor sure does make my day," she admitted, giggling coquettishly. Sebastian realized how few times he'd thanked a nurse for their work and felt instantly ashamed.

"I just have one question—why? You guys always seemed so perfect," Rashawn said after Qiana had left.

"I was . . ." Sebastian thought back to the time, which, since revisiting Stormy, felt like yesterday. "I thought I was going to live forever," he answered, still feeling the lingering feelings of humility from his conversation with Qiana. "I thought I had forever for forgiveness."

"Don't we all at one time or another." Rashawn sighed, remembering when her life was at the mercy of a homicidal maniac. For that second in time, before Rashawn pulled the trigger of her father's .45, emptying it into her attacker, Rashawn thought she would die that night, but instead, she took a life.

"Uncle, you want me to tell you a story?" Rashawn's daughter asked, toddling into the room with a small book in her arms. Rashawn interceded, picking her up.

"Not tonight, babydoll, Uncle is gonna sleep, and then maybe in the morning you can tell him a waking-up story," Rashawn assured the cute little tike, who grinned, happy with the bargain.

"Yes, Rainey, in the morning," he said to her.

"Well, can I kiss you comfort?" she asked, repeating the lesson learned from being sick and her mother, Rashawn, kissing her forehead to comfort her.

"Yes, you can kiss me comfort." Sebastian chuckled, allowing his forehead to be kissed by her soft little sticky lips. Rashawn noticed the jelly stuck on his forehead when Rainey pulled away. She burst into laughter.

"Well that's the sweetest kiss I've had in a while." Sebastian laughed too.

Darrell felt his mother staring at him. He looked at his father, who only concentrated on his dinner and then at his sisters, Lashay and Shequetta, who surely paid their mother no mind, even when she was speaking to them.

"Why you staring at me?" Darrell asked. Stormy's eyes cleared as her mind came back to the now.

"I wasn't staring at you," she lied.

"Maybe she thinks you're pretty," Lashay popped off.

"Yeah, and that's why she's not lookin' at you," Darrell smarted.

"Maaaa!" Lashay howled.

"Stop it now, y'all." Stormy got the table back under control.

"I'm going on the road again, Stormy," Jerry announced, catching everyone off guard.

"The road?" Stormy asked.

"Just a short one this time . . . a coupla months," he assured.

Jerry was a musician. He'd given up the road when they married; however, over the years, his promise faded into a memory with an out-of-town concert every now and then, a little road trip here and there until finally, he took on a full tour a few years back.

Stormy wanted to complain, but Jerry was a talented vocalist. He was very good at what he did; besides, the money he made performing with the band was needed. With the cry for retro, hot and heavy over the last ten years, he was definitely the breadwinner here. Wearing his calico denim, dark shades, and full afro, looking like he just stepped from a *Superfly* flick, he was ready to roll at a moment's notice.

"You mad?" he asked her, noticing her silence.

"No, I'm just wondering why now?" she asked, thinking that maybe he was giving her room . . . space . . . time to be with Sebastian. He had to know she would take it—she was only human. Jerry smiled at her knowingly. He did indeed know her well.

"I figured it was a good time for us. I mean, we could sure use the extra money." He leaned close to Shequetta's ear. "With Christmas just around the corner and somebody wanting all kinds of stuff," he whispered. Shequetta squealed excitedly.

"And you know I want all kinds of stuff too," Darrell added, trying to sound grown up but unable to resist begging.

"Negro, you gotta job; get yo' own stuff."

"Yeah, get cha own stuff," Lashay taunted.

"You too!" Jerry said, turning his attention to her. "What? You're fifteen. Oh yeah, you can get a good job in construction or something like that," Jerry added.

"No way, Daddy!" Lashay cried.

Stormy smiled, watching Jerry with the children. He had been such a good father. She would never want to hurt him. He loved her so much. He'd taken her and Darrell in when she thought a lifetime of struggle would be her only lot. She knew then, at that very moment, no matter what, she would not betray his love and trust with Sebastian York. Still, she knew peace had to come for both her and *Mr. York*—for all of them. She would see this thing through with Sebastian and take it as far as she could. She owed herself that much— she owed her marriage to Jerry that much. She owed Darrell even more.

Precious handed her father the gift she had spent all day searching for. It was a peace offering more than anything. They needed to make peace, the two of them.

"Thank you, baby. How special is this." He smiled, holding the small wrapped box in both of his hands as if knowing it was fragile even before she told him.

"I saw it and knew you would like it," she said, easing into the large recliner next to him. He put his arm around her and kissed her cheek before setting it on the coffee table.

"Are you going to open it?"

"No." He smiled.

"No? Why, Daddy? I wanted to see your face when you unwrapped it."

"I trust you."

"What?"

"You said it's perfect and that I'm gonna love it. I trust you," he said softly.

"But I spent all day looking for just the right thing for you. I wanted—"

"The best for me?" he asked. She nodded. "And I trust you. But, Precious, I'm going to disappoint you and decide for myself when I should open it."

"Daaaddy," she whined, "it's not supposed to go like that."

"You tell me how it's supposed to go, then," he requested.

"I go through the effort to do something that is going to make you happy, and you're supposed to reciprocate by . . . being happy."

"I am."

"No, in front of me—show me that you appreciate the gift I gave you," she insisted.

"So, you worked hard to get me the perfect gift, wrapped it all pretty, presented it in the best way, and now you are hurt that I want to open it another time—an inappropriate time."

Suddenly Precious realized what her father was saying, what he was teaching her—about life, about herself and the choice she made when she gave her priceless virginity to Drake. Sure, it was her body, but she was forced now to think about all the effort her father had put into grooming her for just the right man, the right time, the right circumstance.

Tears welled up in her eyes. "Daddy, I will always appreciate what you have done for me. I never meant to make you feel as though you let me down in any way. I didn't mean to let you down."

He looked at her straight on; the closeness of the chair made their intimate conversation easy.

"I know, baby," he whispered in her ear, feeling her tear fall on his cheek.

"I'm so sorry I opened my gift at the wrong time," she cried, tucking her face on his shoulder.

"Precious, it was the wrong time for me. But, honey, it was your gift," he explained, trying to ease her mind on her life's choices up until now. "Just like this one is mine," he said, reaching over and taking up the small box.

"Don't open it now," Precious requested. She wiped her tears away.

He shook his head. "No, I want to." He smiled. "I'm ready. I can handle it. And remember, Precious, it's my decision, and when you decide to do something, make sure it's what you want to do and that you are prepared for the consequences of your actions."

She nodded, watching him tear away the pretty paper to reveal the miniature crystal statue of a father, mother, and daughter holding hands, forming a circle of love.

He wiped at the tears that formed in his eyes.

Ta'Rae called Rashawn as soon as she got in from the hospital. She ignored the flashing message lights. The avoided calls were probably just her service with calls for prescriptions; she'd fill them in the morning. She had no friends calling anymore—not for months. Not since this all had begun.

It was a warm night, and Ta'Rae opened the windows while waiting for Rashawn to pick up the phone.

"Hi, kiddo, I was calling about Sebby. Wanted to check on him tonight," she inquired.

"You want to talk to him? He's—"

"No, no, just wanted to see how he's doing and if he needed anything," Ta'Rae asked, trying to hide the loneliness from her voice.

"He's fine, Ta'Rae. Precious was here earlier; then he and Rainey visited for a minute and now he's in his room resting. I wish you would come see him. I hate this house being a war zone between the two of you. I miss you."

"I know, and heaven knows I think this is crazy, but I don't know what else to do," Ta'Rae admitted.

"Get over here and see your husband," Rashawn demanded, her voice getting a little loud. Her husband, Chance, noticed and so did her son Reggie. "Look, I'ma get off. I have to do some work for school tomorrow. Sebastian is fine," she said, hanging up.

"Rashawn, you're getting too involved," Chance suggested.

"No, it's never too much for your family, Chance," she assured.

He nodded understandingly. "But look here; you're not being fair, kid," he said, speaking to her softly, using the tone he always took when hoping to reason with her. He outstretched his hand for her to join him on the sofa, which she did.

"You don't understand, Chance, really," Rashawn began, hoping not to be forced to tell Sebastian's secret; however, the look on Chance's face told her he might already know.

"Baby, you're gonna have to let Ta'Rae and Sebastian work this out—crash and burn if they have to. And besides, who's to say they won't come out of this thing triumphant."

Rashawn shook her head. "Tomorrow I'm going to

meet her at the hospital and have a serious talk with her."

Ta'Rae hung up and then went up the stairs to Precious's room. She was lying across her bed, reading.

"Hey, sweetie," Ta'Rae called, pleased that Precious hadn't locked the door. Their relationship seemed to be improving a little. It had been a lifetime ago, it seemed, since Precious and that *man-child* had broken up. Ta'Rae figured that had to be what had happened, as Precious had not been using her cell phone minutes nor leaving the house much except to visit with her father.

Summer vacation was upon them, and in a last-ditch effort, Precious had even brought her grades up enough to avoid summer school. Yes, she was turning it around.

"How about we catch a movie tonight?" Ta'Rae offered.

Precious looked up from the book. "Not tonight. I'm going to get ready to stay this weekend at Auntie's so that I can be close to Daddy."

"Don't you think that's a lot of people at Rashawn's house? I mean, it's not that big and—"

"No, I'm staying at Aunt Rita's, it's just down the street. I love that everybody is so close like that. Well, except us and Aunt Lotty, but you know Aunt Lotty, she drives like a bat outta . . . well, you know, that alone cuts the travel time in half, and then, too, her restaurant is close by there."

"Yeah," Ta'Rae said in an undertone, not really wanting to agree.

"And also, Daddy said the house was gonna clear escrow on Monday, and the contractors are gonna be coming to start on the remodeling. He's moving really fast on the house, ya know." She paused, and then taking a deep breath, as if to shove the negatives back, she continued, "Anywhoo, they are tearing out that old Brady Bunch—looking stuff, and he's putting in, like, surround sound to play his funky old music, and he's putting Pergo on the floor, 'so he can dance,' he said. I was like, 'What next, a disco ball?'" Precious went on, sounding bubbly and excited. "He's all, 'Why not?'"

"A disco ball?" Ta'Rae asked, trying to hide her immediate feelings of exclusion. Sebastian had not even asked her again to come see the house, let alone help him in the decorating. "I think that must be your Aunt Trina in that mix."

"Well, I told him if he put all that in there, I was not going to be living there." She raised her hand in mock protest. "I swear—"

"You're planning to live there?" Ta'Rae interrupted.

Precious sat up on the bed and stared at her. "Of course, Mom," she answered, sounding serious and mature.

"I . . . I didn't know."

"Why wouldn't I?"

"Why would you?"

"I'm not going to say anything else because right at this moment, my emotions just got jumbled all up . . . No, wait, I'm going to say this. I love Daddy. And I'm going to be with him every day until . . ." Precious fought the tears bravely, winning for the moment.

Ta'Rae hugged her tight and then went out of the room, unable to keep her own tears from falling.

* * *

Sebastian stepped out onto the porch and took a deep breath. City smells quickly assaulted his nostrils, or maybe just his memory.

He strained to see the top of his house, over the mature trees, on the next street directly behind the house of Ta'Rae's cousin Jody. He was eager to get started on it. He was feeling stronger every day. A remission was coming; he felt it—he believed it. The chemo treatments were getting easier, and he felt soon they would end. It'd been long enough—forever even. They had to end soon. He'd had enough. His hair was thinning terribly, and he knew the time to let it all go was fast approaching.

"Change gone come," the voice of his mother said, sounding as clear as day in his head. Lately she'd been on his mind. She and the man he believed was his father—Hendrix.

Once as a boy, Sebastian remembered seeing the picture, deep in her jewelry box, of a fair-skinned Creole man, who was close to white except for his ethnic hair and thick features. Turning the picture over, all he saw was the name, Hendrix. He never knew if that was a first or last name, but it didn't matter. Sebastian knew in his heart that this man was his father. Why else would his mother hide the picture among her other precious things? Soon he got over the fascination with finding out, and never did he tell his mother he had seen the picture. When she died, that jewelry box was one of the first things he gathered for preservation.

The thought brought his attention to Rita and Terrell's house. Surely Terrell knew of some private investigators who could find out who Hendrix was. One trip to his safety deposit box would retrieve the picture from her jewelry box and that would be it—he would know the answers to another of his pressing questions. Sebastian mentally placed that project on his growing list of things to do before dying.

"Wanna take a walk?" Trina asked, joining him on the porch with Rainey in tow. Trina stayed there with Rashawn and her family providing day care for Reggie and Rainey. She was not much more than a big kid herself, and the kids adored her.

"Well . . . actually, yes, I wanted to see my house," Sebastian admitted.

"I normally walk a lot faster, but for you, I'll poke along," she ragged, putting Rainey down and slipping her arm through his.

"Oh please, you'd be eating my dust if it weren't for Rainey," Sebastian defended. Rainey laughed along with them, despite her lack of understanding.

"How are Qiana and Nigel doing with the baby?" Sebastian asked as they strolled past their house next door.

"Nigel don't know a thing about babies. He's pathetic," Trina fussed. Sebastian snickered.

They strolled on.

"I think Rita is gonna kill that nanny," Trina said as they continued past Rita and Terrell's house.

"Why?" Sebastian asked. Trina began to tell the tale along with many others, catching Sebastian up on all the family happenings as they passed each house—each with a story that spoke of their family closeness—until, finally, they reached his house, empty and wanting to start gathering memories of its own.

Mrs. Blinky had come in ambulatory the night before and was on a respirator. She was in ICU, and her condition was not promising. When Ta'Rae arrived at the hospital this morning, she was nearly panic stricken upon hearing the news.

"Pneumonia? Why didn't they call me?" Ta'Rae asked, a sigh following her words. She felt hopeless and wondered now about the blinking message lights she'd neglected.

Chaz slid up to the table where Ta'Rae sat in deep thought.

"What's on your mind?"

"My patient . . . she's"—Ta'Rae swallowed the words—"she's not doing well," she minimized, keeping her words professional.

"You seem very disturbed by the news," Chaz noticed.

"Well, yes, Chaz, she's my patient!" Ta'Rae's words sounded blunt and a little harsh.

"Whoa, not me . . . I'm not the one." Chaz leaned back, feeling the heat.

Ta'Rae shook her head and then buried it in her hands. Chaz reached over and moved her bangs behind her ears. She raised her head, looked at him, and then looked around.

"It's a very private booth, Ta'Rae," he said, kissing her hand softly, quickly.

"No, Chaz. Every time I'm unhappy, you can't come to my aid," she told him.

"Why?" he asked.

"Because you are not her husband!" Rashawn interrupted, hearing the intimate exchange as she walked up. She pulled Ta'Rae's hand free from his. "And this booth isn't as private as you think!"

"Rashawn," Ta'Rae gasped, thinking maybe something was wrong with Sebastian. "What's happened? Is it Sebastian?" she asked.

Rashawn's eyes blazed like a volcano. Ta'Rae's words only seemed to fuel the eruption.

Chaz felt the heat from this woman, who he could only guess was a relative of Ta'Rae's by her resemblance. She was beautiful as well . . . even when angry. And she was very angry.

"No! Your man is fine. You'd know for yourself if you were with him," she spat, glaring at Chaz hatefully.

"Oh good." Ta'Rae sighed. "Oh, excuse me, Shawnie. This is Cha—"

"Don't Shawnie me. I don't give a good gotdamn who this is," she growled, keeping her voice low, yet showing her full feelings on the situation she believed to be unfolding in front of her.

Chaz stood. "Well, ladies," he began, clearing his throat and checking his pager.

"No, wait, I'm sorry, Chaz. My sister has misunderstood—"

"I have eyes, Ta'Rae! I didn't mis-see, misunderstand . . . miss anything," she added, looking Chaz up and down.

Chaz held up his hands in surrender at that point and then patted Ta'Rae on the shoulder. "I'll call you later . . . Rae," he added for the final dig.

Ta'Rae sighed. He'd hammered the nails in deep now.

"Who the fuck are you, calling her that?" Rashawn asked, losing all professional language now.

"Rashawn, don't!" Ta'Rae started, realizing that this was between Rashawn and Chaz now. He'd fronted her by his words and basically challenged her. Chaz was a young fool and would regret this.

"Well, Shawnie, I'm Dr. Chaz Baker . . . and—"

"Well you graduated a little too soon, because apparently you didn't do the homework assignment on manners, young man," Rashawn went on. "Because my name is Mrs. Chance Davis. I'm a professor at Moorman University, and this woman here is Doctor Ta'Rae York—Mrs. Sebastian York to be exact." Rashawn's neck jerked from side to side as she spoke, her finger fanning in front of his face as she continued to tell him off, this way and that way, up and down. Soon his face blushed red, and he stormed off, unable to listen anymore.

Then Rashawn turned her heat to Ta'Rae. "What are you thinking?" Rashawn said, unable to hide her disgust.

"I'm thinking that you are the rudest—"

"Oh my God, Ta'Rae, shut the hell up. What is wrong with you, woman? Are you brain dead, or are you just that horny that you have to mess around while the man is still livin' . . . or are you just lining one up?" she asked, leaning close, her words coming in a low rumble.

"God, you sound like Carlotta." Ta'Rae stood now.

Rashawn pushed her back down in the seat and then quickly sat across from her. "What is wrong with you? Tell me you know what you are doing is wrong?"

"I'm not doing anything. I'm just . . . He's just a friend," Ta'Rae explained, trying to look nonchalant. Rashawn sighed heavily. "Shawnie," Ta'Rae began then, sounding sheepish now. "Please don't tell Sebastian. He's just a friend, really. This is not what you think."

Neither was Stormy; Rashawn knew that. Sebastian had been totally honest about his past and the woman therein. But this thing with Ta'Rae felt wrong for some

reason, much more than an indiscretion. But then, like
Chance said, maybe Rashawn was playing favorites
here. Maybe she was favoring Sebastian over Ta'Rae,
understanding his needs over those of her own sister's.
Rashawn shook her head and then huffed again. Actually
she was feeling a little proud of herself for nipping that
in the bud. "Well the way I told him off, you probably
don't really have friendship with him anymore anyway."

"Probably not," Ta'Rae agreed, hiding her sadness at
the loss.

Sebastian was anxious. He felt foolish. He felt excited. He felt criminal.

"Hello." A familiar-sounding male voice answered
the phone. Sebastian knew it wasn't Jerry. The voice
was youthful, changing, tussling with hormones with
the manly side winning out.

"Yes, this is Dr. York. I'm calling for Stormy Gunther,"
Sebastian said, trying to sound as official as he could.

"Hold on, please," said the boy, sounding polite and
well taught on phone manners.

There was a pause, allowing Sebastian to calm
down. He'd done it. He'd called Stormy's house. It wasn't
that big of a deal, obviously. She had given him the
number when she left him a message, telling him to
call. Surely if there was going to be drama, she would
not have left him the message to call.

"Hello, Doctor," Stormy greeted before they heard
the other phone being placed back in the cradle.

"You called?" he asked. He wanted to set the record
straight right off the bat—she called him; not the other
way around.

Stormy chuckled, knowing immediately the game he played. "Yes, Doctor, I called you. Sheesh." She laughed. "Loosen up. You're the stalker. You can dish it but you can't take it, huh?"

"I haven't stalked you," he denied.

"Oh please. Did I come to your job?" she asked. There was only silence between them until Sebastian had to agree that his persistence had been a bit much.

They laughed about their awkward reunion and then got to the matter at hand. "I told Jerry about um . . . us," she said hesitantly.

"Us?"

"You know what I mean, Sebastian. Don't make this harder than it is . . . or more than it is," she said, her voice showing a bit of growing tension.

"I'm just wondering what *us* means. Can't I get a full understanding of something before I agree to be a part of it?"

"Us, Sebastian—you and me."

"I'm not so sure that's the correct terminology for what is going on here."

"Damn, Sebastian. Why are you making this so complicated?" she screeched, her voice rising abruptly. "I'm not trying to have another affair with you!" she yelled.

"Calm down, Stormy, calm down," he blurted, hoping she wasn't over there getting loud—being overheard.

"You are one crazy man . . . damn," she huffed, calming a little.

"I guess what I'm saying is, I don't want to hurt you again. I don't want you to ever think something about me that's not actually the way it is."

There was a long silence before Stormy spoke.

"Once there was this girl. She was sweet and innocent; you know, just a round-the-way kinda young lady. One day, she met this man. Oh my God, was this a good-looking man or what. Smooth talking, flashy—you know the type. Anyway, he could charm the shell off a turtle . . . and he did. That girl, thinking she saw something in the man, gave him everything she had—her bed, her love, her self-respect, and more. When she woke up, she realized the man was leaving. She thought to herself, 'Oh hell nah, I'm not letting this wonderful, caring man get away from me.' So she chased him and almost caught him before she realized he was a ghost, because when she, like, reached out for him, she fell through the image and hit her head on the wall, really hard. She thought she was dead for a minute, but she wasn't. She just found out that her vision was defective. She was just seeing things that weren't really there."

"And so what happened to that girl?" Sebastian asked, suspecting that he already knew the answer.

"Oh, she grew up, got herself some *good* glasses. I mean, you know, she got herself some twenty-twenty vision—all the way around. That includes hindsight, ya feel me? She don't miss nothin' now, and I'll be damned if she's gonna walk herself into another wall following after something that was only make-believe in the first place."

"So, I think I understand what you're saying," Sebastian admitted, feeling regret at his presumptions.

"Good. Remember, just like back then, you came to me. Only this time, Sebastian, you are not going to just get what you need and walk away. Ya feel me?" she smarted off. "If this is gonna work, I'm gonna get something out of it too."

"Yeah." He chuckled. "I feel ya."

"I'm serious. You want to find peace? Okay, we're gonna do this."

Sebastian let her words sink in a minute before he spoke. "Are you ready? I mean, are you really ready for this? One minute you seem okay that I came back into your life; the next you act like I rose from hell. Put it like this—I'm not asking for drama. I'm not trying to bring you drama or take you to the verge of anything."

"Don't flatter yourself, Sebastian. I want closure as much as you do. I've wanted it for a long time. I'm readier than you could ever imagine."

The week passed, and soon the weekend came again. It was the first Sunday of the month, and as was tradition, Carlotta held her barbeque. Everyone piled into cars and headed to the hills—the Richmond Hills, that is—where she and Scott lived. Their home was immense, with swimming pool, Jacuzzi, and all the other amenities that made living comfortable.

Sebastian had been feeling better with each day. The work starting on his new house had definitely played a factor. Without that positive project to keep his mind occupied, he would have been in bad shape both physically and mentally because dealing with the chemotherapy had been nothing less than difficult.

"And your hair, well, we just need to cut it off," Trina told him frankly. "I mean, you're so handsome. It won't look bad; actually, it'll be kind of sexy," Trina teased. Sebastian felt the heat come to his face as he chuckled.

Precious, overhearing, joined in. "Go for it, Daddy. I agree, you'll look hot," she added, licking the sauce from her fingers and biting into her hot dog, barely thinking about her words, sounding like a typical teenager, easily distracted.

"No, no, I'm not ready," Sebastian reneged.

"Oh my gosh, vanity is rearing its ugly head," Scott groaned.

"I'm not vain. I don't see you bald-n it up around here," Sebastian remarked challengingly.

"Tell you what, you cut your hair, I'll cut mine," Scott challenged.

"Can I have a piece of that?" Phil added in. He'd been visiting Sebastian regularly lately and had even been doing a little carpentry work on the house. It was his favorite pastime, and in his words, why not spend it with a friend.

"Oh, that's easy for you, Mr. Comb-over," Sebastian teased Phil with fun intended. Phil laughed.

"No, seriously, if you cut it off, I'll do mine," Scott went on.

About that time, Terrell and Nigel strolled up with their babies in arms.

"Oh, the baby daddies," Scott jeered. Both men groaned.

"What's the challenge? We want in," Terrell blurted.

"Oh, you do?"

"Wait, you guys; you don't even know what's on the table," Sebastian said between laughter.

"Doesn't matter; we're up for it," Nigel added, showing their need to get back in the ring doing *manly man* things.

"So not even knowing, you want in?" Sebastian asked.

"Yep," both men agreed.

"Well, damn, I can't pass this up! Cut the shit off, then," exclaimed Sebastian excitedly.

"Waaait a minute, cut what shit? Ain't nobody cuttin' my shit," Terrell began, backpedaling.

"Ohhh no." Scott pointed. "You said it; now it's going!"

"Trina!" Sebastian called out.

About that time, Trina came slinking out of the house. She was dressed in thug gear complete with the bling-bling and earring in her ear. She had on a skullcap, wielding the hair clippers over her head while singing the latest hip-hop tune.

When she reached the deck where the men were standing, she whipped off the cap, exposing what looked like a bald head. Carlotta, spying her, screamed. She called on the Lord to save her sister from her own insanity. Precious followed close behind, dancing to the song Trina sang as if in full accomplice with her aunt's new appearance. Laughter mixed with hysterical tears filled the backyard as Trina did her scalping dance around Sebastian, ending in a full battle cry complete with chest beating before she snatched off the disguise, freeing her head full of hair.

Carlotta cursed and spat with tears running down her face at being made so upset. Rashawn screamed with laughter, tears pouring down her face as well. No one was sure why all of the tears ran—some from true amusement, some from sorrow, as today Sebastian conceded to the first battle with the cancer.

The challengers went first. Everyone's eyes were on Sebastian as he watched. Terrell went out kicking and screaming the loudest, cursing at being tricked into losing what he called his mane of manliness, to which Rita quickly corrected, his "crop of nappiness."

Chance was already bald. Having accepted his thinning hair last year, he'd long since been clean-shaven on top, trading it for a full beard. Scott then went, followed by Phil and then Nigel. Qiana groaned watching Nigel's falling hair dance around his shoulders, and then it was Sebastian's turn.

"Looks so good," said Trina after she finished, handing him a mirror. She then kissed him tenderly on the top of the head. Precious, too quickly anointed his smooth dome with love.

"Hey, we didn't get none," Terrell fussed playfully.

"Yeah, where's the love, ladies?" Nigel whined, rubbing his newly bald head as all the women hugged Sebastian tight.

"And then Daddy was, like, doing this Shaft impression. Oh my God, he was hilarious," Precious related that night over the phone. "He did the voice—you know, all deep and stuff—'shut cho mouf,'"

Ta'Rae sipped her wine while listening in silence. She was stunned for the most part. "So he's bald?" she asked again.

"I just said that, Mom. He's totally bald. Oh my goodness, he looks really good too. You know he's lost a little weight, but it only makes him look, like, I don't know, I guess sexy. That's what Trina called him. Anyway, I know that's weird to say about Dad, but whatever, I'm just glad he did it. I'm so proud of him."

"So, he's happy?"

"Yes. He's happy. Why wouldn't he be? We're moving into the house next week. You know the house is next to your cousin Aurora," Precious added.

"I didn't know that," Ta'Rae admitted.

Aurora was a widow; her husband had been killed in a work-related accident. Aurora was lonely, very lonely, and quite attractive, having held up well for forty-seven.

"Yeah. Aurora already came over. Dad was trying to put up these really ugly curtains, and she was like, '*not even*,' and came back over with these beautiful ones that we put up."

"Together?"

"Together what?"

"You put them up together with Aurora?" Ta'Rae asked, finishing the wine now with a gulp.

"No, we made her do it by herself. Of course we did it together. We made Dad hold the chair, though, while she got up there, because you know Dad—he would have fell all on his head." She burst into laughter. "Anyway, then she cooked dinner for us. She's really nice. Why haven't I met her before?" Precious asked. "Alls I know is I've met so many folks around here. They all say I'm a true Ams. They say I look like Grandma Zenobia—booty and all." Precious giggled.

"You're a York," Ta'Rae said, trying to sound as though that meant something. Precious ignored her comment and went on bubbling about the Ams family.

Sebastian saw two patients and called it a day. He was exhausted, and all he had done was talk to them. But he refused to give up his practice. He'd worked so hard building it up.

He'd been given the green light to return to the office and took it, running. Now at high noon, he was crawling across the street to the hospital, headed to the cafeteria for a bite to eat.

Several of his colleagues stopped by and commented on his shaved head, and others inquired about his chemo. Surprisingly enough, talking about it all was easy, and he felt no separation from the topic. He didn't even attempt to pretend they were not in fact talking about him and *his* cancer. He ate heartily, enjoying the newfound freedom within his mind and heart. Maybe he would make it through all of this after all. Even Hilton had noticed a change in his countenance. She assured him his mission was *getting there.* He'd not mentioned Stormy to her yet; he knew he would have to soon.

Just then, the familiar sound of laughter hit his ear. It was Ta'Rae. Sebastian strained to see over the shrubs. He needed to look. Her laughter sounded healthy, and he wanted to see her face. It had been so long since he'd heard her laughter. Rashawn had told him she'd called every day; however, still she had not spoken to him directly. Once she'd even stopped by to drop off some more of his things, yet she did not even come inside. She was being foolish and stubborn, and he didn't understand it—that is, until he finally saw her . . . with him.

Sebastian sat back in his seat, his mind spinning as to what to do next.

"What am I doing? He's a colleague," Sebastian reasoned quickly, relaxing just a little. The tension had jumped into his shoulders, making them instantly tight. "You're the one with the guilty conscience. Ta'Rae hasn't ever given you a reason to doubt her loyalty to you, ya fool," he scolded himself.

Sure enough, as if planned, Ta'Rae and her lunch date sat on the opposite side of the large shrub. He could hear everything they said.

"So what's next for Mrs. Blinky?" Chaz asked.

"She's just not responding to the antibiotics at all," Ta'Rae answered with a heavy sigh.

"So, we still gonna catch that movie tonight?"

"God no. I'm not going to any more movies with you. That last one was horrible." She giggled. Flirt was in her voice. Sebastian heard that loud and clear.

"Then let's do something else," Chaz responded, sounding flirtatious too.

Ta'Rae giggled coquettishly. "Like what?"

"Tell you what, I'll stop by at eight, and we'll go from there," Chaz said, nearly whispering.

What the hell . . .

Sebastian jumped up. "Ta'Rae! I was correct. It is you," Sebastian said, trying to sound professional and above his inner feelings.

"Sebastian." Ta'Rae gasped in surprise at seeing him. "Your hair . . . it's gone."

"Yeah, well, Trina cut it," he said, not taking his eyes off Chaz.

Chaz rolled his eyes, ready to take on more heat. *This woman has more barricades than a fort,* he thought.

"You let Trina cut your hair?"

"Sebastian York," Sebastian said, introducing himself to Chaz.

"You remember Chaz Baker," Ta'Rae said.

"First year interning?" Sebastian insulted, blatantly referring to his age.

"No, actually I—"

"Sebastian, you know he's not an intern. You've met Chaz before," Ta'Rae jumped in, defending him.

"Ah. Well, anyway, Ta'Rae, I was just about to call you. Rashawn said you'd been calling every night and well, I'm actually free this evening. How about we have dinner at Singers and—" Sebastian began.

"Singers is a really nice place—much better than a lousy three-buck movie at the Pioneer," Chaz said, conceding early, saving himself further humiliation.

"I called your office. Didn't Jasmine tell you?" asked Sebastian, ignoring the fact that Chaz had taken her to the trendy local young folks' hangout, featuring three-buck classic noir films and a connecting coffee house. Despite the low price, it was a very hip and happening place with the thirty-something folks.

"Actually . . ." Ta'Rae stumbled.

"Well, no matter, I should have known you'd be here. It's Monday. I guess I should have waited before eating." Sebastian chuckled. "What was I thinking? How about I make it up tonight at Singers, and then . . ." Sebastian's tone took on an air of romance.

Chaz stood.

"Whoa, look at the time," he exploded dramatically. "Gotta run. Well, Dr. York, glad to see you up and about," he said, outstretching his hand. Sebastian looked at it and then hesitated. Chaz ran his fingers quickly through his hair and then without looking at Ta'Rae again, he shoved his hands deep into the pocket of his jeans and walked away from the table.

Sebastian came around the tall shrub and sat down in Chaz's seat. Ta'Rae looked tense but played it off well.

"So, Singers, huh? My favorite place."

"I know that," Sebastian said without smiling. "So about seven—I'll make reservations."

"You don't have to keep up your end of this—"

"I always keep up my end," he said acerbically. Standing and with head high, he walked out.

* * *

Ta'Rae changed clothes at least ten times, looking for the perfect outfit. Finally, a quick run to Neiman Marcus had her dressed to kill. She was nervous and felt foolish, but she didn't know how else to feel.

Sebastian was on time as normal and rang the bell. When she opened the door, he looked gorgeous. Despite his slight weight loss and the new diamond stud in his ear, he looked like a Sebastian she had never known before. She could tell he felt the same about her, as his eyes gave him away, covering her from head to toe. She felt the heat. Stepping back from the door, she let him pass.

"Have a drink before we go?" she offered.

"I can't," he answered.

"Well I meant like a soda or something," she fumbled.

"No, you didn't, but it's okay. You're allowed to forget, Ta'Rae."

"I didn't forget," she insisted.

"Relax, baby," Sebastian purred.

Baby.

He called her baby again. There was something about the way he said that word that affected her and not always in a bad way like she had always pretended it did.

"Maybe we should just go, then," she blurted, sounding less than comfortable.

"Hold up now. Don't you think I might want to spend a minute in my home?" he asked.

"Your home? I thought your home was in the Palemos now," she spouted off before stopping herself from saying what she instantly regretted.

"My home is where my wife is," Sebastian quickly

volleyed. "And if you don't know that by now . . . well God help you woman."

"Let's go, please, Sebastian," Ta'Rae pleaded.

Sebastian smiled smugly. "Okay, baby, let's go," he said, holding out his arm for her to leave first. He locked the door behind him.

Singers was crowded; however, their regular table was available. The headwaiter, Grotto, smiled upon seeing them.

"It's been a while, Yorks," he greeted. His English was broken.

"Yes, it has," Sebastian greeted, offering him a manly hug. Grotto was taken aback a little at Sebastian's lack of inhibitions.

Ta'Rae began to relax quickly. She was in her realm. Sebastian could tell. He ordered her favorite wine and their favorite meal, just like old times, and for a second or two, under the dim romantic lights, Sebastian almost thought he saw her smile at him. He thought he almost caught a little want in her golden eyes. He knew he wanted her. With all he was inside, he wanted her.

"You look good tonight," he finally admitted.

She nearly purred with appreciation of his observation. "Oh, this old thing," she flirted.

Yes, she was flirting. He was sure of it.

She reached out and took his hand, turning it over and rubbing his palm. He loved when she did that, admiring his hands. She always liked his hands.

The wine came along with bread and olive oil.

Ta'Rae broke a small piece of bread, dipped it in the oil, and fed it to him. This time she wasn't acting like his nurse; she was acting like a woman who wanted him to bed her down as soon as possible. At least that's what he hoped. He quickly copied her actions, only she allowed his fingers to linger at her lips.

"Do you miss me?" he asked her.

She looked down at her wineglass now, and then took a sip. Tossing her head back, she looked at him without answering, yet answering him loud and clear with her eyes.

Yes!

"Do you still love me?" he asked her.

"Sebastian, can't you see how crazy this is?"

"Then do something about it."

"You started all this."

"But you can end it, if that's how you feel. Then you end it. Don't start something new. That damn Chaz Baker. Ta'Rae, what the hell was that 'maybe we can find something else to do' bullshit. That fucker," Sebastian spat, showing Ta'Rae that he had indeed heard enough to draw the wrong conclusions. "What the hell was that about?"

"So is that what this is truly about? You overheard our conversation and now you're jealous of Chaz?"

"I'm not jealous of nobody. I don't have the time for those kinds of games. Do you?" he asked. His anger now grew as fast as his passion had.

"Sebastian . . . don't do this," she whispered, shaking her head, noting nosy eyes looking their way. "This is our favorite restaurant. Please don't take this good memory away from me," she begged.

"Oh no, you did not say that. Your memories? Oh, that's right, you're gonna need those. Why? Just make some new ones with your new boyfriend," Sebastian growled ferociously. Ta'Rae's eyes widened and filled with water.

"I don't have a desire to help you maintain old memories of us, Ta'Rae. I'm not dead yet. How about we keep working on building new ones," he went on, growing in volume.

Ta'Rae stood, slamming her napkin down in the seat.

"If they are going to be as shitty as this one has turned out to be, you can keep them," she said before tossing her wine into his face. "And add that to them."

She stormed out.

All eyes were on them now as Grotto ran over to the table. "Mr. York!" he exclaimed, helping Sebastian to stand as if the wine had been a fist.

"Looks like I'm going to need two really large doggy bags, Grotto. We're leaving," Sebastian said softly, looking around at the eyes on him. He reached in his pocket and discreetly slipped Grotto a hundred-dollar bill and then used the cloth napkin to dry his face.

When he got outside, Ta'Rae was nowhere in sight. She had no doubt caught a cab. Sebastian took the food and headed back to the Palemos. He was sure Precious would enjoy the meal. Perhaps she would even enjoy it with him. He needed to talk to Stormy. She would set him straight on what he did wrong tonight. She was good at setting him straight on things.

Their peace-making therapy had been going so well, he actually believed he was becoming a changed man. He had actually started to think he had it all under control.

"But I'm not and I don't. I'm still the asshole I've always been." He sighed heavily, turning into the driveway.

* * *

Ta'Rae went to the hospital instead of going home. Heading to her office, she pulled on her lab coat. She could still smell her perfume—Sebastian's favorite scent. She felt the tear fall before she could stop it. She stared at the phone. How she wanted to call Sebastian, apologize, hold him . . . love him—start the evening over. She reached for the phone and called his cell phone. He didn't answer. Heading upstairs, she went to check on Mrs. Blinky.

Reaching the third floor, she turned to head to Mrs. Blinky's room.

"Dr. York?" Dan Stewart, the physician on call, greeted, noticing her about to enter Mrs. Blinky's room. His eyes danced over her.

"Yes." She smiled, hiding her embarrassment of being overdressed under her lab coat. She knew her dangly diamond earrings must have given her away as much as her high heels.

"What are you doing here? I didn't expect you until tomorrow."

"Oh, I was just going to check on Mrs. Blinky. Poor sweetie was feeling so poorly this morning. I wanted to stop in and—"

"Then you didn't get my message."

"What message?" Ta'Rae asked, her stomach tightening a little.

"We lost Mildred at about six forty-five. You just missed her," Dan said.

"Missed her? I didn't release her. Did that daughter of hers take her out of here? Oh my God," Ta'Rae began, fuming. She hurried to the nurse's station and grabbed a phone.

"No, no, you misunderstand. She died at six forty-five," he said. He took the phone from Ta'Rae's hand

and hung it up, obviously seeing her emotions growing instantly upon hearing the news.

"No, that can't be," Ta'Rae exclaimed, looking around at the nurses who didn't seem to hear them speaking.

"How did I miss the call?" she asked, thinking about where she was at that time.

The restaurant.

Tears filled her eyes. "Have they called her daughter?"

"Oh yes, it's all been taken care of," Dan said, sounding almost nonchalant about the whole thing.

How can he take this so lightly?

Ta'Rae broke for the stairwell. She didn't really know where she was going, so she headed up, reaching the seventh floor before she stopped to give way to her tears. *What a night, what a horrible, horrible night,* she thought to herself. She needed to talk to someone. She needed to be held. *Chaz Baker.*

She reached the perinatal floor, and from the stairwell she headed into the back office to call him. To her surprise, she found him as she clicked on the light. He was wrapped around a young blond nurse. They hungrily groped each other, gasping between eager kisses and the hurried sex. Ta'Rae stood stunned for a moment before the two of them fully adjusted to the light and the fact that she was actually standing there.

Pulling quickly away from the woman, who immediately attempted to pull up her scrubs, Chaz stared with his mouth open as well as his fly.

"Rae!" he yelled, louder than intended; however, with passions high, it no doubt could not be helped. He fumbled awkwardly as he speedily tucked away his deflating love rod.

"It's Ta'Rae. Only my husband calls me Rae, Dr. Baker," Ta'Rae said, speaking low, still filled with shock, yet hiding it well.

The intern ran from the office, realizing who Ta'Rae was and how precarious her career suddenly became. Ta'Rae closed the door in her wake.

When she turned back, Chaz was still adjusting his jeans and shirt. His hair was a mess, and he attempted to straighten it by combing it with his fingers.

Ta'Rae watched as he transformed before her, wondering if he was planning to convince her that what she had seen, she had not seen.

She realized she still had Mrs. Blinky's chart in her hand. She laid it on the desk.

"Ta'Rae, it's not what you think," he began.

"Oh yes, it is, Chaz. It's sex." She chuckled sardonically. "This is the second time you've tried to tell me that sex is not sex. At my age, and as long as I've been married, I think I know sex when I see it," she said coolly, folding her arms across her chest.

"Couldn't convince me of that," he smarted off. "I wouldn't think you'd know a dick when you saw one."

Ta'Rae stepped up to him and slapped him hard across the face.

"Sure I would," she said, spinning on her heels and storming out.

Chaz held his cheek.

"Bitch," he mumbled behind her back. Hearing him, she turned around, and then noticing Mrs. Blinky's file, she snatched it up. Staring at him with a heated glare, she continued on her way.

Ta'Rae could barely make it home. She was tired and worn out. She needed something . . . someone. Sebastian.

"Why did it all change?" she asked the only one listening—God.

She looked in the mirror at the empty bed behind her, waiting for her. She imagined she saw Sebastian's face, his concerned brow while he waited to hear her news of the day—the death of her patient, a woman who touched her soul, Mrs. Blinky. Sebastian would have cared. He would have understood her sorrow over that woman's death.

Bursting into tears, Ta'Rae went to her closet. She dug deep to find one of Sebastian's shirts, one she'd hidden away. She slipped it on and felt his presence around her instantly. She inhaled his cologne in the fabric. Holding herself tight, she imagined herself in his embrace.

"That man loves you, Travonya," she heard her mother say.

This time she knew her mother's voice. She'd been hearing it for weeks, ignoring it. But tonight she could ignore it no longer because before her she now saw a vision of her as well, sitting on the floor as she often did, barefoot and tranquil in her facial appearance. Ta'Rae felt no fear, nor did she feel the urge to break down, although tears did continue to leave her eyes.

"I know," she answered, smiling weakly, wiping the tears away.

"And you know why he showed his ass tonight, don't you?"

"Yes, Mama. He was jealous," she whispered, smiling at the thought of Sebastian's face. How he feigned surprise upon seeing her, and his exchange with Chaz. Sebastian had never been as aggressive as he had been the last couple of months. Tonight was the worst.

"Let me tell you something about your man," her

mother went on. "He's fighting death now, with both fists up and ready. He is scared, and he's gonna take it out on you."

"But why me? What did I ever do?"

"Nothing you can put your finger on. Listen, do you remember when I was about to die?"

"Oh, Mama, I don't want to think about that," Ta'Rae said now, turning away from the vision before her.

"No, now sometimes you have to think about things you don't want to think about—face them; stop just getting mad about them. There's no more room for negotiation with this thing—it's not going to change it."

Ta'Rae nodded reluctantly.

"Now listen, remember how your daddy started working those long hours, never coming home until late in the night?"

"Yes. I was so upset with him. I used to wonder why he didn't stay by your side night and day. But I guess he couldn't."

"Right, because I pushed him away, just like through his actions—picking fights and this *buying-a-house-in-the-Palemos* mess—he's pushing you away now. I remember how I acted, but I needed to make my peace, chile, and you have to let Sebastian make his."

"I can't do that," Ta'Rae admitted, sniffing the sleeve of the shirt, again taking in Sebastian's aura.

Shaving his head, putting on that crude bravado act; and it was an act. He was scared and needed her as much as she needed him. Her mother needed to understand.

"He needs me."

"He needs you, but he has demons he has to fight first, and you need to let him fight them."

Ta'Rae knew that there was something coming between her and Sebastian, something she refused to address, maybe even someone else.

"You're right—there was someone else in Sebastian's life," her mother told her now as if reading her thoughts.

Ta'Rae knew it! She could feel it.

"I can tell," she told her mother, sitting down on the bed, defeated. "Mama, I can't do this alone anymore." Ta'Rae sniveled while speaking in the direction of where Sebastian used to lay his head.

"Ta'Rae, you don't have to."

"What do you suggest I do?"

"You think about that for a while and look harder for the answers," her mother told her, and then as quickly as she appeared in Ta'Rae's mind, she left.

Ta'Rae slid into bed, still wearing Sebastian's shirt. She hoped just having it on would bring dreams of him to her sleep tonight.

Before long, she drifted off.

Sebastian couldn't sleep. He stared at the clock, wishing he could bring himself to call Ta'Rae. He knew he could probably talk to Precious right now, and she would be willing to hear everything he had to say and maybe even understand some of it, but he knew she would never understand his relationship with Stormy. He barely did. In a way, he was glad Ta'Rae had decided not to come to the Palemos. It was as if planned because he could take care of this business he felt he had with Stormy. He hated this task, but he had to complete it. He needed his slate clean for Ta'Rae and for the rest of the things on his list. In the end, he wanted Ta'Rae to have all of his heart—undivided. And purging Stormy from his past was the only way. He believed that.

He and Stormy spoke nearly every day—argued, laughed, and once he could have sworn she cried on the phone. She dug deep. Stormy had become his gateway to all of his memories—both good and bad—and she was relentless in her probing of his mind and heart. She was worse than Hilton could ever be in forcing him to admit the ugliest of character flaws within himself. However, he had to admit, the weeks spent talking to her, really talking to her, had purged many things. Although she had not admitted to it, he was certain she, too, had found answers to some lingering questions as well. So much so that their relationship was changing a little, maybe progressing. Who could say?

Sebastian had dreaded the appointment, and he was not disappointed. When it was over, he was tired.

"If only I could have a break. These past few weeks have felt like years," he said to Phil. "I mean, I know it's not going to go away, but just a break," he pleaded.

Phil shook his head. "Remission is not indicated," answered Phil flatly. "I'm sorry, Seb. I wish I had better news," he added, rubbing his newly bald head.

"It's okay, buddy. I know you would tell me if there was hope."

"Even an ounce," Phil admitted.

When he left, Sebastian drove slowly on the inside streets, avoiding the freeway. He thought about stopping in on Stormy, but the goal they had set out to establish had been reached. Last night on the phone, they had run out of things to say; five minutes of dead air had passed between them. He couldn't believe it.

He couldn't really say he had found peace for himself, but he knew he had answered Stormy's years of wondering. Sebastian could tell she didn't love him, not the way she thought she did anyway. If anything, she barely liked him, or so she tried to put on.

The thought of Stormy made him smile. He was glad he had found her again. Without finding her, he would not have found Darrell.

Sebastian drove toward the Palemos and then detoured toward the 680. He needed to get away for a while, out of the city.

Before he realized it, he was entering Davis, near Sacramento. He'd not been there in years. Minutes later, he pulled up at the state capital in downtown Sacramento. He parked, got out, and paid the meter.

"I'ma take a tour of this place. God, been a resident of this state for forty-five years and have never been in here." He chuckled, stating the facts to an older woman who was also entering the building for the tour.

After seeing the building, examining the exhibits as if he was a foreigner in a strange land, he again hit the freeway, headed south. Dark came by the time he had hit all the places of interest along highway 99 between Sacramento and Fresno, which were few and far between. Checking into a hotel, he picked up a map to mark out where he would go the next day.

Settling into his room, he noticed that his cell phone showed fifteen calls. He had been missed. However, he didn't return any of them except Stormy's.

"Where are you?" she asked.

"I'm not sure. Like Madera or something," answered Sebastian while peeking out the window of his hotel room. "It's like five hundred degrees here. I know that," he added, unbuttoning his shirt.

"Sebastian, what are you doing? You know you are too far from your doctor, from home. This is not getting you any closer to what you need to find either," she said after pausing, apparently to choose her words carefully. Sebastian laughed, hearing concern in her voice.

"You ever been here?" he asked, changing the subject.

"On my way to Los Angeles. Once, me, Jerry, and the kids drove through there to go to Disneyland."

"Disneyland? Yeah, that's where I'm going next." Sebastian grew instantly excited, kidlike, with the thought.

"Sebastian, I don't think you should," Stormy warned. "Don't make me call your wife again."

"Again?"

Stormy paused.

"I called her the night you went to the hospital."

"Damn, you did? What happened?"

"Nothing. I hung up before she said anything to me. I wasn't gonna talk to her. I'm not your mistress."

"What are you?" Sebastian asked, lying back on the small uncomfortable bed, sipping from his bottled water.

She paused again. "I'm your friend," she finally answered.

"Yeah, friend," Sebastian reluctantly agreed. "Where is Darrell today?" Sebastian asked then, cutting to the chase, taking their relationship where it needed to go next.

"Why are you asking about my son?" Stormy asked, turning defensive.

"Just asking," Sebastian began, again trying to move forward.

"Let's make a deal. No asking about Darrell."

"Why?"

"Because this is about us," she insisted. "We are not finished with *us*."

"I told you, there is no *us*," he said. "And we are so finished with *us,* it's not even funny," he added. "It's time to move on to the next thing—Darrell. Wanna hear what I think about Darrell?"

"We are not even ready to talk about my son. We will never be ready to talk about my son. He is not involved in this—at all!" she said, her anger showing clearly in her tone.

"Yes, he is. I believe that with all my heart, and you're lying to me."

"Go home to your wife, Sebastian."

"My wife has nothing to do with this. Don't bring her up; don't start getting this thing twisted."

"Fine, then, we'll leave her out and we'll leave Darrell out," she said, dealing a hand to him. "You keep me from her and I won't tell Darrell about you."

"That's not fair."

"It's extremely fair. Why hurt people for no good reason?"

Sebastian cursed bitterly into the receiver, trying to keep his anger under his breath but failing.

"Don't be over there cussing me. We got a deal?" she asked again.

"No," Sebastian answered, waiting for her next comment. It took a minute before he realized the phone line was dead. She'd hung up.

"I don't want to worry her," Rita whispered into the phone to Rashawn.

"You might have to. Sebastian hasn't answered his phone all day, and I'm so worried," Rashawn whispered back.

"But maybe he's just, like, out," Rita whispered again, hoping Precious would not hear. She was such a nosy child.

She'd come over looking for her father earlier and got distracted with the baby and hadn't left yet. Rita didn't know how to get her to spend the night without telling her that her father was missing.

"You going over to Ta'Rae's?" Rita finally asked.

"Rita, I need to tell you something," Rashawn began after a long pause.

"Oh my God," Rita exclaimed, even before she'd heard.

"Stop being so dramatic." Rashawn laughed.

"Well, I needed to get that out of the way." Rita chuckled.

"I think Sebastian is having an affair."

"Shudditup." Rita gasped, genuinely shocked this time.

"No. For real."

"You are lying, so shut up," Rita repeated.

"He told me himself," Rashawn assured.

"He told you he is cheating on my sister. He told you that his black ass is cheating on my sister. Dying or no, I'ma beat—"

"No. Listen," Rashawn interjected. "It was when they first got married. He said when Ta'Rae first got pregnant. He said he cheated."

"You are just, like, so kidding me," Rita went on. "With who? And why do you think he's doing it again?"

"She's the one who took him to the hospital that night."

"He's seeing her again?"

"Well, not like seeing her, just, like, seeing her, ya know?" Rashawn tried to explain. "I've heard him on the phone with her . . . well, with somebody. Before he moved out and well—"

"Were they talking dirty?"

"No, Rita, nothing like that." Rashawn took a defensive stance now. "What makes you think I listened that long?"

"Yeah, anyway, does Ta'Rae know?"

"Don't know; maybe that's why they separated. I really don't know."

"Does Carlotta know?"

"Dunno."

"We need a meeting," Rita finally decided.

"You sound like we're some SWAT team." Rashawn laughed.

"Well, we have a crisis on our hands, one that's just crying for our involvement."

Without telling Precious or the nanny her reason for leaving, Rita slipped out and met up with Rashawn and Trina. They then headed to Carlotta's house. She, too, was just about to get concerned about Sebastian. She had called him a couple of times, and now she grew agitated when her sisters informed her he was indeed missing. "Well, shit; call the police, then! He could be lying dead somewhere!" she bellowed.

"He's not dead," Trina said confidently.

"How do you know?"

"Men who cheat never die. They just misplace themselves for a few hours," Trina said, reliving her own injury; having been jilted by her last husband, the injury was still fresh.

"Cheat!"

"Never mind, Lotty. Trina, nobody said he's cheating," Rita corrected her. Trina smacked her lips and rolled her eyes.

"Anyway, we are wondering about Ta'Rae."

"Ta'Rae doesn't even know he's missing, does she?" Carlotta asked. The women all looked at one another.

Getting past her mood, Ta'Rae danced around her kitchen while making a salad. The sun had shown all day, and she was feeling great. She'd thought about her mother again, and a peace came over her. Just the night before, she had again visited with her in the privacy of her mind, and now Ta'Rae's resolve was solid. She would call Sebastian and get all this behind them. He would come home and they would see this thing through together. She would move into his house, or whatever crazy thing he wanted to do.

Her sisters had called and told her they were on their way over. She was actually feeling pretty good about having the company. She was too out of the loop and hung out to dry. It was time to get this breach between them fixed.

"It'll be good to have them over," she admitted, opening the large loaf of French bread and seasoning it. She was planning to serve pasta when they arrived. She'd even aired out a bottle of Chardonnay.

"I'm not sure I'll tell them about my visits with Mama but . . ." She winked at her own reflection in the refrigerator.

"They are going to be sooo tickled when I tell them

that I'm going to move in with Sebastian." Ta'Rae giggled.

Before long, she heard them pulling up. They were always so loud getting out of a car when they all rode together. It was as if they couldn't go five miles without bickering amongst themselves. Ta'Rae snickered at them through the window, watching Trina pushing Rita, and Carlotta fussing at them, telling them to *act right*.

As soon as she heard the doorbell, the phone rang. She answered it as she opened the door, welcoming her sisters in.

"Hello, York residence," she answered.

"Get off the phone, Ta'Rae. We need to talk to you," Trina fussed, moving past her and on into the kitchen. "Ohhh, it sure smells good. I know you made it all low fat, huh? Just for me," she went on.

"Trina, stop," Rita fussed. "We are not here for that."

Ta'Rae fanned her hand at Rita. "Leave her alone," she said, turning her attention back to the phone now.

"You don't know me, but I'm a friend of Sebastian's," the soft voice spoke, freezing Ta'Rae's smile on her face.

"Excuse me?" Ta'Rae asked, moving her body language accordingly, secretively. Carlotta noticed and her ears perked up. "A friend?"

"Yes, and that's all you really need to know, and the fact that Sebastian is safe. He's in Madera," she said.

"Who are you? Madera?" Ta'Rae asked.

The others gathered around the phone now; even Trina was piqued, crunching on the hard bread while trying to listen in. Again, Ta'Rae moved away from them, yet they eased up on her again while she spoke to the mysterious caller.

"Please, just tell me who you are," Ta'Rae requested, feeling her eyes burning and her blood pressure rising. "I won't get angry. I just need to know."

"I think Sebastian needs to be the one to tell you about me," the woman said.

Ta'Rae's heart sank. She'd made the statement that every wife dreads—the "If he was a real man, he would come clean" statement.

"No, you need to tell us who you are!" Trina spoke through gritted teeth into the phone, pulling it from Ta'Rae's ear.

"Trina!" Ta'Rae screeched, taking the phone back. The woman had hung up.

Ta'Rae dropped to the floor in a bundle of tears.

"Star sixty-nine the heffa!" Carlotta screamed, grabbing the phone now.

"She probably has it blocked," Rita figured, walking in a circle as if formulating a plan. Carlotta cursed—Rita was right. The number didn't ring through.

Rashawn dropped to Ta'Rae's side and held her while she fought her own growing emotions.

"Rashawn . . . why . . . how . . . I don't understand," Ta'Rae cried.

"Call him, just call him," Rashawn said, speaking softly.

"Yeah, just call the nig and see what he lies!" Carlotta said angrily, tossing Rashawn the phone. Rashawn took it hesitantly and dialed Sebastian's number, then handed it to Ta'Rae.

Sebastian answered but upon hearing his voice, Ta'Rae shook her head, unable to speak.

"Rae . . . Rae, is that you?" he asked. "Come on now, stop playin'," Sebastian could be heard saying, his voice sounding light and carefree.

Trina groaned loudly and shoved another piece of bread into her mouth, cursing, "Yeah, we got yo' playin', playa."

Rashawn hung up the phone only to immediately hear the jingle that was programmed for Sebastian's cell number. Ta'Rae waited until the second ring before answering it.

"Ta'Rae, what's wrong with your phone?" he asked, sounding tired but cheery.

"Why are you in Madera?" she asked, forcing her voice to come.

He hesitated. "How do you know I'm in Madera? I mean, I bought a shirt, but that's all. Dang, those credit card companies are tough! Hunt you down faster than the FBI." He started laughing.

"It wasn't the credit card company that called me," Ta'Rae said, sounding serious.

"Oh?"

"She called me."

Sebastian's silence sealed it.

"You're not going to deny it?" she asked.

"No. I have nothing to deny," he said.

Ta'Rae looked up at her sisters and then at Rashawn, whose eyes held no secrets now.

She knew.

Getting to her feet, Ta'Rae held the phone to her chest. "You guys go eat," Ta'Rae said, sounding suddenly sober and strong. The sisters looked at one another, knowing that Ta'Rae had to take care of her business now, and though they wanted to be there for her, their time was not yet. So they went into the kitchen to wait.

"Who is she?"

"Ta'Rae," Sebastian began, rubbing his forehead.

"I just want to know. Am I out of line for that?"

"No, Rae, not out of line."

"Good, because I was gonna say too damn bad, because I want to know," Ta'Rae said.

"What I was going to say . . ." Sebastian began after allowing Ta'Rae a moment to gather herself. He could just picture her standing there with her hand on her hip. Her eyes blazing, her lips tight, her jaw line clenched. "What I was going to say was, she's from my past," Sebastian began.

"I'm your past. Do better than that," Ta'Rae said, feeling the heat rise in her face and her stomach tightening.

"Ta'Rae, please," Sebastian said in a commanding tone he hoped told her to be quiet, for just a second at least. "Stormy is a friend. At one time"—Sebastian paused before finishing, carefully tasting the words, knowing this choice of words and the decision to speak would change his life—"she was more."

There was silence.

"How much more is still under debate, but right now she's my friend—nothing more," Sebastian explained.

"Are you sleeping with her?"

"Did you sleep with Chaz?" Sebastian shot back, foolishly flying off the handle and then listening to his words falling without a net to catch them. He instantly regretted everything.

"You bastard! Is that what this is about? Chaz is a colleague!" Ta'Rae shouted, noticing Rashawn's glance out of the corner of her eye.

"And Stormy is my friend. If you expect me to trust you, then, damnit, you need to trust me!" Sebastian yelled.

"Trust! When was she more, Sebastian? Tell me.

We've been together forever. When did you find time for *more*? Tell me that and then I'll let you know how much trust you deserve."

Again there was silence.

"I don't want to talk anymore over the phone," Sebastian said. "I'll come home tonight." His voice was heavy with shame and remorse.

Ta'Rae's heart was heavy. She began to cry.

"No, you tell me now. I don't ever want to see your face again until you tell me," she said through jagged tears.

Sebastian's stomach turned; he was feeling ill. He wanted to hang up, but he knew he couldn't. The woman he loved more than anyone else on the planet was hurting, and he was the cause. He couldn't even blame Stormy for calling. Apparently she felt threatened and was lashing out, fighting back, protecting what she felt was sacred. She was showing him how it felt to have what you treasured most touched in a careless way.

He didn't know how to fix this. If he lied now, they would be ruined. He could not take that to his grave. But if he told her the truth, she would hate him forever, and that was something he could not live with either.

"Rae," Sebastian began while listening to her sobs. He felt the water coming to his own eyes. He squeezed them closed with his fingers—being strong for the both of them was imperative now. How could he make her understand Stormy's place in their lives? "Have you thought much about life without me?" he began.

There were only sobs.

"I've thought about life without you, and even the thought of heaven is hell without you by my side," he began.

Sebastian was never one to mack or play with false words. He was too serious for that. Ta'Rae knew now, no matter what he was about to say, he was telling the truth.

"I love you. I have always loved you," he began. "But there was a time . . . a time when I didn't love myself. I guess. I was selfish and felt I deserved more than the perfection I already had. But I immediately knew that I was wrong. I was so wrong, Rae," Sebastian said, staving off his tears. He had no right to cry. He knew this.

"Then it's true; you were unfaithful to me," Ta'Rae said, barely able to get her words out.

"It was before Precious was born . . ."

"Before? She was born only a year after we married." Ta'Rae's voice questioned.

Sebastian's voice carried with it even more shame now as his words came with heavy sighs. "You had just found out you were pregnant," he admitted.

"You can't possibly have loved her," Ta'Rae seethed with anger.

"I didn't. I don't. I—"

"What is it, then?" she asked, flailing her arms around.

"I have affected her life badly, Rae. I hurt her really bad. I messed up—"

"You hurt me!"

"No. Now listen. I just now hurt you; she's been hurting for years. Baby, see . . . I have to fix that. God knows I can't go out without fixing that," Sebastian tried to explain. It was so complicated, however, and even he wasn't sure he understood what he felt he owed Stormy Brown-Gunther.

Ta'Rae tried to hear him, beyond his words, but the

pain was too great. Sebastian was a good man. She wanted to believe that, now more than ever. But the pain was just too great. She hung up the phone.

When she looked toward the kitchen, all eyes were on her. She wanted to run but couldn't. Her legs felt like lead. She joined them at the table.

"You wanna talk?" Carlotta asked. Ta'Rae took a deep breath and then shook her head.

"You wanna eat?" Trina asked. Again, Ta'Rae shook her head.

"You wanna hug?" Rita asked, grabbing her quickly before she could turn it down. Ta'Rae, covering her face, buried her head into Rita's shoulder and cried.

Sebastian needed a drink. He stepped out of the hotel into the sweltering heat of the San Joaquin Valley. He called Phil.

"I'm feeling just fine," Sebastian told him, answering his inquiry.

"Stay out of the sun as much as ya can. I know it's hot as hell where you are right now. My dad doesn't live far from there," Phil said.

"I didn't know you were a country boy." Sebastian chuckled.

"Yeah, sho' 'nuff." Phil laughed heartily as if having a flashback to a happier time in his life.

Just talking to Phil about such a light topic eased Sebastian's mind. "I'm a city boy," Sebastian admitted. "This is all new to me. The smell is killing me."

Phil laughed, remembering the dairy air.

"My dad didn't speak to me for a month when he realized the college I wanted to go to was actually in the city—Los Angeles at that. Oh my," Phil went on, laughing again at the memories.

"Well, at least it was only a month. My father hasn't spoken to me in, oh, forty-five years."

"Sorry to hear that, Seb," Phil said, sounding serious now, realizing Sebastian's state of mind.

"It's okay. I've had Rae's family. They've been a great substitute."

"Nothing substitutes a father," Phil said flatly.

"You think I haven't thought about that?"

"I'm sorry. I didn't mean to—"

"No, no, Phil. It's okay."

Sebastian spent the next few days driving. He'd freed his mind of many things and eased his mind on many others. He needed to prioritize things. "I have to get things organized," he told Precious over the phone.

"Like that other woman?" she asked cautiously.

"There is no other woman, not like it sounds," he answered.

"Mom thinks there is. She thinks you're with her," Precious told him.

Sebastian sat quietly for a moment. His eyes burned with frustration. He and Stormy had covered so much ground. They had made so much progress until now in regard to self-discovery. He knew this. She had come to realize that, in reality, she was quite happy with herself and her life. She had realized her love for Jerry was based on more than her feelings of low self-esteem. Within their many discussions, Sebastian had told her how he grew up, poor and without much more than a dream of success to keep him going, and how once reaching his goals, why he felt the need to act better than those around him—high and mighty. "It's hard to let that past go, that fear of falling behind," he had confessed. He'd never told anyone that. It felt good to get it out in the open.

"Precious, I want you to understand something. I love your mother more than any woman on this earth. I always have and always will. This woman Stormy, she and I had some unfinished business that I—we—desperately needed to attend to, and I've done that. I'm so sorry that your mother had to get hurt this way, but in the end . . . In the end, this time apart will make us better," he explained. "I'll come back a more together man."

Precious was silent. Sebastian wasn't sure if she understood or not, but he had told her the truth, and that was the best he could do for now.

"Is she with you?"

"No . . . No, she's not with me. I would never do something like that. She's got a husband and a family and . . ." Sebastian paused, almost letting it slip about Darrell. The time was not right to talk about Darrell. That was the only issue he and Stormy still had to work out, and Stormy was unyielding, vicious, where Darrell was concerned; he didn't want Precious getting bit by her next.

"So where are you today?" Precious asked, changing the subject abruptly.

Sebastian looked over the desert outside the restaurant window. "The desert." He laughed.

"You taking your medication?"

"Yeah, Phil called me in a prescription when I got to Santa Barbara, so I picked it up. I'm cool," he told her.

"Mom . . ." Precious paused.

"What about your mom?" Sebastian asked, showing eagerness in his voice.

"She's been really . . ." Precious paused.

"What?" Sebastian asked excitedly, hoping that maybe Ta'Rae had sent a message to him via Precious.

"Sheesh, Dad." Precious chuckled.

"Well I wanna know. I mean . . ." He paused.

"She's weird. I mean, weirder than normal—if that's possible. She's been working and all that, but . . . Well, I think she's been in her room talking to herself and then she's been like . . . knitting," Precious finally said, as if the concept was so foreign, she couldn't bring herself to face it.

"Knitting?" Sebastian asked, totally surprised.

"Yeah, she just starting coming in from the hospital at night, getting all comfy in that big rocker and, well, she knits! She said her mother told her it would help."

"Her mother?"

"Yeah, Dad, Grandma Zenobia. Dad, please come home as soon as you can."

After Precious and he spoke, Sebastian wanted to call Ta'Rae but couldn't bring himself to. He needed just a little more time to work out some things; apparently, she did too.

"Her mother? Knitting?" he heard himself ask.

Could she forgive him? That was the question that filled Ta'Rae's brain to capacity. Ta'Rae knew it was only she and her mother who could figure it out and come up with the answer—not Carlotta, Rita, Rashawn, or Shelby, although they all had been trying, prying.

Ta'Rae knew she appeared crazy to them, working like a madwoman, doubling rounds at the hospital and then spending all her downtime rocking and knitting. But they would never understand, and there was no way she could explain to them the need for this time with Zenobia. The internal exchanges between them were deep and enlightening and to a certain degree, healing.

They married on a warm June day. Everything was perfect. She remembered how handsome Sebastian was and how proud she felt—maybe even a little haughty that she had nabbed a man like him. He was gorgeous, talented, and more than any woman could want. "But he had that side of him, that mysterious side," Ta'Rae told her mother.

"It wasn't a mystery, Ta'Rae. You just didn't want to figure it out. You just didn't want to look that deep, for fear you would see something dark lying there."

"Dark?"

"You never asked any question about his family— his mother, his father, his life before meeting you," Zenobia explained, straightening out the yarn while sitting on the floor in front of the rocker.

She wore her country's ethnic garb, colorful and bright. Her hair was braided high on her head, and her smile was youthful.

"I guess I figured that he would have told me about his past, if in fact he had one," Ta'Rae reasoned, only to see her mother shaking her head vehemently.

"Men don't volunteer things like that, especially if the memories are painful, and I think . . . I think Sebastian had a lot of pain and anger in his past."

"Pain? Anger?"

"And now he has to face it, all of it, and find peace and forgiveness before he dies."

Ta'Rae sat down her project and pondered the thought of Sebastian being unhappy, angry. She had never thought about him in that light.

"Do you think I was the reason he . . ." Ta'Rae paused, unable to finish the sentence.

"No, I don't think you were the reason he did that, but you weren't the reason he didn't. Not everything people do is for the reasons everyone else thinks they do it."

"If he loved me, Mama, he wouldn't have done what he did," Ta'Rae insisted.

"Maybe, maybe not, but think about this. You don't have forever to figure it out. You don't have forever to forgive him."

"If he cared about his vows, he wouldn't have broken them."

"If he didn't care about his vows, he wouldn't be tryin' his damnedist to get back to them."

Their eyes met, and with understanding, Ta'Rae's heart eased of the hurt just a little more. All she could hope was that Sebastian made it back in time.

The heat bore down on Sebastian as he cleared the border into Mexico. He didn't know what brought him there, but he knew he needed to be there.

Sebastian had never been superstitious, but there was something magical about Mexico. He remembered the year he and Ta'Rae had gone there on vacation— Las Cruces, that's where they were, and now he was there.

He remembered the little store where he'd met the old man, the man with the riddled words. Sebastian promised he would return once he figured out the meaning of the man's words, and now he felt he had.

The man was old even back then, and Sebastian feared he was dead now. But he'd come all this way, and there was no way he was turning back now, not without at least finding out, not without a chance to tell the man what he knew about life and what he was learning about death.

The door jingled when he entered. The smell of fresh tobacco filled his nose, rich and full-bodied. From behind the curtain stepped a lovely young Mexican woman. She was dressed in traditional clothing, bright and festive. Her hair was long and thick, her smile warm.

"Buenos días, señor," she greeted.

"Buenos días," Sebastian greeted back.

"Can I help you?" she asked in broken English.

"I'm looking for an old man. He was here the last time I came. But it's been a long time. He's an Indian I think. He was a medicine man," Sebastian asked awkwardly. His question brought a bright smile to the girl's face.

"Joe, yes, he's here."

Sebastian's heart leapt.

Yes, he'd come to see the old man. He'd come to answer the old man's riddle and learn more of what the old man taught. He came to believe in the old Indian's medicine.

Sebastian needed to believe. He needed something to cling to. The young girl led him behind the heavy curtain and into a room lit only by candles.

"Siéntese abajo, por favor," she instructed, pointing to a fringed rug. Sebastian obeyed.

Soon the back curtain opened, and Joe walked in, looking no older than he had the last time Sebastian had seen him. It was truly amazing.

"Hello, my friend," the Indian greeted. Sebastian reached out and took his hand.

The old man upon touching him looked instantly sad. "You've been sick," he stated assuredly.

Sebastian, stunned and amazed, just nodded. "Very," he admitted.

"You are here for strong medicine," Joe said, leaning close to him, smiling.

Sebastian just smiled back, feeling less than certain about why he was there.

During the night, Ta'Rae had fitful sleep. She'd dreamed about her mother again, and Sebastian. Her dreams filled with visions and symbols that no doubt had meaning beyond her comprehension. She tossed and turned, waking in a sweat. It was a warm night. "But not that warm," she panted, throwing the covers off.

The bay had sent a breeze over its waters, so there was not really any true summer there in the Bay Area, so Ta'Rae was confused a little.

"This is more than a hot flash," she thought aloud, admitting to herself that she indeed felt invaded, exposed—violated.

Where was Sebastian? No one had heard from him in weeks.

Finally, she did resort to looking at the credit card statements, but the last one was over two weeks old now, useless. She'd even called his cell phone. He'd not answered.

Giving in to the insomnia, she began to wander the house. First she peeked in on Precious, who slept like an infant. Ta'Rae then ventured downstairs to the kitchen where, by the light of the open fridge, she poured herself a tall glass of juice.

Maybe her mind was too cluttered. Perhaps a little knitting would clear it. "That's what Mama's been telling me anyway." Ta'Rae chuckled, realizing how the therapy of visiting with her mother was easing much sadness and loneliness for her. And actually, so far, knitting was working out pretty good too. She'd nearly finished a nice-looking afghan.

When she turned to head to her favorite chair in the living room, she saw a shadowy figure there, showing against the moonlight coming in from the large bay window.

"Travonya," he said with a voice, deep and rumbling, familiar yet . . .

She screamed, her volume matched by the juice glass crashing into the bricks of the fireplace as it left her hand. Sebastian stood and quickly clicked on the lamp. "Baby, it's me, Sebastian. You walked right past me when you went into the kitchen."

Ta'Rae held her heart as it beat madly in her chest. Precious, too, came flying down the stairs with tennis racket in hand and eyes widened in fear and excitement.

Sebastian chuckled upon seeing the women in his life ready to defend themselves against prowlers.

Ta'Rae's body jerked with an instant need to go to him to hold him, yet Precious's reflexes were faster. She flew into her father's arms.

"Daddy! You're all right. I was so worried," she cried, her tears of joy coming like water. Ta'Rae noticed a pouch hanging from a strip of leather around his neck. Precious noticed it too. "What's this?" she asked.

Sebastian loosened his hold on her without taking his eyes off Ta'Rae during the entire exchange. "Sweetie, let me and Mom have a minute, okay," he said.

Precious looked at her mother and then at her father, realizing then how different he looked. He'd even gained a little weight it seemed. She stepped back from him. "I'm just gonna be upstairs. Let me know if you, ummm, if we're gonna go to the house, I mean, I wanna go with you," Precious spoke cautiously before turning and running back upstairs. "Don't leave me . . . if you go," she called over her shoulder.

The moment between Ta'Rae and Sebastian lasted nearly a whole minute, forever it seemed, before he stepped forward, meeting her halfway as she fell into his arms. They kissed like young lovers. Ta'Rae didn't care about anything but being in his arms. He felt strong and alive, virile and healthy. Ta'Rae knew she was not dreaming this. "Where have you been?" she asked, barely able to speak.

"I'll tell you in the morning," he said, leading her up the stairs.

Ta'Rae followed without asking any more questions.

They undressed slowly, Sebastian removing Ta'Rae's gown easily, kissing her breasts as he pulled it over her head. He then stood admiring her body, turning her around slowly as if looking at her for the first time.

Ta'Rae could not speak. It had been so long since she'd felt his touch. She knew her words could only lessen what she felt.

The sea breeze could not cool the heat Sebastian was creating as he laid her back on the bed. His kisses were slow, lingering, his lips delicious, decadent. She ran her hands over his smooth head, indulging him as he explored her body, taking his time.

He kissed her face, her neck; his hands wandered to

all the familiar places, bringing back all the familiar feelings. She reciprocated, hoping for the same.

Sebastian had been impotent for most of the year, and she worried about tonight. However, reaching his thighs and running her hands between them, she found a strong erection growing.

Closing his eyes, his smile lingered on his face as she stroked his manhood, caressing it, owning it, guiding it home.

Forgiveness came easy as they both declared their eternal love for each other in this world and into the next. Nothing else mattered except their oneness tonight.

He took her deep and thoroughly, not missing any spots. He was thick with desire for her, and she wanted him. Calling his name over and over, she told him as much.

Sebastian knew tonight was only for tonight. They had not solved or resolved any of their issues, but fortunately, loving each other was never a problem for them.

Ta'Rae's body felt like a dream, closing around his—the perfect fit. How could he tell her that the years spent with her had made his life worth living—and made dying nearly impossible to accept. How could he explain what he had done to extend his life just a moment longer? Would she believe it anyway? Would she believe as strongly as he did right now the magic of an old man from Mexico?

She buried her face against his chest, giving in to an orgasm, one that shook her whole body.

He didn't know how long his virility would last, but tonight he wanted to make the best of the medicine man's juju.

"No man should die without a woman's tears to

mourn him," the man had said, handing him the pouch.
"And a woman cannot mourn a man who has not loved
her with all his might," he added.

Ta'Rae had three more orgasms before finally
Sebastian could hold back no longer. His release was
tremendous, causing him to give way to voice.

They giggled in their afterglow, hoping only that
Precious was not listening.

"What's this?" Ta'Rae asked, still lying under
Sebastian as they relaxed in the residual of the best sex
they'd had in a long time.

Sebastian held it up so she could see it closer. "I
really don't know, but I've been taking it for two
weeks," Sebastian confessed.

"You don't know?" Ta'Rae asked.

"I think it's monkey turds or something like that."
He chuckled. Ta'Rae burst into laughter.

It was good to hear her laugh.

"No, seriously, I got it in Mexico."

"You went to Mexico?"

"Yeah," Sebastian answered, saying no more about
it, although his tone spoke degrees. Ta'Rae didn't ask
any more. Whatever happened in Mexico had brought
him home, if even for one night. She would accept that
and ask no questions.

The few months that followed were blissful for the
York family. They had almost forgotten about the
demon that sat at the back door . . . waiting . . . panting
in his evil, for just the right moment to strike, to push
them off the top.

* * *

Terrell sat at his desk pondering his household situation. It was bad. He really needed to get rid of Kenita. She was a psychopath. No one wanted to believe him. But he was a lawyer; he was trained to spot the crazies, and she was one of them. At this point in time, Terrell couldn't put his finger on why he thought that way, but he really believed that she was trying to kill him.

About that time, he looked up to find Sebastian entering his office. He looked perky enough. *What a trooper he is. Brave as hell too*, Terrell thought to himself.

Terrell had to admit that he wouldn't know how to act if he was going through what Sebastian was going through. According to Rita, he was dealing with his past and his present with the absence of a future. It had to be tough.

"What's up?" Terrell asked, greeting his brother-in-law with a manly hug. They tapped fists, and Sebastian sat down, making himself comfortable.

Silence fell over him for a moment or two. Sebastian looked almost regretful for coming in. Suddenly Terrell realized what he was possibly there for. His chest tightened, and he suddenly found it hard to swallow, to speak. Terrell wanted no part of writing Sebastian's will.

"What can I do for ya?" Terrell asked after taking in some air. Sebastian smiled that sly smile of his.

Even with the thinning face and smooth head, he was still a handsome man. He'd always had it so together. It was hard watching him, knowing that on the outside, he was one way, but inside he was being eaten alive.

Over the past few months, Terrell figured Sebastian had been in some kind of remission, but it was anyone's guess how long that would last. Some folks stayed in one for years, others just enough time to get them excited about living. Terrell feared the latter in Sebastian's case, because lately Sebastian had been looking rather tired, and he was losing weight again.

"I have a job for you . . . well, for your investigator. You have one of those working for you, right?"

"Yes, I do," answered Terrell, his interest piqued and his heart lightened. Writing Sebastian's will was not a task he was looking forward to. He actually hoped that Sebastian already had that taken care of.

"Is he good?"

"Yeah, he's worth his pay."

Sebastian reached in his back pocket and pulled out his wallet. From the billfold, he pulled out an aged picture of what looked to Terrell to be a young white man.

"Do you think he can find this man?" Sebastian asked, holding up the picture. Terrell took the small old photo from him and looked on the back. It was dated in pencil along with the word *Hendrix*.

"Who is it?"

"My father."

Terrell gawked at the picture, looking closer, and then at Sebastian. "Your father?"

"Yes. I need to find him before I die. I need to at least see his face before I die," Sebastian said, repeating himself for conviction. "I've got this list, see, of things I would like to do before—"

"I understand."

"Finding this man is one of them," Sebastian said, tapping the picture.

"Do you know where I would start?"

"No. I was hoping your investigator would know how to proceed. I was born in San Francisco and raised in Oakland. Somewhere between there and here lies this man, Hendrix."

"Well, okay," Terrell said now, picking up the phone and dialing his ace detective, Adam Sage. Adam used to be a personal attendant to the rich and famous. He gave it all up for his first love—detective work.

"And this Negro is not cheap," Terrell went on, rating Adam's qualifications based on his fee.

"Oh, I'll pay," said Sebastian, reaching for his wallet that was on the desk. Terrell held up his hand.

"You know your money is no good here in this office." Terrell frowned as if insulted. "Your money is only good on a football bet or a fancy restaurant bill."

Sebastian laughed.

"Adam, Terrell McAlister. I have a job for you," Terrell said into the phone.

Sebastian went over his list in his mind. *Whew, got all that little stuff out of the way*, he thought, thinking over the menial tasks listed there. He'd gotten to the meatier issues, Hendrix and Darrell, and of course the issue of revising his will. *I'll wait on that one a little longer*. He put his mind on Darrell. He'd called to speak with Stormy just the day before, and Darrell had answered the phone. Just hearing the boy's voice was enough for Sebastian's heart to confirm the thoughts in his head.

Ta'Rae had not brought up the issue of his affair with Stormy. Sebastian wasn't sure if she was over it or just avoiding it. Who could ever know with Rae?

Sebastian looked over at her sleeping, appearing carefree. He kissed her forehead. She had said nothing about the night before and his inability to perform again. They both knew this would be the way it was from now on.

Now on. The thought made him laugh inside. His *now on* was today, but for Ta'Rae, she still had tomorrow. One day she would even find another lover to take his place in her bed. *Maybe even this bed*, he thought.

Sebastian thought about the days with Stormy. It was funny that no matter how many times he thought back, he could never remember how she felt, how the sex felt. It was strange how much he took for granted back then. So much he had put at stake to gain not so much as a decent memory. He glanced at Ta'Rae again. How he hoped she would have memories of him—good memories of him, lasting ones. How he wished they could have another child.

How he wished he could penetrate her one more time.

"How do I beat this thing?" he asked himself. "There's got to be a way. I've never lost anything before in my life. This will not beat me—this will not beat us," he added, whispering the words into Ta'Rae's ear softly, wanting the words to travel into her subconscious. He wanted the words to arm her to be his backup, to reinforce her, to gird her up and ready her for anything.

Not knowing if she heard him or not, he watched her awaken, her exotic eyes opening slowly to meet the gray morning. She turned and glanced at him over her bare shoulder. He kissed her there.

"Why are you watching me sleep?" she asked, quickly rubbing the sleep from her face, smoothing back her hair.

"I watch you sleep a lot," he confessed.

She smiled and then glanced at the clock. "You let

me sleep too long. I have to get to the hospital," she said, throwing back the blankets.

He held her back for a moment. "Do you have to go in?"

"Of course I do." She chuckled.

"It's been getting lonely around here without you," he admitted, allowing his insecurity to come up.

"Sebastian, what are we going to do today? It's Monday, dear," she replied sweetly.

"We could find some things to do," he flirted. Ta'Rae smiled at him, patting his hand almost patronizingly before climbing out of the bed anyway and heading into the bathroom to shower.

Sebastian welled up with emotion. He was impotent, and Ta'Rae was pretending she didn't notice or care. Ta'Rae and her pretences . . . He couldn't go through it, not again.

Adam Sage was good at his job. He could find anyone, anywhere.

Stepping into the bar in Chico, California, on the corner of Main and Third, he spied a man who looked very much like the man in the photo—with forty hard years on him. He was a tall, thin man with long white hair that he wore in a ponytail. Heavy lines and scars marred his once-handsome face.

Wiping the bar with the rag, he watched Adam as he slid up to the counter. "What can I do you for?" he asked, sounding gruff and rugged, nothing like the man he'd met in Terrell's office.

Sebastian York was cultured, refined, and despite his failing health, was the epitome of a man's man. This dude was rough. He'd seen the hard end of many situations, even the law. From his research, Adam had found out many unpleasant things about Sebastian Hendrix— Henny as he was now known.

Henny had done time for murder—apparently going to prison the year Sebastian was born. He'd been free for about fifteen years; however, living aboveboard was not in his calling—he'd been in and out over the years for minor things, from drug possession to assault and battery. He owned this bar true enough, but blood money had paid for it.

From the looks of things overall, Dr. Sebastian York was going to be very disappointed in what Adam Sage had found this day.

"I'm looking for someone," Adam said, pulling out the photo he carried of Hendrix . . . a lifetime ago.

The old man held the photo up to the dim light. An iniquitous smile flashed across his lips and then ran and hid behind the gruff exterior that owned his face and normally hid his true feelings. "Never seen him," he lied.

"Really, because my sources tell me he owns this bar," Adam went on, baiting him.

"Well, that's pretty fuckin' funny because I own this bar," he barked, and went back to wiping the counter. "So you need to get your sources straight on that," he added.

"Oh, they are pretty straight," Adam went on.

"And who might your sources be?"

"That man's son," Adam said, pointing at the picture that the man had laid down on the bar. Adam watched for a reaction. There was none. He was good.

"Yeah, seems like this picture is all this man has of his father, after his mother died."

The gruff man flinched.

Got him.

"Yeah, when his mother died a few years back, he found this picture among her treasures. I guess she felt something for this guy and—"

"What's the son's name?"

"Sebastian, like his father," Adam said, hoping still to corner the man, Sebastian Hendrix, into admittance.

The man again released a crooked smile that his face immediately punished for appearing without permission. "Why would he want to find a father who hadn't been around for so long?" the man asked, a slight accent escaping in his words. Adam picked up the dialect—Louisianan.

"Because the man I'm working for is dying, and he wanted some closure. He wanted to make an accounting," Adam told him.

The rough man's eyes now caught Adam's in a death grip that caused his heart to race. The man's eyes caused Adam to take account of himself—his gun, his car, his means of escape.

"What would a father want with a dying son? Why in the hell would he want to meet him now?"

"Closure, Mr. Hendrix, that's all."

"My name is Claude, my friends call me Henny. You know, like the drink." He coughed now, hacking from the years of smoking and bad living.

"Yes, I know the drink."

"Good, then you know me," Hendrix said flatly, his foul breath hitting Adam in the face.

Adam slid a copy of Sebastian York's photo toward the man, along with a card that had Sebastian's information on it. "Closure is all he asks for, and from what I've gathered, it's the least you could do," Adam said, turning to walk out of the musty place.

"Hey," Henny called. Adam turned to him, hoping he had convinced the man to see Sebastian, and maybe at the same time, hoping in his heart that this man Henny left Sebastian alone.

"What's he dying of?"

"Cancer," Adam answered flatly. Sebastian had given him the green light to offer up whatever information he saw fit. So he did, and for a second, Adam again saw Henny react to the news, but then, once more, the battered face stiffened and he simply grunted his response. "Well, if you see the man I'm looking for, give him my message, okay?" Adam requested. Again Henny grunted and went back to the counter. Adam Sage didn't realize until he got outside how hard it had been to breathe.

Precious had actually done it. She'd voluntarily chosen college preparatory classes for the fall. After looking over all the hard courses she'd chosen, she rolled her eyes and groaned.

"What am I thinking?" she asked herself, shoving the paper deep into the pocket of her jeans.

"Problem?" a nice-looking boy asked her. His smile was familiar, but for the life of her, she couldn't place him. Of course, so many of the nerdy guys were coming back simply gorgeous this year, as if they'd all spent the summer at some magical pond of good looks. But she was certain she didn't know this guy.

"Nah, just, like, getting ready to take my brain on a mystery tour." She groaned. He chuckled. "You going here? You new?" she asked.

"Oh no, I go to Central," he admitted. She nodded as they slowly began to stroll toward her car.

"That's an okay school," she told him. The school itself sucked, but every year Central's track team kicked their track team's butt and left them eating serious dust, so that had to account for something. It was the only time the private school interacted with the public school and, well, frankly, it was never worth their time.

She stopped walking and stared at him.

"Do you know me?"

"No," he told her.

The silence between them was thick now. He was cute and all, but Precious felt no initial attraction beyond that. Maybe it was still her broken heart left over from Drake; who knows, but getting to know another boy *that way* this soon was out of the question. She was glad this boy wasn't inspiring anything remotely romantic to come up inside her.

"I don't date," she told him.

He waved his hand. "Okay."

The boy stood quiet for a long time as if he'd said all the wrong things now and didn't know how to fix them. They reached her car, where she awkwardly hoped he could see that she had to leave now, but instead of getting the hint and walking away, he stood looking around as if wanting to say more.

"Do you want my phone number or something?" she asked, thinking that might be his purpose for lingering.

"No," he answered flatly.

"Look, you're kinda creeping me out. At least tell me your name."

"Oh, cheeesus." He chuckled, sounding even more familiar now. "My name is Darrell—I thought you knew that."

"How could I know that if I've never met you?"

"Never mind. Look, I don't even know what I'm doing here. I just wanted to meet you and now I have, so—"

"You came all the way from Central just to meet me?"

"Yeah, and now I did and well, I gotta go." He turned to leave.

"Wait," Precious called to him. He was a curious boy, and he intrigued her.

"What?" he asked, stopping in his tracks as if suddenly very disturbed and upset with himself for having gone through with this.

"I feel like I do know you," she told him. "Are you sure we haven't met before?"

Darrell smiled and shook his head. "No, Precious, we've never met before," he answered.

"How do you know my name?" she asked, only to have Darrell continue on his way.

Singers was crowded tonight. Sebastian had asked everyone to join him and Ta'Rae at the restaurant for their anniversary celebration.

"It could be our last," he told them.

Scott had insisted on picking up the tab. "My gift," he said.

The music was soothing, and the company was pleasant as they ate their meal and visited together as a family. Everyone was avoiding the obvious conversation topic—Sebastian's pending demise.

"Okay, nobody wants to talk about it, but I will," Terrell finally blurted as all eyes fixed on him, wondering what he would say. Terrell had never been known for his tact.

"Kenita is trying to kill me," he said, getting sighs of

relief, hidden behind groans of sarcasm. He was in true form tonight—fortunately.

"Look, T, I told you that girl is minding her own business. You are being paranoid," Rita told him.

"Now, now, she might be trying to take him out. Let's hear what he did to her," Carlotta requested, bringing rounds of laughter from the table. Sebastian, too, joined in the folly, glancing just briefly at Ta'Rae, who seemed distracted, looking around sighing heavily. He would give anything to know what was on her mind.

The conversation about the homicidal nanny continued without Sebastian paying any further attention. He was drawn to Ta'Rae and what was possibly on her mind. She didn't see him staring at her. She was just that deep in her thoughts, playing with her earring, sipping her wine, looking around while the others laughed and talked among themselves. Suddenly there was a tinkling of crystal, and Sebastian was drawn back to the group. Scott was standing, preparing a toast to the anniversary couple.

"To Ta'Rae and Sebastian, the two most loveable, loving, and lovely people I've ever met," he toasted.

"Here! Here!"

"Ta'Rac and Sebastian!"

"To my sister and her man." The toasts continued.

"Here! Here!"

Around the table the toasts went until they came to Ta'Rae, who now looked at Sebastian for the first time this evening. Her eyes covered his face as if she now faced a stranger. Someone she didn't know who had possessed the man she once loved. *Once loved?* Sebastian asked himself, watching Ta'Rae stand and smile at everyone at the table and then back at him. Her words seemed stuck in her throat as if tangled in her heartstrings.

"To Sebastian," she began, clearing her voice. "To Sebastian," she began again, her sound level, almost a whisper.

"The man whose life was shared with me . . . and who I would give anything to share my life with . . . forever," she said before setting down the glass and rushing to the ladies' room. Rashawn and Trina went after her.

The table was silent with all eyes on Sebastian, who straightened his collar, showing a little uneasiness with the attention suddenly shown him. Rita quickly wiped her tears and smiled at him.

"These chicks sure know how to mess up a party," Terrell said in his usual crass manner, attempting to lighten a tense situation. Scott and Sebastian laughed.

Ta'Rae woke up and reached over for Sebastian. He was missing from his side of the bed—it was cool where he normally laid. She shot up and looked around for him.

"Sebastian!" she called out.

No answer.

"Sebastian!" she called again while slipping into her house shoes and checking the bathroom. He wasn't there. She went down the hall calling for him while looking over the banister, unintentionally waking Precious, who came out of her room.

"Mom, what's the matter?"

"Nothing, sweetie . . . nothing," Ta'Rae lied, rushing down the stairs, following the kitchen light.

When she reached the breakfast nook, she found

Sebastian on the floor in the fetal position, gripping his belly. He was clearly hanging on to consciousness by a thread. His face twisted with pain that she knew was no doubt nearly unbearable. She glanced around, noticing his spilled glass of water and his medication on the floor.

"It's okay, Sebastian. I'm here now," she told him. He nodded slightly and then slowly closed his eyes in relief, so thankful she had arrived when she did.

Without panicking, Ta'Rae instructed Precious to call 911 and then Phil. "Tell Phil's service it's Dr. York calling. We're having a crisis," she said, sounding cool and calm, under control. Precious, who only hung on by her mother's strength, quickly obeyed. "And then get my bag," Ta'Rae further instructed Precious.

Sebastian groaned in agony while Ta'Rae quickly tended to his pain with an injection of morphine. "You're going to be fine, Sebastian," she assured him, sounding strong and brave—for the both of them.

Two weeks later, Sebastian was back home. He knew things would never be the same again. He just had no clue how bad it was going to be from here on out. He didn't want to know but had a feeling he was about to find out. A sadistic play was about to come on his life's stage—with him as the star.

"How is he doing?" Carlotta asked.

"He's okay . . . cranky," Ta'Rae answered.

"Cranky?" Carlotta asked, thinking the word was an odd choice.

"Wouldn't you be?" Ta'Rae answered abruptly.

"Ta'Rae, what are you going to do? I mean, have you made any plans?" Carlotta asked cautiously.

"No! What kind of question is that?"

"Look, you need to stop all these stupid—" Carlotta caught her temper. "You need to start thinking about the future."

"How can you suggest that? What are you saying?"

Carlotta looked around and then back at Ta'Rae. "I wish we were at my place, because I want to seriously slap the black offa you right now," Carlotta growled under her breath.

"The answer is nothing. I'm not going to do anything. I'm already doing something," Ta'Rae explained.

Carlotta huffed.

"Have you thought about what you would do if Scott died?" Ta'Rae asked, thinking she had hit pay dirt in the get-her-back department. But Carlotta smiled instead.

"Yes. As a matter a fact, I have thought about it. Me and Scott talked about it, and I know exactly what I'm going to do," Carlotta answered, taking a long sip of her Diet Coke and saying no more on the topic.

Ta'Rae was dumbfounded and for a moment was forced to reflect on her own situation. "Well, I still have my practice," she began.

"And that's good, because you are gonna need the money. And you need to sell that big-ass house you're living in. I know having money all these years has been wonderful, and you two have always afforded whatever your heart's desired, but listen Ta'Rae, it's not going to be the same on one income; it's just not. You need to start downsizing just a little."

"Never—"

"And you need to take Precious out of that damn

private school for her last year. Let her get a taste of the real life, because an expensive college may not be in her cards. She may actually have to pay her own way through college."

"No way." Ta'Rae fanned her hand in the air, as if Carlotta's words were obscene. "We have her college fund."

"You need to sell one of those cars. Sebastian isn't going on any road trips for a while. You have three; the insurance alone is probably a small house note. Speaking of which—"

"Next you'll say to give up the time-share."

"Scott was just talking about that. He's got a buyer if you and Sebastian are interested. Be honest—when will you ever use that time-share again?"

Ta'Rae was floored. She swallowed the thick lump of humility that had formed in her throat.

Terrell looked in the mirror. The lines in his face were deepening; maybe it was just worry. Maybe he was being poisoned. He'd heard that some poisons could distort the face, wrinkle it all up and stuff like that.

Just then, he heard the door jingle and Nigel's voice greeting Sebastian. He quickly came from the bathroom.

"Hey, man," he greeted, shaking Sebastian's hand. Sebastian looked around uncomfortably before sitting down. Terrell knew today was the day.

"I want to write my will today," Sebastian said to the both of them.

Terrell began to sweat. His breathing shortened, and he immediately felt ill. He had wondered how he would feel when the time came, and now he knew.

"Nigel is a pro at this kind of thing, man," Terrell said, reneging from the duty, heading for the door, grabbing his sports jacket off the rack before busting out the door. Once stepping outside, Terrell took a deep cleansing breath and headed to his car.

Sebastian's inevitable death had not fully hit Terrell until now, and it was too much to take. Terrell walked into his house, looking around at the toys all scattered about. He could hear the children screaming in the kitchen while Kenita was preparing their lunch. When the boys heard the door close, they all ran to the living room. Terrell squatted for them to jump into his arms and hugged them all tight. His eyes burned with held-back tears. He was sad and could no longer help but feel it. He was helpless to change what was going on around him. He could do nothing but continue living while Sebastian died.

Death never sat well with Terrell, having lost both of his parents as a small boy. Terrell knew what he missed not having a father. He could not imagine his boys' lives without him. Terrell knew then what he was going to do—spend more time at home with Rita and the kids. He was going to start building some meaningful memories for them.

Just then, Kenita came from the kitchen holding Zenobia, smiling at him. "Kenita, I think by month's end we are going to make other arrangements for the care of the kids," he said to her.

Her face dropped. "What?" she asked.

"Other arrangements . . . we are going to make . . ." He stumbled, noticing her face distorting with growing anger. Terrell's feeling of remorse and gloominess suddenly turned to a little alarm. "Why don't you put Zenny down," he suggested seriously. Kenita didn't move.

"Put my daughter down, Kenita," Terrell repeated, only now it was a firm order.

"Put Zenny down," one of the twins repeated.

Suddenly, as if returning to her normal self, Kenita smiled and quickly sat the baby down. "It's okay, honey," she said to Zenny. "Daddy didn't mean it," she purred.

"Oh yeah, Daddy meant it," Terrell said, wanting her to turn to face him. Instead, she went to her room and slammed the door. Terrell heard it lock. He cursed under his breath. This was bad.

Startled, Stormy awoke; she was sweating and shaking all over. Her abrupt jolt woke Jerry as well.

"What's wrong?" he asked, sleep still holding tight to his senses. Stormy jumped out of the bed and scrambled for her shoes. Jerry joined her, still in a fog but right on her heels.

"Stormy, what is going on?"

"He hasn't called me in weeks. Weeks!" she yelled.

"What are you talking about? Who are you talking about?"

"Sebastian! I need to go get the paper. I need to see the obituaries. What if he's dead?"

"Stormy, stop," Jerry said, grabbing her arms, keeping her from putting on her coat and going out into the cold. He wasn't sure if she was even fully awake. She was acting far too erratic to be thinking clearly.

Instantly she broke down in tears. "Who would call me? There is no way I would know. They don't know about me," she cried. Jerry held her tight. "He could be dead!"

"He's not dead, Stormy."

She sobbed into his chest. "Oh, Jerry, I had such a horrible dream," she cried.

Jerry stroked her hair, tugging lightly on one of her braids. "He's not dead," he repeated.

"How do you know?"

"I just know," Jerry admitted, trying to avoid a full confession.

Stormy looked at him closer now, her brow dipped as she read the guilt on his face. She rubbed the nightmare from her eyes. "Jerry, what are you trying not to tell me?" she asked.

"I'm trying not to tell you a couple of things," he confessed. "First, I'm trying not to tell you how jealous I am that he's got your dreams tied up like this. Second thing is that the gig I had didn't pay as much as we had planned, and so I've been doing some solos for some extra money."

"Jerry, why didn't you tell me?"

"Wait," said Jerry, shushing her gently. "I'm doing solos at Singers, you know, that real expensive place in the city. Well, a couple of weeks ago I saw a dude and his wife. I mean, I figured it was his wife, the way they were together, you know. It was them and a few other couples. Looked like family, you know," Jerry went on.

"Go on," Stormy requested as if she needed to pause for a second to gather her mental notes, connect the dots correctly. She didn't know Jerry even knew what Sebastian looked like. There would be a couple of things to address when Jerry finished his story—she knew that.

Jerry shook his head and chuckled apprehensively. "Singers," he continued. "They were just there like it wasn't nothing to afford a place like that. They had to have laid out over a grand just for dinner and drinks. They had bottles of champagne flowin' and all that."

"You sure it was him?"

"Yeah, it was Dude. I saw the picture, Stormy," Jerry admitted, confessing to an invasion of her privacy. Jerry knew she had the picture hidden. It wasn't like he didn't have to dig for it. It was a picture taken during the summer. He didn't ask when they had been together at Fisherman's Wharf, but apparently they had been there and gotten their picture taken together.

"How did he look?" she asked, not noticing Jerry's fallen expression.

"He looked in love with his wife, Stormy," Jerry told her, waiting to see if the words hurt. He wanted them to hurt, just a little.

Suddenly she stopped speaking and held him tight. "And here you are trying to hold us together and look at me—I'm acting crazy over another man. Jerry, what's wrong with me?" she asked.

"Stormy," Jerry began, holding her head to his chest, rocking her gently, feeling instant regret over doubting her love for him, "baby, if you didn't ask about that dude, I would wonder about you. I knew when I got with you, there was somebody else in your heart. I mean, hell, I could tell the way you looked at Darrell that you were still in love with his daddy."

"You're Darrell's daddy, Jerry."

Jerry lifted her face to his. "But I'm not this father."

Stormy ended his words with a kiss, a long one that spoke to him beyond words.

"But you are his daddy—always," Stormy finally said.

"Always is promised to nobody, love," Jerry told her.

"Love is always promised to us," Stormy responded, pulling him back to the bed.

Fall brought in early rain and many fallen leaves. Sebastian worked at his house, cleaning the drains so that he would not run into problems come winter. His mind was on so many things yet nothing all at once. Everything seemed to be back to normal after that last incident. It was almost scary.

Ta'Rae had been nothing but perfect. Precious had started her senior year in school, and by the looks of it, her grades to date had *scholarship* written all over them. He so wanted her to continue her education, maybe even become a doctor. It was better than any of the other options he could think of for her.

Drake. The name hadn't come to his mind in months, and he quickly shook it away now. Even a hint that Precious would end up with a man like that shook Sebastian's core.

"I'd have to keep living to prevent that from happenin'." He chuckled. If only it was that easy of a deal to make.

Sebastian enjoyed tinkering at his second home, although he still could not convince Ta'Rae to share his excitement over it. Sebastian would work on the house every weekend, with or without Precious helping him. Laying the Pergo had turned into quite the project.

Ta'Rae worked just about every day now. He'd noticed that she had even taken on some clinic time at the hospital. It was almost as if she was worried about money. Sebastian hated the thought of her worrying about anything.

Today Sebastian messed around on the roof, despite

Phil's warning about overdoing it. Phil had been talking about chemo again. "I won't do it again. I won't," Sebastian insisted, mumbling to himself.

Down below on the deck, his stereo played old-school R & B. The air was brisk and fresh. From his vantage point there on the roof, he could see Rashawn's house as well as Rita and Terrell's place. "Chemo . . . Phil is nuts," he grumbled on, thinking about how well everything was going. Even his hair was coming back in; only it was coming in perfectly white. It was a natural phenomenon from the chemo, Phil explained. Sebastian wasn't sure he liked it, but it was getting cool at night, and his bald head needed a little something.

His hair, although white, was growing back in short soft waves, which had him resembling the man in the picture, the one from his mother's jewelry box—Hendrix.

Shaking the memory of the picture from his mind, he quickly filled his mind with thoughts of Darrell. He'd been sneaking around, seeing the boy.

Sebastian knew if Stormy found out she would have him arrested. "For something," he griped.

"But what if he is my son?" he asked himself, knowing the answer. The way Stormy would flip out every time he barely mentioned the prospects only strengthened his convictions. He'd been calling Stormy again—at the store—unbeknownst to Ta'Rae and to the total irritation of Stormy. At first she seemed relieved that he had called, as if she was actually worried or something. But then he mentioned Darrell and she hit the roof, all niceties gone.

"I'm not trying to get between you and Jerry," he said aloud, as if speaking to her about the matter—

again. "You act like doing that would help me any. Besides, I'm not calling to get to know *you* any better. I'm calling to get to the truth about Darrell," Sebastian went on in his one-sided argument with Stormy. He'd been thinking long and hard about having it out with her all week. The more time that passed, the more he wanted to know the truth. He wanted to know if Darrell was his son. It was on his list of things to get done before dying.

"We need to get to the bottom of this. Stormy, I held up my end of the bargain. I told Ta'Rae about you; now you need to tell Darrell about me," he reasoned out loud. That was what he had planned to say to Stormy the next time he called. He had it all arranged.

Stormy had been happy to hear that he and Ta'Rae had gotten back together. She was happy to hear that they were making their family strong and had renewed their vows to each other. She seemed content to call their deal square, done. She felt that she had accomplished what Sebastian said he needed her to do for him. "We're done," she'd said.

"We're not done!" he told her flat out. She just sighed heavily and hung up on him.

"She was all happy about things in my marriage and then she tells me we're done, like I was some pity case she was working on. Who does she think she is? She needs to be happy that I want to claim my son! Who's to say he's even mine?" Sebastian ranted. "Am I wrong? Am I wrong for the way I'm thinking? Just let me know if I'm wrong." Sebastian loudly challenged the voices in his head.

"Who are you talking to?" Ta'Rae asked, suddenly catching him off guard.

Sebastian looked down from the roof to see Ta'Rae

standing on the deck. He'd not realized he was talking that loudly.

No doubt she'd come by for lunch. It was Monday, after all. She was still wearing her white clinic coat.

But how long had she been there? What all had she heard? he wondered, panic growing instantly, showing in his voice. "What are you doing here?" he asked her.

"I came to see your progress. Who are you talking to?" she asked again.

Before he could answer, his foot slipped. The last thing he heard were Ta'Rae's screams.

DEPRESSION

The fall had been a setback—of the major kind.

"It's more than a broken leg—his spirit is broken, his . . ." Ta'Rae sighed heavily. "He acts like he's being punished."

Rashawn took a sip of her cocktail, then said, "Why do you think that? He doesn't seem so down in the mouth to me. He was laughing and joking—"

"Not with me he's not. He's stressing over that man that he thinks is his father and all that mess. He's just, like, acting troubled about stuff, anxious," Ta'Rae said, leaving out their personal bedroom issues. "You know that he's homebound now, in that chair and all. But yet, he doesn't argue with me about anything, but he's—"

"Why does it always end up about you? Why do you always judge Sebastian's feelings based on how he interacts with you?"

"Well, that's cruel to say," Ta'Rae responded, feeling instantly hurt. "That's not what I meant."

"Have you asked Sebastian if he's feeling broken?

Have you even tried to get inside his head and see what might be wrong with him?" Rashawn asked.

"I get the feeling that you've already done that," Ta'Rae replied, noticing Rashawn's tone changing to that of the ethics professor and sociology major that she was.

"We've spoken," Rashawn responded coyly.

"What did he say?"

"I think you need to ask him."

"No, I think you need to tell me," Ta'Rae said, her tone becoming determined. "You need to tell me what he's feeling . . . what I'm feeling . . . what I'm supposed to feel. Since you know so damn much, just fuckin' tell me."

Rashawn pulled back her attack. It was unfounded and she knew it. Everyone was tense lately. Everyone was catching up with the emotions they all had left to feel. She of all people could understand the stages all had to go through before finding peace with the situation they were in.

For so long they had all been guilty of jumping in and out of Ta'Rae and Sebastian's peace-finding mission. They had come in and out at will. Rashawn knew she was guilty of it. She'd chosen Sebastian to comfort and depended on her other sisters to come to Ta'Rae's aid, or maybe all the so-called friends that Ta'Rae claimed to have, the ones who had been a no-show since the news of Sebastian hit the airwaves. But it was now that Rashawn was forced to realize that Ta'Rae had no one to catch her emotional fall. She was hanging on by a thread with no net beneath her.

Rashawn noticed the dark circles under Ta'Rae's eyes and how thin she had gotten. She felt bad for the part she might have played in Ta'Rae's emotional neglect. "I don't know what Sebastian is feeling, Ta'Rae. I really don't," she confessed.

Ta'Rae curled her lips and then dug her chip into some salsa. Rashawn was surprised Ta'Rae didn't get up and leave but instead continued to eat her lunch. There was no drama, no Ms. High Society sitting here today. There was only Ta'Rae. Maybe she realized how defeated she was. It was a conquest that Rashawn wished she hadn't had a share in.

"Have you thought about . . ." Ta'Rae stopped herself.

"What?"

"That woman. Have you thought about her?" Ta'Rae asked.

"Why would I think about her?"

Ta'Rae shrugged and continued eating while speaking. "I wonder if he needs to see her to cheer him up?"

"Are you crazy?"

"No," Ta'Rae answered, taking a large bite of her burrito.

"I guess I didn't understand the question, then."

"I wonder if Sebastian needs to see her to cheer him up. It's obvious that he's not happy anymore, and I can't stand it," Ta'Rae confessed. "Sorry to again talk about how I feel, but I mean, I can't help it. I can't stand it anymore, and I want to make him happy."

She was beginning to sound a little manic and Rashawn grew concerned. "No, Ta'Rae, he doesn't need her. He needs you," Rashawn told her.

Ta'Rae shrugged nonchalantly and took a gulp of her margarita. She then rubbed her temples quickly. "Whoa, brain freeze," she said, laughing crazily, crossing her eyes.

Rashawn just stared at her. Never had she seen

Ta'Rae so untogether—she was falling apart right in front of her. "Ta'Rae, you can't start looking for ways to make Sebastian happy. He needs to come to grips with everything, accept things for the way they are. I know it sounds cold, but he has to come to acceptance about all that is to come. And so do you," Rashawn added, reaching over the table and holding her hand.

It had been weeks since the fall from the roof. So many things rolled around Sebastian's head. He was running out of time—he knew it; he could feel it. He'd not kept up to his end of the bargain, and now he would pay the price for his arrogance. The deal was to find peace. And he'd not found it. He'd not even begun to touch on it. He'd not even slept at night, pondering his discontentment. Yet, peace seemed so close, so very close.

"Just a little bit longer," he prayed. He'd not done that in years—prayed. And maybe he really didn't consider himself officially praying now, but for some reason he felt as if he had an audience. He felt heard.

Sebastian wanted to talk to Ta'Rae about his feelings, but how could he? He was in a wheelchair. The leg wasn't healing well at all, and Phil didn't think he'd be standing on it for a long time. There had been complications due to the cancer having moved to the bones. "I had hoped it had not progressed to this stage. You were doing so well," Phil explained.

"I'm not doing chemo again, Phil. I already told you," Sebastian hurriedly spat.

Phil raised his hand. "It's up to you, Sebastian," Phil responded coolly.

Sebastian swallowed hard, realizing what Phil had just implied.

"Oh."

"You can be as comfortable as you want to be. I'm going to up your dosage of morphine for the pain," Phil said, casually pulling out a pad and scribbling down a prescription.

"Keep me comfortable. That's where we are now? Damn." Sebastian gasped.

"It's time we came to grips with where we are in the stream of time, Sebastian."

"And where are we, Phil?"

"Without chemo, I'm afraid we're there."

Sebastian swallowed the lump that had formed in his throat. He looked around for an escape and finally found one—the door. Spinning his chair around, he hurried out with Phil calling for him to stop.

Down the hall, Sebastian sped in the chair, glancing back only once, glaring at Phil hatefully before boarding the elevator.

The cool outside air hit his face, and he immediately regretted his actions.

"Phil," he said over the phone, having called his private cell.

"Yes, Sebastian," Phil answered.

"I'm sorry, my friend—"

"Me too. I'll see you next week. Then you'll do the chemo?"

"Sure." Sebastian surrendered.

Stormy realized right at the moment that her thinking was way off. She ran her hand over the soft fabric of the sports jacket and thought about Sebastian. How could she be thinking about that man when Jerry, right now, was out on the road again trying to make a living to support her and the kids?

So many nights, years ago, she had cried while holding the jacket that Sebastian had left at her apartment. She had lied to him when he came by looking for it. She swore to him that he had come by wearing something else. Maybe she knew then he was going to run out on her, leaving her without anything to hold on to—at least anything he knew about. But she kept that jacket and cried into it many nights. Even after Darrell came and she got busy being a single mother, she ran across it in her closet every now and then and gave it a moment of her attention.

It was years later before she realized the jacket was gone. She never asked Jerry what happened to it, assuming he had disposed of it. She had simply gone on with life.

Today, touching the jacket on the rack, she caught herself. She was feeling way more for Sebastian York than she should. It was more than pity, but less than lust . . . love, maybe? She forcibly dismissed the thought. She had told Sebastian that she no longer felt anything toward him. That she was purged and free. She had even told him never to call her again. She regretted her arrogance now because seeing him one more time would make her day, her night, her life, complete.

Just then, she thought she saw Sebastian coming through the door; she knew she was seeing things as this Sebastian was younger, stronger . . .

"Hey, Mom," Darrell said with a grin, walking through a rack of sports coats.

Shaking her head, she grinned, mostly at him, but partly at her thoughts. "What is it, boy?"

"Money, what else?"

"I can't believe you came all the way down here to jack me," Stormy said, laughing at her child whose practiced look of innocence always made her crack up.

"Me? Never, but twenty bucks would just about cover what I want next door at GameStop."

Stormy needed to redirect her feelings. She needed to get a grip and quit playing around with her life, her family—her security. This was no game here; there were innocent people involved in the fallout of what she and Sebastian had done. Regret was all they were to each other—one big fat ball of regret.

Realizing then how heavy her heart was, she decided to take a break and join her son on his twenty-dollar shopping spree. Surely that would make her feel better, and by the look on Darrell's face when she suggested joining him, she knew he would feel great by the time they left GameStop.

Chaz Baker sat in the cafeteria. He was reading his hospital newsletter without much on his mind, or so he thought. Ta'Rae was always somewhere in his head. There was something about that woman that drove him crazy.

"And what a prick I've been, now I've lost her," he self-bashed. About that time, he looked up to see Sebastian headed toward him in a motorized wheelchair. He looked bad, nothing like Chaz remembered. He had aged at least ten years in the last few months. Chaz wanted to turn away, but Sebastian was apparently coming to speak to him.

"Chaz Baker." He smiled, outstretching his hand.

Chaz nearly jumped to his feet, surprised at the greeting. "Dr. York," Chaz greeted, shaking his hand.

"Call me Sebastian."

"Sebastian." Chaz relaxed a little, getting comfortable in his seat again.

"Have you seen my wife?" Sebastian asked, glancing around as if looking for her.

The question hit Chaz as odd, considering Ta'Rae was never at the hospital on Thursday. "No. I figure she's in her office, or maybe the Midtown clinic," Chaz answered.

"So you know her schedule, do you?" Sebastian asked, rubbing his bushy chin. He was unshaven. He was far from smooth looking, Chaz noticed.

"No, it's just—"

Sebastian chuckled. "Easy boy, I'm yankin' your chain," Sebastian admitted.

Chaz was really uncomfortable now. "Yanking my chain?" Chaz asked, knowing that Sebastian York was not the chain-yankin' sort of guy.

"Can I ask you something? And I want an honest answer. It's not going to affect anything, change anything, or probably even really matter except for one reason, and that's purely for my own satisfaction," Sebastian led in.

"Shoot," Chaz responded, accepting the possible challenge.

"Did you sleep with my wife?"

"No," Chaz answered quickly, curling his lip unconsciously, the look of defeat showing.

Sebastian saw it and smiled. "But you wanted to?"

"Honest answer?" Chaz asked now.

"What am I gonna do, jump up and fight cha?" Sebastian asked, slapping the sides of the chair.

Chaz smiled, accepting Sebastian's dark humor. "You might, because, man, I wanted your wife in the worst way," Chaz confessed.

"Worst?"

"Best . . . worst . . . I mean, does it make a difference? She shot me down," Chaz admitted.

"Because she was married or because—"

"Why are you asking me this?" Chaz interrupted.

"Because . . ." Sebastian hesitated. "Maybe I'm just a crazy dying man, but I want to make sure that Ta'Rae is going to be all right . . . after."

"All right?"

"Yes, *all right*—I want her to be . . ." Sebastian flailed his hands while stumbling with the words. He wanted Chaz to understand him without him having to just come right out with the words.

"Taken care of," Chaz assisted.

Sebastian nodded now, without opening his eyes. "I'm . . ." Sebastian paused.

"Sebastian." Chaz sat back in his seat, running his fingers through his hair and then folding his arms across his chest. He tried hard to hear what he wanted to hear, and then hear what was really being said.

"All I'm saying is I won't stand in your way. Hell, I can't stand in your way," Sebastian added with more than a little sarcasm coming forth.

Chaz suddenly realized what was happening. "I could never do that. I understand what you're trying to do, but . . ." Chaz looked around the room and then at the broken man in the chair. He was clearly at the end of his rope. "You can't just hand your wife off like that, man. Ta'Rae is worth more than that."

"Don't you think I know that?"

"I'm not going to—"

"She needs to know that she has a future. She needs to know she's beautiful. That—"

"Then fuckin' tell her, man. Don't give her to another man; don't throw her away like that," Chaz jumped in, standing quickly, speaking from his heart and not his lower head—for a change.

Silence between the two men was thick now, as Chaz was unable to talk about it anymore. Deep inside he wanted to jump for joy. He wanted to shake Sebastian's hand. But under it all, he knew this was surrender talking.

Walking away, Chaz tried to get the proposition out of his mind, but he knew he would be unable to. The chance to pursue Ta'Rae York again was a burning that had yet to go out. But the chance coming from the lips of Sebastian York was all just a little too surreal.

Precious watched her mother fold her clothes and put them in her drawer. "Mom, why are you doing my laundry?" she asked.

Ta'Rae turned to her slightly but kept doing the chore. "Well, honey, I let Hanna go. You know that, and somebody's got to do this," she answered.

Precious quickly put down her textbook and rushed over to the pile of clothes, taking from her mother what she had in her hand. "I can do my own clothes. I can do more than you think around here."

"I know, Precious. You can do whatever you set your mind to," Ta'Rae said to her, standing and looking at her straight on.

Precious looked her mother over—she was beautiful, even without make-up, without effort. She'd changed her hairstyle from one needing so much care to one a bit simpler, pulled back with a colorful band. Although she was losing weight and it showed in her face, it didn't mar her beauty and soft elegance. Precious could only hope that she looked like her.

"Mom, are we going to be all right?"

"Sure, sweetie. I know it seems like we are bucking up to struggle, but we aren't. We're just simplifying, getting needless things off our plate so we can concentrate on the more important things in life. I mean, we have insurance, I have my practice, and Daddy put away some money for—"

"No." Precious blinked slowly, rushing her mother's words to the back of her thoughts. "That's not what I meant. I want to know if we—you and me—are going to be all right."

"Ohhh, you mean us," Ta'Rae asked, pointing at Precious and then back at herself. She then took a deep breath as if she hadn't given it much thought lately.

"Well, I would say yes, because I love you."

"Because you love me?"

"Yes, and I know that you have to make decisions on your own and decide for yourself what is the best next move, for yourself."

"So what I do is up to me?"

Ta'Rae smiled tightly and then nodded yes before starting for the door. But then, before walking out, she spun on her heels. The fake smile was gone and her brow furrowed. "No. No, Precious, it's not. I'm lying to you. For years, I've tried to be the perfect mom and wife and person, but it's not working. I don't have the energy anymore to play this game we've been playing as a family. You are a child, and I'll be damned if I'm going to let you just ruin your life making dumb choices like you did having sex with that boy, that man,

Drake. And if I had my way about it, he would be in jail right now for statutory rape. Feel me? But Sebastian just wasn't up for all that kind of mess, so we let it go. But your life, it's still our—no, my—responsibility, and I plan to tighten up a lot. I plan to do my job a whole lot better." Ta'Rae spoke sternly. Precious stood still, holding her fresh-smelling top with both hands, nodding slowly.

"Right now, I have to think about your father and do what's best for him, and I expect you to be doing the same. I expect you to continue working hard in school and keeping your life on track for the time when you will have to make decisions and live with the consequences because, honey, blink and you're grown. But for now, you're just my little girl . . . *my* little girl," Ta'Rae explained. "So yeah, I could use your help around here, more than ever. I let Hanna go last week because having her here made me uncomfortable. We've for years used the luxuries that our money could buy to keep from dealing one on one with each other, but this is our time to touch and feel, get down and dirty with this thing called a family, so now you and I have to handle all of this, and you're old enough to know what needs to be done."

"I do."

"Then hop to it because I have a feeling we are gonna be downsizing a whole lot more, real soon," Ta'Rae admitted, saying it out loud for the first time. Admitting for the first time that life as they had come to know it was about to change. Simplifying, what a concept. But they had lived a surreal life for way too long, and it was time to touch down and deal with the basics. She and Sebastian hadn't really sat down and discussed it, but it was an easy call for Ta'Rae. Her friends and the life she'd lived before had no meat, as her father used to say. It had no depth. It was shallow and meaningless. She needed to make some changes, get in touch with what was important, and soon. What all the changes would be, she had no idea, but she knew they would be major ones, and she didn't feel like dealing with a bunch of materialistic foolishness while she figured everything else in her life out.

Heading back to her office through the hospital annex the next day, Ta'Rae heard a familiar voice calling her. She turned to see Chaz. It had been months since she'd run into him and wondered now if maybe she had just not seen him or he had been avoiding her. It didn't matter; there were far too many things on her mind to worry about that horny little boy.

"You look tired. How are things?" he asked, reaching her and joining her quick stride, easily keeping up.

"Well, you look . . . ," she began, looking for something about him to insult; however, he looked tanned and well kept. She could find nothing wrong. Sighing, she just fanned her hand in surrender to his arrogance.

"I guess that was rude of me," he apologized. "I meant to say—"

"Never mind what you meant, Chaz," Ta'Rae said, sounding as tired as she apparently looked.

He shook his head. "I meant to say, I'm sorry," he said, sounding sheepish and sincere. Ta'Rae nodded acceptance of the apology. "You needed a friend, and I betrayed that," he admitted as if perhaps waiting for just the right time to say this to her.

"Yes, I did need a friend—back then. But now—"

"Now you need what?" he asked, interrupting her. There was eagerness in his tone. "I can be that for you. Whatever you need, Ta'Rae," he said, speaking in a low voice, looking around to make sure they were not overheard. "I can be whatever you need—now. Give me another chance, Ta'Rae. Please," he begged.

Ta'Rae's eyes widened in surprise. She pushed the elevator button. The door opened. With eyes still wide with disbelief, she stepped quickly into the elevator, staring at the handsome young doctor standing there with his hands in the pockets of his lab coat, looking lost and lonely, until the door closed. Her heart was pounding a hundred miles an hour.

"Now? What did he mean by that?" she asked herself.

Sebastian's hands wandered although Ta'Rae pretended to be asleep. This routine was becoming humiliating, for both of them, but especially for Sebastian. Ta'Rae knew how much he wanted her. It was obvious. But the cancer was beating him. It was beating them.

Still Sebastian would not submit to it. He was not going to give in. However, this losing battle was taking its toll on them intimately. Ta'Rae almost dreaded the nights.

"I want to please you," he whispered in her ear.

Still she kept her eyes closed.

He'd made a trip to the *Naughty Palace* adult store a couple of weeks ago, bringing home many intimate toys to try out, and she wasn't sure how using them together, with Sebastian at the helm, made her feel. At first she felt desperate and agreed to it. She was so hurt at the loss of his virility, she was willing to try anything, hoping to arouse him again. But then it hit her how low they had fallen—sunken. Replacing the real for the artificial this way; it was humiliating. It would be different perhaps if this sex play was for enhance- ment of the real thing, but that large black dildo was to replace Sebastian's manhood. The thought made Ta'Rae wince. Nothing could replace Sebastian's manhood. Nothing could replace Sebastian.

She could only imagine how he must have appeared, cruising into the porn shops in the wheelchair, looking scruffy and unkempt, buying sex toys. The thought made her cringe. What would be next for them?

She heard him rummaging about, opening the drawer of the bureau. She just knew he was looking for the vi- brator. He'd named it and everything. Quickly Ta'Rae turned to him in the dark. "I don't want to . . . ," she began before realizing that Sebastian had laid back in the bed with his hands folded behind his head, in thought.

"When's the last time you saw that doctor you were seeing while we were separated?" he asked.

Guilt instantly covered her. The irony of the ques- tion was more than coincidental.

"Seeing him? I was never seeing him," she de- fended.

"Well whatever the situation was, whatever you were doing with him, when was the last time you did it?"

Ta'Rae sat up.

"Sebby, I have never been unfaithful to you— never," she stated matter-of-factly.

Sebastian shushed her, pulling himself up to a more comfortable position against the headboard. "I'm not accusing you. I'm . . . I'm not," Sebastian admitted, sounding meek and humble in the darkness of their room.

"Then what?"

"Listen to me. Don't say anything until I'm finished," he instructed.

"I want you to sleep with Chaz Baker," he began, after taking a deep breath. Ta'Rae could hear the air he sucked in deeply as if he needed the force to push the words out. Ta'Rae was speechless. Had he already spoken to Chaz Baker? Was that what Chaz meant at the elevator? Had Sebastian already arranged it?

"Are you crazy?" Ta'Rae asked.

"No, I'm not. I want you to be happy."

Ta'Rae instantly thought about her lunch with Rashawn, about her own thoughts of bringing Stormy into their lives—for Sebastian's sake. And now, here Sebastian was offering her someone for the same reasons.

"I don't need that. I don't need this," she insisted, touching his flaccid appendage. Sebastian smacked his lips, turning away from her, embarrassed slightly. "I need you. What do you need?" she asked him.

After a moment, he looked at her and smiled. Ta'Rae smiled back, taking his large hand and guiding it between her legs where he slowly created a fire sliding his fingers inside her. Exploring the familiar, he brought her to a mild orgasm.

"Remember when we first met?" she purred, satisfied.

"Yeah, I do." He grinned, inhaling her scent on his fingertips.

"You were always so nasty," she teased.

He laughed out loud. "But you loved it."

"I loved you, that's why. I do love you," she said, kissing him passionately.

They giggled and reminisced like young lovers until Sebastian got tired and drifted off to sleep. Lying beside him, Ta'Rae stroked his chest as she, too, dozed. She fought the thoughts of Chaz Baker and the possibilities.

Memories were all she needed, right?

"What the hell did you just say?" Carlotta screamed.

"Sebastian wants me to have an affair," Ta'Rae repeated, looking around.

"You both have lost your damn minds," Carlotta whispered, scrubbing the counter harder than necessary.

"I'm not thinking about it," Ta'Rae lied. She'd done nothing but think about the possibilities—an outlet for her frustration, somewhere else to put her mind for just a few moments.

"You bet your ass you're not thinking about it! What would Mama think of you if she was living? Oh my God, Ta'Rae, and with who, that boy you were seeing?"

Ta'Rae wasn't aware that Carlotta knew about Chaz. Again, the sister-vine was up and running. And now Carlotta was bringing Mama into it.

"Like I said, I'm not even thinking about it. I just wanted to tell you and—"

"Ta'Rae, you and Sebastian need to hold it together. Y'all need to pull on family instead of all this crazy mess. You guys aren't swingers, are you?" Carlotta asked now, looking closer at Ta'Rae's face, hunting for a lie.

"No, no, it's not like that. He just felt that I needed to maybe get the pressure off. All this worry about him and well, I even thought about him needing to see that woman Stormy again. Maybe we both just need to release some tension and—"

"Shut it up!" Carlotta insisted, holding her hand close to Ta'Rae mouth.

The smell of bleach burned her senses. She moved Carlotta's hand away. "Don't tell me to shut up. You don't know what we're going through. You don't know what we need to make it . . . to make it through this."

"You need Jesus . . . shit!"

Ta'Rae slid quickly from the stool and grabbed her bag, opening her change purse. "Let me pay for my lunch."

"Since when do you pay your sister for your lunch? What? My telling you what you need to hear suddenly makes you a patron? Damnit, Ta'Rae! You need to fix yourself. You're broken, girl. You're messed up in the head!" Carlotta went on.

"Look, Carlotta, I thought I could talk to you. I've tried for months to deal with you guys—"

"Deal with us? Deal with us?" Carlotta's eyes glowed with growing heat. "Don't make me come over this counter and black your eye," Carlotta threatened. This time Ta'Rae didn't move. Instead, she slammed her purse on the counter and raised her fist, taking a fighting stance.

"Come on!" she challenged.

Carlotta stepped back as if slapped.

"Come on!" Ta'Rae screamed, drawing attention to them.

"Get out!" Carlotta screamed. "Get out and don't come back until the crazy bitch that is wearing your body is gone!"

"No problem!" Ta'Rae yelled, grabbing her bag and storming out.

Reaching her car, her cell phone rang. She prayed it was Sebastian, but again her prayers were misdirected. It was Chaz. She stared at the number, heard the jingle she'd programmed for his numbered slot on her phone. The day she'd programmed the playful tune began with Chaz as a light fantasy; now that tune represented an option—a dark option given to her by her husband. Closing her eyes tight, one tear squeezed out and ran down her cheek. She envied its escape.

Glancing back at Carlotta's diner, she climbed behind the wheel and locked her door.

"Hello, Chaz," she answered.

"Hello," he said, sounding as if he'd been nervously pacing before making the call.

"Chaz, before you speak, I would like to meet you," Ta'Rae requested. The phone line was silent.

"Okay," he finally answered.

"Let's go to church," Ta'Rae suggested one rainy Sunday morning. Sebastian glanced at her over the newspaper and then went back to reading. He'd been cranky lately—they all had.

He was unshaven, and his white tresses sat on his shoulders. He rolled his eyes as if reacting to a privately told bad joke.

"Yeah," Ta'Rae went on, sounding perky. "Let's all go get on our fancy duds and go to church."

Precious smacked her lips, tossing the unfinished wedge of honeydew melon onto her plate. "Mom, stop it."

"Stop what? I'm just thinking, it's nearly Thanksgiving, and we should maybe go to church and give thanks for what we have." Ta'Rae reached over for Sebastian's hand. He pulled away from her and shuffled his newspaper again, continuing to read. "Okay . . . Well, maybe we can go to Carlotta's for dinner," she suggested.

"Aunt Lotty canceled it because she knew Dad couldn't make it," Precious said, sounding almost resentful. She was getting fed up with the way things were going—school, housework, it was taking its toll.

"I coulda made it," Sebastian growled, sounding old and angry.

"Well that's good that Aunt Lotty is thinking about stuff like that," Ta'Rae said, hiding the truth, hiding the fact that she and Carlotta had exchanged words and she'd not spoken to Carlotta since that afternoon at the diner.

"What's got you in such a"—Sebastian twisted his lip—"mood?" he said, smirking.

Ta'Rae knew what he was implying. He was noticing her cheery air, her lighter spirit. He was assuming she was sleeping with Chaz Baker. Especially since she'd not been intimate with him since the night they spoke about Chaz. Ta'Rae knew that had to be what he thought.

True, she'd met with Chaz the day he called her. She met with him to tell him to forget even the thought that she would sleep with him—for any reason. She spoke in anger when they conversed on the subject, taking out all her frustrations from the encounter with Carlotta on the young doctor. She first explained, in the frankest of ways, her love for Sebastian and how that alone was going to prevent this perversion from happening.

Secondly, she told him, "You are nothing than a weak-minded opportunist with the morals of a snake." She pointed her finger in his face. "I can't believe you were ready to take advantage of me like that. But then again, you've more than once proved to me what a dick really looks like." At that point, he had cussed her, she had cussed him, and then she had called Trina.

Trina was into everything, from ceramics to transcendental meditation. Ta'Rae knew Trina was the person she needed right now in her life, and Trina welcomed Ta'Rae's attention. Over the next couple of weeks, she turned Ta'Rae onto Tae Bo and yoga. They'd meet every Monday and Thursday at the YWCA. Strenuous and exerting exercise had aided Ta'Rae in working off much of her frustrations and sexual pressure. By the time she got home after those classes with Trina, she was sweaty and worn out, dropping off to sleep as soon as her head hit the pillow.

Ta'Rae felt in her heart that Sebastian just knew she was romping with the young buck, Chaz, allowing him to twist her this way and that until spent and exhausted, but no, it wasn't that way at all.

"My mood? What about yours, Mr. Sourpuss?" Ta'Rae said, winking slyly, scooping what was left of the melon and putting it in a bowl, covering it for storage.

"Mom, don't," Precious pleaded, knowing what her mother was doing these nights—her father, during one of his fits of anger and bitter resentment, had told her.

"Don't what?" Ta'Rae asked her, sensing that Precious had the same thoughts as Sebastian had about what she was doing with her time these days.

"Don't gloat," Sebastian said with a sneer in his words, folding down the paper and dropping it to the floor before wheeling away from the table.

"You left something, Seb. I mean, this is not a hotel, sweetie," she called after him sarcastically.

"Can't the two of you stop this?" Precious cried out.

"Stop what?"

"Acting like you have time for all of this," she went on. Ta'Rae instantly felt sorry for burdening Precious with her and Sebastian's immature actions. "Can't you just accept what's going on in the real world without bringing the bags and bags of garbage from your little fantasy worlds into the mix? Can't you just stop carrying on like you have time for all of this stupid shit? I know you both are wishing you could just make everything bad go away, but you can't. And hurting each other is not going to fix a damn thing," she screamed. Precious was beside herself. Never had she felt such rage inside her, so much anger toward her parents—both of them. Why were they acting this way toward each other? Why now, when they needed to pull together, were they acting like such idiots, pretending they had all the time in the world to fix things?

"I know you are not trying to go off on me. How dare you." Ta'Rae was surprised how calm she was, considering Precious's lack of respect, cursing at her this way.

"How dare me?" Precious went on, flailing her arms and stomping around the breakfast nook. "Can we do a recap of this last year? Can we?"

"No, let's not, Precious." Ta'Rae moved past her and into the kitchen, opening the refrigerator, tossing the other covered Tupperware bowls with leftovers in them out of the way so she could put the new leftovers in. Their eating had been erratic and just downright poor.

"Mom, Dad is dying. He's in pain constantly. He's acting like he's okay, but he's not okay," Precious explained. "You have to know this; you're a doctor, for crying out loud."

Ta'Rae thought about Precious's words while she stood staring into the open icebox, feeling the cool air on her face. She didn't want to stand up. She didn't want to face her daughter. She didn't want to cry anymore.

Soon she heard the sliding door to the deck open. Precious had walked out. Ta'Rae knew she would have to fix their relationship. Or maybe there was nothing to fix. Who could know anymore? So much was broken.

Ta'Rae went to the phone. She picked it up and started to dial Carlotta's number before remembering their last conversation. How she had closed Carlotta out—slammed the door was more like it.

She called out to Sebastian. He didn't answer—again. He was being so stubborn, shutting her out this way.

"Shutting *you* out?" her mother asked.

"Yes, Mama, shutting me out."

Ta'Rae knew how it felt to be shut out, and it didn't feel very good; however, she couldn't make Sebastian let her into his world. Could she? He was hurting, not just physically, but mentally too. It was obvious. He had given her over to another man and inside felt she had taken the bait. Why she hadn't told him she hadn't taken Chaz as a lover was still a mystery to her; however, she did know that there was no way she could completely understand what he was going through.

Although she had not seen Sebastian's list, she'd heard about it. And apparently Sebastian had some serious matters left to deal with on there. That woman. That man Hendrix. And who knew what else.

What Sebastian was going through was more than Ta'Rae could even imagine him dealing with in a lifetime, let alone just a few months. It was as if Sebastian had asked for a little extra time in order to square away everything in his life, his past, his future, and his present, all at once, and he got it—all at once.

"I've been faithful. I've been true. I deserve his attention. I've forgiven and . . . and I'm trying like hell to forget," Ta'Rae argued with her mother challengingly. "This was supposed to be our time, Mama. Our time to . . ." She tried to finish the sentence but couldn't.

Stepping from the kitchen back into the breakfast nook, she noticed Sebastian in the entryway. She could see the sadness in his eyes, the regret. "I'm so sorry, Ta'Rae—for everything," he whispered, moving quickly out of her view.

Her heart gained a hundred pounds.

Ta'Rae took a seat in Hilton's office. She had rehearsed over and over what she intended to divulge and what she did not. "I can't believe I'm doing this," she said, starting out the visit with tension in her voice. "You see, I had this patient . . . she fell. I mean, sure she fell somewhat hard, but what I'm getting at is that her initial injuries had long time healed but still she was . . . She couldn't get up," Ta'Rae explained, her eyes burning, fighting a losing battle with tears. They came slowly, and she attempted to fight them off before they built into something she could not control. All the while, Hilton said nothing.

"Well, at first I didn't understand what was happening. I figured she was just depressed, right. But the more time that went by and the more the woman deteriorated, I wondered, What is going on? Why can't I help her?" Ta'Rae let out a loud sniff, closing her eyes tighter with the growing ache in her heart.

"What happened to her?" Hilton asked.

"Well, she kept coming into my office, and her daughter, well, her daughter finally stopped coming with her . . . thank goodness, but the woman—my patient—kept coming in on her own, sometimes even without an appointment. She just wanted to talk, ya know. She would sometimes even invent something aching or hurting but then would spend the entire visit talking about her husband, the man she'd spent her whole life with," Ta'Rae went on. "She eventually caught this really bad cold. It complicated and she died of pneumonia."

"How did that make you feel?"

"I don't know . . . angry, I guess."

"Why?"

"Her daughter—I'm thinking, why didn't she want to believe that her mother was hurting? Why, just because she couldn't see it?"

"You mean like Sebastian?"

"Sebastian?"

"You can see that Sebastian is hurting, right?"

"Yes, oh God yes," Ta'Rae answered, growing in emotions yet still holding it together tightly. The tears were stayed for the most part.

"But what about you—don't you hurt?"

"I don't get you. I . . . no, I don't."

"You don't?"

Ta'Rae looked away. The pain in her chest instantly increased. She put her hand there to massage her organ to keep it beating. "I don't have a right to hurt."

"But, Ta'Rae, you do hurt. Your life has crashed around you, and you are barely hanging on. Am I right?"

Ta'Rae gave up. She started crying again, tears streaking her smoothly powdered cheeks. After a minute or two, she sighed heavily. Her body was shaking and rattled from the internal turmoil. "I feel . . . I feel like Mrs. Blinky. I feel like I'm falling, and God, Hilton, I don't want to hit the ground like that woman did. I don't want to fall all the way to the ground," Ta'Rae admitted.

Hilton looked at her watch. "Talk to someone about it, then," she said coolly.

"I'm talking to you," Ta'Rae answered in a low voice, close to mumbling.

"No, you need to talk to those who are holding the other end of the rope, those who can catch you before you hit bottom."

Ta'Rae knew who Hilton meant. Her family—those wonderful, troublesome, meddling, ghetto-fabulous women who she'd turned her back on so often.

Could she really turn to them? After everything she'd taken them through, would they even want to catch her?

"Your time is up," Hilton then said.

"It is?"

"Yes, it is, Ta'Rae," Hilton said, sounding totally sober and together.

Ta'Rae stood obediently and gathered her things. She fought with all her might to gather herself together before she would have to face those remaining in the waiting room. There was no way she would show them her pain, her weakness. She was almost regretting having shown Hilton. *And for what? To be dismissed after an hour?* Ta'Rae asked herself.

Ta'Rae then looked at her watch. It had only been forty-five minutes. "My hour isn't up," she said.

Hilton smiled. "I didn't say it was."

Ta'Rae immediately understood.

ACCEPTANCE

Christmas was coming fast, yet the Yorks had no tree, no trimmings, and no lights. Again, Sebastian had beaten the odds and had managed to get back on his feet. He'd managed with the past few weeks of therapy to use a walker, with anticipation that soon he would only need a cane. His strength and self-will were phenomenal, in Ta'Rae's opinion, although, afraid of a jinx, she never told him that.

Maybe it was anger or just frustration or just plain pigheadedness, but whatever the reason, he was fighting again. She could hear him moving through the hallway coming from the spare room that they now used as their bedroom. She sat in the library looking over their expenses for the last year. Her head swooned at the sight of the digits in the medical bills. Their insurance was covering most of it, but still . . .

Then there was the mortgage on both homes . . .

Precious's school . . .

Credit cards . . .

The time-share . . .

Triple car notes and the insurance polices on them . . .

Finally Ta'Rae moved the bills to the side and buried her head in her hands. Perhaps giving up their book-keeper was taking this *downsizing, simplifying* thing too far. All of this hands-on paperwork was getting to be a bit much. Just then, she noticed an unfamiliar form from their bank; she pulled it from the stack to read it.

Sebastian was sitting in the big chair reading in front of the fire when he heard Ta'Rae coming down the hall into the living room. It had been a quiet evening, not surprisingly. Aside from casual conversation, Precious was in her room most of the time and Ta'Rae hadn't been very talkative these days. It was okay, though, as he had things yet to deal with . . . his list.

He'd been calling Stormy again, and she'd been avoiding him like the plague. *Acting like I really want to talk to her,* Sebastian fussed internally, knowing that he wanted nothing more than to talk to her. He needed to get to the bottom of the issue surrounding Darrell. If she didn't start talking soon, he was going to take matters into his own hands.

Just then, Ta'Rae stood over him with a paper in her hand. She looked like a raging maniac, and Sebastian guarded himself wondering if he would receive a blow in addition to the paper being thrown in his face.

"What is this?" she screamed.

Sebastian fumbled around trying to catch the paper that fluttered in the wind of her anger. He finally caught it and looked at it. "Damn," he mumbled. He could not hide his guilt. There was no place for it to run, except across his face.

"Is that all you can say?" she asked.

"Well, I was going to tell you about this," he began.

"Oh, sure you were," she yelled, flopping down on the coffee table in front of him.

"I'm still trying to get this all settled with Stormy, but as you know, it's not like I have years to get this matter all ironed out, and she's refusing to speak to me over the phone. So I had to make a decision. I had to—"

"You chose to finance this boy's education without telling me about it—about him? When were you going to tell me about him, Sebastian?" She stood and began to pace in circles as if she were a caged animal looking for a way out of the room.

"Ta'Rae, I had an affair when we first got married, and out of that affair I have reason to believe that I have a son. His name is Darrell and—"

"Ohhh, Sebastian, I just can't handle this anymore." Ta'Rae groaned. Finding her escape, she ran upstairs and locked herself in the bedroom.

"Stormy," Sebastian said calmly over the phone.

"What is it, Sebastian?" Stormy answered, hearing the surrender in his tone. He'd called the store and was able to get her to the phone this time.

"We need to talk."

"About what?"

"I told Ta'Rae about Darrell."

"Well you shouldn't have done that. You've hurt her for no good reason," Stormy said calmly, coolly.

Sebastian rubbed his temples with his thumbs. His

head was throbbing. "Can you stop this? I've put my marriage on the line again for you," he said bluntly.

"No, Sebastian, you put your marriage on the line for you. Jerry is the father of my children, and as for me, I've made my peace with what has occurred between us in the past. You said you had too. You have to quit lying to yourself and to other people. You need—"

"Look! You need to stop this game!" Sebastian yelled into the small cell phone. He didn't care anymore who heard him. "You need to . . ." He paused to calm himself but it didn't work. "Look, let's get a blood test then, and I'm not asking—I demand it!"

"No. Darrell is not your son, and I'm not going to subject my son to this just to have you leave his life in the end. You are not going to just up and leave my son like you did me."

"Is that it? I'm being punished for what I did to you? It was a mistake, Stormy. What happened between you and I was a mistake," he yelled. "You can't tell me that now, after admitting it, dealing with it, facing all this . . . this shit, that I don't deserve my son!" he yelled. "I don't have years to make it up to you. I'm sorry about that, but I don't."

"Don't be stupid. It's not that simple, and you know it. How can you say that to me?" Stormy spoke angrily, yet her tone was low as if making sure she was not overheard by anyone on her end that might be in earshot.

"I want to spend some time with him—"

"No."

"Look, you can't stop me. Get a restraining order if you think you have to, but I will get to know Darrell," Sebastian fussed on.

"Don't do this, Sebastian. Don't put my son through this. It's wrong what you are doing—"

He hung up. The phone rang back. It was Stormy. He ignored it.

Just then, he saw Precious standing in the doorway. "Did you say Darrell?" she asked. Sebastian just stared at her and then, ignoring her inquiry, he went back to his paper, shuffling it loudly showing pure unmitigated frustration.

Sebastian wasn't going to need Adam Sage to find out where Darrell would be and when; he'd already gotten that information. Darrell worked at the sandwich shop near the school he attended. It was also near his physical therapist. Sebastian had found him by chance but considered it destiny and started hanging out there a couple of days a week. At first, it was awkward finding a common interest but after a couple of weeks going there, it got easier to strike up conversation. Darrell was a bright boy with much potential, and Sebastian wanted to make sure he would be able to reach it. Darrell was open to talk with him while wiping tables and during the slow periods. They bonded quickly. It was obvious to them both what the truth was even without a full disclosure on Sebastian's part on how well he actually knew Stormy.

How could Stormy say what he was doing was wrong? How could she expect him to just accept the fact that he had a son on this planet who would never know about him?

* * *

Ta'Rae didn't argue when Sebastian packed up a few things and moved back into his house in the Palemos. They'd not slept in the same room since the night she found out about Darrell, so it made sense to her that he would want to go. She knew the phone would ring off the hook that night with her sisters' questions, so she unplugged it and turned off her cell phone too.

Precious had come back from assisting Sebastian with his move. She was angry and let it show. "So what happens now?" she asked.

"I really don't know," Ta'Rae answered. She had just finished going over the bills again. She found herself scrutinizing them closer now after finding the money Sebastian had diverted from their joint savings to fund Darrell Gunther's education. Why hadn't he told her about his plans? Why was he trying to handle all of this by himself? Had he learned nothing from what they had been going through? But then again, the way she had blown up when she found out about Darrell, how could he share this with her?

"How could he?" she asked herself, her inner thoughts coming out louder than she intended.

"How could he not?" Precious answered her.

Ta'Rae looked up at her. "What are you saying?"

"You asked how could Daddy just leave you, and I'm thinking . . . well . . ."

"Precious, leave me alone," Ta'Rae said with a disapproving scowl on her face. She had been avoiding conversation with Precious about the issues she and Sebastian were having. Despite what was obvious, Ta'Rae felt none of it really concerned her.

"Oh, now you want me out of your life too? Why? So you and your little boyfriend can—"

Ta'Rae slapped Precious's face faster than she realized she could move. Precious stood stunned for a moment before she backed away.

"You don't know who you are fooling with, girl. Don't make the Zenobia Ams in me come out, because I will slap the black smoove off you," Ta'Rae said now, her eyes shooting darts that Precious almost felt. Her eyes blinked rapidly. "Now, listen to me. I am the mother, you are the child. You better learn your place and learn it fast. If you need a book to help you, I got one for your ass. It's called Mama101."

Precious said nothing. She shed no tears either. She just stared as if the woman standing there was no longer her mother but someone else; someone she'd only heard about but had never met—her grandmother, Zenobia Ams.

"Now, you go to your room. I'm sure you have something in there you can do instead of being out here running your lips on things that are not your concern," Ta'Rae said, moving outside to the deck. The brisk air would do her good because she was finished speaking.

Precious stood quietly for a moment longer before running up the stairs to her room. She thought about calling someone, her aunts. "Like they would help me. They've been threatening for months to beat my ass. Now with Mom on their side, it might actually happen." Precious thought about her father. "No, he's already got stuff going on." Giving up on options, she climbed into bed and pulled the covers up high around her neck and for the first time in months, she thought about Drake. Drake was gone. She accepted that. But still, it was hard to face sometimes.

* * *

Sebastian sat at the sandwich shop waiting for Darrell to come in. It was the normal time of his shift, yet he'd not arrived. "Must be his day off," Sebastian reasoned. He wasn't about to ask anyone about the boy. It was bad enough he felt that he looked like some kind of pedophile for hanging around the boy so much. To not be conspicuous, however, he bought a sandwich before leaving.

"I need to go to Stormy's job, give her a piece of my mind," he told himself, getting comfortable in his car. He'd filed the subpoena for her to present Darrell's DNA sample to the courts, and she had not yet complied, nor was Darrell the wiser as to what was going on. Still, he didn't seem to have a clue that Sebastian was anything more than just this guy who used to be a doctor but who now had a lot of time on his hands to shoot the breeze.

Preparing the sandwich to eat, Sebastian realized he was indeed hungry, but before taking a bite, suddenly there was a hard knock on his window. His heart jumped into his mouth before it registered that the person banging on the glass was just some old man—no doubt homeless and wanting money.

"Move on!" Sebastian called through the closed window. The man refused, hitting the window again. Sebastian turned the key and allowed the window to crack just enough for his voice to carry through.

"Get the hell away from my car!" Sebastian ordered him.

"Open the gotdamned door," the gruff man barked.

"Are you crazy? I'ma call the cops," Sebastian told him. "Or better yet, run your ass over," he added smartly.

"You can't kill me. Shit, you'd have to live a lot longer than what you're gonna live to take me out," the old man said.

"What do you mean by that?" Sebastian asked, instantly feeling a little strange, feeling affected by the old man's words.

"You don't even know who I am," the old man said. "See, that's what I'm saying. Of what point was all of this? You went through all that to find me, and I'm here now, and you don't even know me."

Sebastian's heart raced as he lowered the window farther.

"Look at cha, scared shitless of your old man."

"I'm not afraid," Sebastian lied. He unlocked the door, and Hendrix climbed into the passenger seat. He grinned at Sebastian before looking longingly at the sandwich Sebastian had yet to tear into.

"Ain't ja gonna be polite? I came all this way," he said, his Southern diction slipping out. Sebastian caught it while handing over the food. The man tore into the sandwich as if he hadn't eaten in a day. Wiping his mouth with the back of his hand, he looked around the car. "Nice vehicle."

"Thank you," Sebastian answered.

"That's my truck over thea." He pointed a crooked index finger. On it was a large ring made of onyx and silver. Sebastian didn't turn away; he continued to stare at the man whose face became painful to look at.

"You're Hendrix, aren't you?"

"Call me Henny, everybody does."

"How did you . . . well, I guess I know."

"Adam Sage," they both said at the same time.

"Took me a while to make up my mind to do this. I mean, with you about to croak and all, I had to reason . . .

why bother? But then, when he told me you had cancer of the colon, I felt bad for you cuz that's what killed my brother. I got ta thinkin', maybe if youda knowed, maybe . . . aw well." He looked Sebastian up and down. "Damn, it's gotta be miserable. I knowed my Jack was miserable like a dog before he finally died."

Sebastian was speechless.

"Looka this, your hair is white, like mine. Ain't that a bitch." Henny cackled. "I guess you really are my son. So, See-bas-tian," he said, pronouncing his name in three, long-drawn-out syllables, "what do you want to know about me?" He looked at his watch. "I don't have much time, but then again, neither do you."

"Get the hell outta my car," Sebastian finally said after only seconds longer in the devil's presence.

"What? This isn't what you thought it would be? I'm not what you thought I would be? Funny, that's what your mother found out too, bless her sweet—"

"Get out of my car," Sebastian repeated. Henny looked at him. The stare down was intense.

Henny opened the door. "Before I say good-bye, I need to tell you one thing. You only get one life. While you live it, you only get so much time to change so many things. And now you know for certain I am nobody you needed to bother with. If I were you, I'd be spending my time on someone or something a bit more mattersome—like the little bit of future you got left," he said, pointing at the picture of Ta'Rae Sebastian had tucked on the side of his speedometer.

Henny climbed out of the car and slammed the door, walking off while lighting a cigarette. Sebastian watched him until he climbed in his beat-up truck and drove away.

What was that? Why had it happened like that?

What kind of father shows up just to say good-bye? he asked himself. Suddenly he realized something. Showing up to say good-bye was exactly what he was doing to Darrell. Tears came before Sebastian could stop them.

Ta'Rae walked in to Rita's house. All of her sisters were there. Even Shelby had flown in. Ta'Rae hid her hurt well, yet she knew they saw it. It was bigger than she was at this moment.

"So, nobody was gonna tell me about the Christmas meeting?" she asked. The sisters looked at each other, feeling guilty and yet within their rights for excluding her this year. Every year at this time, a week before Christmas, was when they held a family meeting, a brunch, to discuss the holiday celebration. Every year they spent the holidays together, so they would meet to decide where and what to cook, etcetera. This year they had not even called Ta'Rae to let her know what time they would meet.

It was obvious to everyone that Sebastian had moved back into the house around the corner. It was obvious that Ta'Rae was back to handling this situation on her own, back to being stubborn. So why call her?

"No," Carlotta finally answered.

"What? I'm not a sister anymore?" Ta'Rae asked, moving her seat up to the table, taking a small plate from the stack and placing a croissant on it.

"Are you?" Carlotta asked. It was obvious to the others that this was between the two of them more than anything, so they sat quietly waiting to see what would happen next.

"Carlotta, I've got no excuses that haven't been used

and abused over the last, what, year?" Ta'Rae admitted.

"Yes, so please, don't even go there. We've heard it all before." Carlotta groaned. Rita gasped at Carlotta's remark—she was going for the jugular. This was getting nasty.

"Lotty, now that's not fair," Trina began.

Ta'Rae raised her hand. "It's okay, Trina. Carlotta is angry at me because she thinks I had an affair," Ta'Rae explained, noticing Rashawn rubbing her forehead. It was clear that the thought had crossed her mind as well. "I didn't."

"You didn't sleep with Chaz Baker?" Qiana asked, knowing as much about their family business as any sister would, besides the fact that she probably had heard about Chaz—his escapades and hospital romps — being a nurse there.

"Please, Qiana, I don't have time for that sort of mess. I did spend time with him, talking, but nothing more," she confessed, hearing the sighs of relief. "When this all started, I felt as though I was falling, and there was nothing . . . nothing to hang on to. I thought I had the strength within myself to deal with all that came at me. But I see now that I don't. I probably never did. Hell, I can barely handle Precious by myself, any second now and I think we are gonna get ta boxin'," Ta'Rae confessed further, getting a hearty nod from Carlotta.

"But love, that I do know about, and know this—in the end, I know where my love is. I've always known."

"Where is that?" Rashawn asked as if needing to hear it, maybe for her own reasons.

"With my sisters, with my child, with my man," Ta'Rae answered quickly. "I have learned many things during all of this. I'm sure we all have," she said, looking around at all them. Each had involved themselves in her situation to some degree and had taken something away from it, something they would never forget. They each had taken something to add to their own rope cords, thickening it for the time when they, too, would need to hang on for dear life. Ta'Rae realized she had all the strength she needed right in front of her all the time, and yet she had waited until she was hanging by a thread to see it.

Her mother had told her in a vision to *look harder* and now she understood.

"Ta'Rae—" Rita began before bursting into tears, unable to finish.

"What are you crying for, Rita?" Rashawn asked.

"I thought we had lost her. I thought, not only do we have to accept the loss of Sebastian but of Ta'Rae too," Rita admitted.

"You can't lose me. I'm not so old that I forgot my way home," Ta'Rae said, smiling.

Carlotta huffed playfully. "Yeah, but you forgot to do something with that mop on your head," she remarked tauntingly.

Ta'Rae gasped, grabbing at her hair. "What you trying to say?"

"The shop—you overdue big time."

The laughter erupted.

Stormy took the mail from the box. There was a letter there from Sebastian. She hesitated before opening it. "It's not from a lawyer, that's good." She snickered, thinking about Sebastian's threat followed by the subpoena. She hoped he was all air and wasn't really thinking she was going to follow through with his demands.

> *Dear Stormy,*
>
> *I've spent half a day putting this letter together and this unfortunately is the best I can do.*
>
> *It's come to my attention, painfully so, that what I'm insisting on has been wrong. It's wrong for me to insist on finding out the true paternity of Darrell. It's been wrong from the start. Hell, it was wrong coming back into your life, period. For what? Just to leave as abruptly as I did the first time? But I think finding you again was kismet, and I won't take the complete blame for that.*
>
> *Let me get to the point. I have made arrangements with my attorney to make sure you are notified when the time comes, as I will not be contacting you again. I have also made provisions for Darrell's schooling; just call it a scholarship from the Good Doctor. He's a bright boy, and I want to help him grab hold of what he's reaching for. It means something to me to do this.*
>
> *You won't hear from me anymore and that's good. I mean, how will you have peace with me always bothering you, right? And how will I have peace unless I let you go.*
>
> *The least I can do, however, is more than I did the first time, and that is to say good-bye.*
>
> *Good-bye, Stormy Brown-Gunther. You will always be the best mistake a man could have ever made.*
>
> *Forever a heel,*
> *S. York*

She dialed his number only to find it disconnected. Stormy dropped down on her porch in a heap of tears.

Sebastian milled around that house of his; it felt very large today despite the fact that the house and the entire lot it sat on could fit inside the one he had shared with Ta'Rae. Perhaps this one felt oversized because he wasn't sharing it—not with Ta'Rae anyway.

Tomorrow was Christmas, big party day for the Ams folks. He wondered if Ta'Rae was going to be a part of the festivities. He wondered if he would be.

Precious had moved in again, and it was feeling better at night, not so cold. However, he and Precious still had some issues, ones that he wasn't even sure he wanted to address. She was growing up faster than he had planned, and the timing wasn't good for it. Rethinking his last thought made him smile.

It's not a good time for too many things, my friend, he internally reminded himself.

It was hard being a parent, a husband, a man, even under the best of conditions, and Sebastian was going to need more time if he was going to fix everything. Another remission was the only hope for him—one he clung to with everything he had. However, he had accepted the other possibilities . . . fully.

He was tired. He was dying. Yes, he accepted it. He needed to find his comfort zone right now, his peace of mind. It was funny how he thought he needed to complete everything on his list in order to reach this level in himself.

The need to find his father had proven only to make it clear to him that the past held nothing for him but lessons, some hard, some not so, but all designed with one purpose—to move forward and only forward. Meeting his father taught him one thing that was for sure—you just can't change anything.

Stormy Brown-Gunther. Going after Stormy with questions had only led him back to Ta'Rae for the answers. Stormy had made him see that, clearly. From the first time he laid eyes on her all those years ago, she only showed him what true love was—Ta'Rae. The thought made him chuckle. "And what a mess I made figuring out that whole thing," he said aloud, shaking his head at the memories of his meetings with Stormy. How he haunted that woman, plagued her, and for what? To gain something for himself that was not even his to have. It was Stormy who needed the closure on that chapter in her life, not him. He had closed the door when he walked away, abandoning that woman like an old shoe. He was ashamed of his actions and so glad she'd finally forgiven him. He'd grappled with that angel named Stormy Brown and finally received absolution from her—and maybe a little blessing, too, in Darrell.

What a wonderful woman she was, what a *good* mistake she had turned out to be. Of course, he would never believe that Darrell was not his son. But as Stormy brought out, what good would it do to push that issue any further? All Sebastian really hoped was that if indeed Darrell was his son, that one day she told him and on that day, she had good things to say. Whatever the case, he'd put some money aside for the boy to have, and he felt good about that.

And Ta'Rae. What is it I need from Ta'Rae?

"Sebastian," he heard.

Spinning around, his eyes burned immediately. It

was her. He couldn't believe it; he had to have wished her up just that quickly.

Fighting emotion, he stood his ground, however. It wasn't pride that kept him footed; it was fear—fear of rejection. Fear of all that Ta'Rae kept inside might come out. He'd hurt her again with his secrets, but he had to be honest; he just didn't know if he could handle all it would take to fix it with her. *What am I thinking? There's nothing we can't conquer if we just couple our minds.*

He would work until his last breath to fix whatever was broken between them. He loved her. When he fell for her, he fell hard. Falling for her all over again would be the easiest thing for him to do, he'd do it again and again until he got it right. He no longer cared about the silly things he cared about before—his trivial needs, his demands. He would take whatever affection she could muster; whatever she could give him, he would take.

Maybe what he really wanted from Ta'Rae was so simple she'd already given it to him and he'd missed it somewhere along the way.

"Sebastian," she said again, taking a step forward. The air was thick between them, and Sebastian shifted his weight onto his cane. "Baby, I'm so sorry for everything. I'm sorry for what hurts you. I'm sorry for what I've done . . . what I've not done," Ta'Rae began. "I know we may not have a lot of time to fix everything. But, baby, it doesn't matter," she said. Sebastian started to speak but she stopped him. "No . . . no, let me finish," Ta'Rae interrupted. "And about Precious, she's just angry. She's a teenager, they are all angry about something," Ta'Rae went on, and then rolled her eyes as if again feeling the heat from Precious's last diatribe. "She and I can work out whatever it is. And that woman, Stormy Gunther, I have to get past that, I do. Darrell too," Ta'Rae said without hesitation or second thought. "I have worked that out in my mind a million times, and it's just not worth losing a minute of time with you. We can get beyond all that. Baby, we can get through it all. There's nothing we can't do if we put our minds together," Ta'Rae said, touching his face tenderly. "You know why? Because we love each other. I know I have always loved you. You have made me feel whole. Complete. Every time I see your face, your picture, hear your voice, think about you, I fall. I fall in love with you all over again."

She kissed him on his forehead, his cheek, his lips, and leaning back from the kiss, she saw that Sebastian's expression took his face far away, to a pleasant place somewhere in his mind. His expression struck her as strange. "What?" she asked him. "Why are you smiling like that?"

"You just took care of the last thing on my list." He smiled.

"What was that?" she asked, holding him tight.

"You don't even know."

"No, I guess I don't. Tell me what I did that was so wonderful it made your list."

"You called me, 'baby,'" he told her, his smile broadening, taking the edge of pain away.

"Oh, Sebastian." Ta'Rae giggled, kissing him with all the passion she had.

PEACE

The flowers were arranged perfectly. Trina had a way with things like that. Smooth jazz played in the background while the room filled with friends, colleagues, and family.

Despite Carlotta's pushing, there was no choir. Sebastian had never been a religious man. All of Ta'Rae's sisters were bossy, headstrong, and intrusive. Where would she and Sebastian have been without them these last few months?

Sebastian had, a long time ago, claimed Ta'Rae's family as his own; it had just taken her a long time to realize how he, too, depended on their strength—in the end more than ever.

The months leading up to this day had taken everyone to the pinnacle of his or her emotions, but never did anyone run out of love. There was never a time when she or Sebastian's needs were not met—with a *quickness*.

However, everything moved in slow motion for

Ta'Rae this day. She wasn't even aware of what she wore, as Rashawn and Rita had dressed her that morning.

"Basic black and pearls," Rashawn had said to Rita while going through Ta'Rae's closet a few days back, or maybe it was that morning—who could know? Each day had blended into the next since Sebastian closed his eyes for the last time.

He died in the early morning hours; in the bed they shared all their life together. He was born that time of day, Ta'Rae remembered, so everything was all in balance now.

At peace . . .

The pain was lifted. Ta'Rae felt the relief as soon as he passed. The heavy weight gave way. He had said good-bye with a tender kiss of eternal love that Ta'Rae felt down to her tocs. She knew then he was letting go.

Precious had been staying with Carlotta and had to be called when Sebastian died. Once the words left her lips, Ta'Rae could only hear the silence until Carlotta picked up the receiver and told her Precious had broken down. Carlotta then said she would gather everyone together and all of them would be on their way. Within minutes, the house filled with loving arms, tears, and the uniforms of the men who took Sebastian's body away. Ta'Rae's days had been in a fog ever since.

Looking around now, Ta'Rae came to focus on the voice of Phil, Sebastian's friend and his personal physician. He was speaking of a time when together they played golf and Sebastian hit a hole in one.

There were smiles on all the faces. Even on the face of a woman Ta'Rae had never seen before. In the back of the room, near the window, she stood—cute, youthful-looking with dimples showing in her round face. She wore black, basic black, as if she, too, mourned. Ta'Rae stared until the woman looked at her.

The woman's lips curved into a slight smile, and then her face straightened abruptly. Ta'Rae knew immediately who she was.

Stormy Gunther. She had to be!

At first sight, Stormy appeared to be a woman like herself, and Ta'Rae waited for the normal emotions of jealousy and rage to come; however, instead of anger, Ta'Rae felt a new feeling, one she'd not felt before. It went beyond any human emotion she had ever experienced before.

No one seemed to notice Stormy as she moved through the crowd toward her, and for a moment Ta'Rae felt faint, but then again, maybe that wasn't the feeling she was experiencing, maybe it was something more.

"Ta'Rae," Stormy said with the soft voice of an angel. Ta'Rae could barely hear her and leaned closer, straining. It was a voice she wanted to hear clearly and remember forever. It was different from the one she remembered from the phone calls. "I am so sorry," she said, touching Ta'Rae's arm.

Ta'Rae looked at her hands, small and newly manicured, long acrylics painted with gold designs embedded. Ta'Rae looked again at her face, perfectly made up. Her hair was fresh from the shop, done up in an elaborate style with glittery flakes of gold sprinkled within the thick plaits. She was downright urban with an ethnic beauty that spoke to a side of Sebastian that Ta'Rae had not been made privy to.

Stormy resembled Sebastian's mother a little.

Ta'Rae had only met her once, but she would never forget that woman's face, and now she was seeing it again, only younger. Maybe that's what Stormy was to Sebastian, a bridge to his past, a magnet that he could not help but be drawn to. The thought made Ta'Rae smile inside.

Another answer for you, Sebby.

Stormy hugged her tightly, as if they were kin, as if through Sebastian they now had a bond. Ta'Rae could not speak; she just stared at the woman, who still smiled and spoke as if her presence was not abnormal, even a little odd.

"You are so beautiful," Stormy finally said, nearly blushing, as if she had fantasized this moment for a long time.

Just then, Rashawn appeared. "Hello, I don't believe we've met. I'm Ta'Rae's sister," Rashawn introduced.

Stormy's face was stricken with instant panic, and her eyes quickly swept the room. "Excuse me," she said, immediately walking away.

Rashawn, in her confusion, looked to Ta'Rae for an explanation. "Who was that, Ta'Rae?"

"Someone I need to know. Hang on a sec. Stormy! Stormy!" Ta'Rae called out, rushing after the fleeing woman. She caught her right before she made her escape. "I want to call you. I want to talk."

"Ta'Rae, I don't know. This now feels strange."

"What does it feel like?" Ta'Rae asked, wondering if their feelings were matched. Stormy just shook her head, fighting the onslaught of tears.

"I can't do this," Stormy cried. She used both hands to wipe away her tears. Her make-up smeared just a little.

"Then why did you come?"

"I had to see you. I had to see the woman he loved," Stormy went on, before glancing over Ta'Rae's shoulder at another guest approaching, interrupting.

During the interchange, Stormy made her getaway.

It was a few months before Ta'Rae felt like doing much of anything. Her first outing was with Trina. She had gotten ready for it. When she heard the doorbell, she assumed it was her. Gathering up her bag, she yelled for her to enter. The door opened slowly.

"Hello . . ." the familiar voice called.

Ta'Rae gasped and her head swooned before she turned and saw the young man, whose looks were Sebastian reincarnate.

"Who are you?" she asked, barely able to hold her emotions in tact.

"I'm Darrell. My mother said we needed to meet," he said. "You're Dr. York's wife and I—"

Ta'Rae could not hold back her smile. It was warm and sincere.

"Come in, please," she offered, moving him deeper into the house, to the living room. She noticed him looking at all the pictures. The pictures of the man who he'd met on a few occasions, the man who was his father, although, Ta'Rae was still uncertain as to whether either of them knew for sure or not.

"Your husband gave me a scholarship for college," Darrell explained.

Clearing any words from her throat, Ta'Rae replaced them with a smile. She then took one of the better pictures off the mantel and handed it to him. "This is the best one of him, I think. But then again, I'm somewhat prejudiced that way." She giggled.

Darrell looked at the picture and then at her. He smiled slightly. "I know he was my father," he said after a moment longer of looking at the pictures. "I know he was."

Ta'Rae sighed heavily and then nodded, confirming Darrell's thoughts. He smiled broadly. "Do you hate me?" he asked then, looking at her with Sebastian's deep soul-searching eyes. Ta'Rae's heart tugged.

"No, no, I could never hate you," she confessed.

"Because I didn't come here to bug you. I was just, like, curious, you know," the boy went on, apparently wanting to wander, yet confining himself to a circle. He turned back to her and faced her square on. "My mother lied to him and me. I guess she was scared of what might happen," Darrell told her. "But I heard her once on the phone telling him to leave me alone, that I was not his son. But it's more than obvious," Darrell went on, while holding up the picture.

"Yes, it is." She smiled. "He wanted you to know, but he realized it wasn't really fair—not to you, not to your father, Jerry."

Darrell smiled and nodded. "Dr. York was cool. I mean, really nice," Darrell said, attempting formal language.

Ta'Rae just watched his mouth move for a second before speaking. "Yes, Sebastian was very cool," she said, smiling broadly. Darrell laughed, relaxing a little more.

"Darrell, we have so much ground to cover, and I hope we have time. I hope you will allow me . . . time," Ta'Rae requested. Darrell nodded.

Just then, the door burst open and Trina came in. She glanced at the boy and Ta'Rae, who now had tears in her eyes. It didn't take a genius to figure out what was happening. "Hello," Trina said, greeting the boy openly and full of friendliness.

Darrell nodded shyly.

"This is Sebastian's son, Darrell," Ta'Rae introduced, wiping away the tears as they fell.

"Just like Sebastian, playin' all shy. Come here and give your auntie a hug. You better get used to it. We're family now."

EPILOGUE

The day finally came. Ta'Rae had mixed feelings, but she knew it was inevitable. Precious was too good of a student not to get a full-ride scholarship.

Stormy and her husband had accepted Sebastian's financial assistance in Darrell's education as, not surprisingly, he had skills of his own, and he, too, had been accepted to NYU.

The past year, rebuilding her life, had been made a lot easier for Ta'Rae with Darrell around. Precious felt it too. Having Darrell in their life had definitely filled a void.

He and Precious going away to school together was going to be a wonderful experience and something that, being the family man that he was, Sebastian would have approved of. Ta'Rae knew that.

At the station, tears were everywhere as Ta'Rae watched her family hugging the two young people about to start their journey. They had taken Darrell in as if he were Ta'Rae's own son. If he felt anything bad about how things had turned out—not finding Sebastian until too late—it didn't show.

Just then, Ta'Rae thought about Sebastian's list. She'd found a draft of it in the glove box of his car. She remembered the order of importance he had placed on things. He had only three categories:

Family.

Love.

Life.

How unpredictably simple the most important issues to resolve were for him. Love and family and the need for these two things in his life, that's what it all came down to.

Ta'Rae planned to hold on tight to Darrell now that she had him. He was a part of Sebastian's love—Darrell was Sebastian's family. He was an unexpected cord on the rope she held on to, the one that she depended on to pull her back from the edge, to save her from the fall.